SANTA FE WOMAN

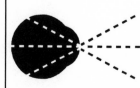

This Large Print Book carries the
Seal of Approval of N.A.V.H.

SANTA FE WOMAN

GILBERT MORRIS

THORNDIKE PRESS

An imprint of Thomson Gale, a part of The Thomson Corporation

Detroit • New York • San Francisco • New Haven, Conn. • Waterville, Maine • London

LIBRARY OF CONGRESS CATALOGING-IN-PUBLICATION DATA

Morris, Gilbert.
   Santa Fe woman / by Gilbert Morris.
     p. cm. — (Thorndike Press large print Christian historical fiction)
   ISBN-13: 978-0-7862-9417-6 (alk. paper)
   ISBN-10: 0-7862-9417-5 (alk. paper)
   1. Overland journeys to the Pacific — Fiction. 2. Frontier and pioneer life — Fiction. 3. West (U.S.) — Fiction. 4. Large type books. I. Title.
PS3563.O8742S26 2006
813'.54—dc22
                                                  2006102648

Published in 2007 by arrangement with Broadman & Holman Publishers.

Printed in the United States of America on permanent paper
10 9 8 7 6 5 4 3 2 1

to Mike Hollingshead

This is a dark world we are living in,
but from time to time I meet someone
whose spirit produces a light.
Thanks, Mike, for being one of those
rare individuals who gives off a glow.
You are a friend indeed, and I am
thankful for your friendship.

■ ■ ■ ■

PART ONE:
END OF A LIFE

■ ■ ■ ■

CHAPTER ONE

As Jori Hayden emerged from the house, she was met by a sharp, cold wind. The winter of 1822 had struck Arkansas with a blunt force, so that now all around Little Rock the creeks and rivers were frozen hard enough to support a heavily laden wagon. She noted thick columns of smoke rising straight from chimney tops only to be blown into formless masses that immingled with low-lying clouds.

Ignoring the freezing wind, Jori moved toward the stable, noting the breath of the cattle in the fields rising in little puffs. Entering the stable, she greeted the man who turned to face her. "Good morning, Caleb."

"Not so good, Miss Jori." Caleb House shook his head glumly. He was a short man with the shoulders of a wrestler. He stroked his droopy mustache with his thick fingers, adding, "Too cold for you to ride this morning. You could get pneumonia."

"You're a prophet of doom, Caleb," Jori smiled. "It's a fine day for a ride." At the age of twenty-two, she had a curved, womanly figure with brilliant black hair. Her face was too square for beauty, but her eyes were so unusual that most never noticed that. Large, well spaced, and shaped like almonds, her eyes were a striking shade of sea green with flecks of gray. They were sharp and alert, at times flaring with anger, but now were dancing with humor. "Your favorite book in the Bible must be Lamentations, Caleb. It's a beautiful world, and you need to see it."

"When you've been flattened by this 'beautiful' world a few times, you'll see it different," Caleb said morosely. "I suppose you want me to saddle the mare?"

"Yes, please." Turning to make her way to a stall, she reached out and stroked the silky nose of the mare that arched her neck over the gate. "Ready for a run, girl?" She laughed as the mare nibbled her fingers, then reached into her side pocket and brought out the quartered slices of apple. She stepped aside and watched as Caleb put on the saddle and bridle, then, without waiting, hoisted herself at once into the saddle. "Thanks, Caleb," she called, then shot out of the stable, putting the mare into a fast gallop.

Caleb stared after the young woman dolefully, then shook his head. "Going to break her neck riding like that! She's had it too easy and thinks the world's a playground. She'll get that knocked out of her one day — just like we all do." He spoke to the large, mustard-colored dog who sat watching him, then turned and moved down into the depths of the stable.

The cold had roughed Jori's cheeks and put a sparkle in her eyes. She was a young woman of great vitality, generous and capable of robust emotion. She loved challenges, and now her blood was up as the mare drove forward. Jori felt the strength of the horse flowing up, touching her legs, and coursing through her body. "Go, Princess!" she cried, and leaned forward delighting in the speed of the mare. She was vaguely aware of the trees on each side that stood stiffly reaching upward and of the gusting wind that sent up the dead leaves in a whirlwind cloud. It was a gaunt world, but when Jori was astride a fine horse, weather meant nothing.

Looking up, Jori saw Gerald Carter, her fiancé, and Clyde Hammond waiting for her. Pulling Princess up shortly, she kicked her feet free from the stirrups and slid to the ground still holding the reins tightly. Her face was flushed, and she made an attractive picture as she stood there. Her black hair escaped from beneath her green cap, and her green eyes were sparkling. "Gerald, did you see us?"

"Should think I did, but you moved so fast I almost missed you." Gerald Carter was no more than five eight, exactly Jori's height. He was not particularly good-looking but had a pleasant, thin face. His eyes were well shaped and of an attractive blue color, and there was an air of gentleness about him. He was wearing a dark brown overcoat and a hat made out of prime beaver. A large diamond sparkled from his left hand as he raised it and stroked his cheek. "A bit cold for trying out horses," he suggested.

"No, any day's a good day for fine horse flesh." Clyde Hammond was a large man made more bulky by multiple sweaters covered by a buffalo overcoat. The tip of his cigar made a red dot against the gray surroundings. His nose was lined with veins, and his eyes were red rimmed. The odor of alcohol was strong on him, but despite his drinking habits, he was known as the best judge of horse flesh in the state. He had brought the mare to the Hayden stables in hopes of selling her. "How did you like her, Miss Jori?"

"She's a fine one, Clyde," Jori said, her eyes dancing. She reached up and patted the horse on the neck. "I've got to have her! Come now, give me a good price."

Hammond took his cigar out, examined it thoughtfully as if the price lay there, then shrugged his beefy shoulders. "Couldn't part with her for less than fifteen hundred."

"Fifteen hundred dollars!" Gerald Carter was shocked. He was generally shocked at the price of horses, for he knew almost nothing about them. For him, horses were a means of getting from one place to another, and he could never understand how Jori loved them with such passion. "Why, you could buy a nice house for that!"

Jori handed the lines of the mare over to Clyde and took Gerald's arm. She enjoyed making bargains, and both the men were aware of the rich, racy current of vitality in her. "But you couldn't ride a house the way I've just ridden Princess there."

"No, but if that animal got sick and died, you'd be out fifteen hundred dollars."

"Oh, don't be such a fussbudget, Gerald!" Turning to Hammond, Jori said, "I'll think about it, Clyde. You'll have to do a little bit better on the price."

"Not for this animal, Miss Jori," Hammond shook his head woefully. "I'll be losing money on her as it is."

"That'll be the day when you lose money on a horse! Come along, Gerald."

The two left, and as they made their way toward the buggy that waited over by the stable, Jori spoke enthusiastically about the speed and the beauty of the mare. "She's exactly what I want, Gerald. Surely you can see that."

"She costs too much."

"Oh, don't be so miserly!"

Gerald handed her into the buggy, then walked around and got inside. He took up the lines, but before he spoke to the horse, he turned to her. "You know, Jori, this has been a bad year for business. A lot of them have gone down. You need to be more careful about money."

"You worry too much." Jori suddenly reached over, took his chin, and turning his head to face her, she gave him a light kiss. "After we're married I'll be demanding all kinds of expensive things."

Gerald could only grin in a doubtful fashion. He knew the two of them were very different and, at times, felt uneasy about how they would get on. But now the dance of laughter in her green eyes and the humor in the set of her lips caught at him. "I expect that's your plan. But it won't be like that. You can do as you please before we're married, but afterward I will expect you to be a beautiful wife, meek and humble."

Jori was feeling exuberant after her ride and paid no heed to Gerald's warning. She reached over and took the line from him. "Let me drive," she said.

"You drive too fast."

"There's no such thing as driving too fast." Jori spoke to the horse sharply and slapped the lines against his back, and the two were thrown backward as the horse leaned forward suddenly against the harness.

The ride home was quicker than if Gerald had been driving. When they pulled into the circular driveway in front of her home, Gerald heaved a sigh of relief. "Well, we didn't get killed." He took the lines from her, but for a moment he sat there looking at the house. "That's a beautiful home your family has."

"Been in our family forever. My great-grandfather built it for my great-grandmother. He was very romantic."

The structure was a very large three-story

frame house painted a lucent white, featuring a gambrel roof and a large interior chimney. The windows were all narrow but very long with dark green shutters flanking each side, and the front entrance to the house featured fluted white columns on either side of the massive door.

Gerald admired the house momentarily, then turned to her and said, "Jori, I really don't think you should buy that horse. Have you been reading the papers lately? A lot of businesses have gone belly-up."

"Things are going to get better. They always do."

"Well, you will have the horse, I suppose. Your father hasn't refused you anything since you were six years old."

"Oh, long before that! I'm totally spoiled."

Gerald resisted the temptation to agree wholeheartedly. Instead he put his arms around her and drew her close. "When are you going to set the date, Jori?"

Jori saw he was serious. She often wished that he was not *quite* so serious. Spending your life with a man who had so little sense of humor was one problem with marrying Gerald Carter. On the other hand, he came from a good family with a great deal of money, more than the Haydens by far! His courtship had been sedate enough, and she had been vaguely disappointed that he was not more daring. It would have given her pleasure to have repelled all borders, so to speak. But he was the more proper one of the two of them.

"I'll marry you when the leaves fall."

"You string me up and let me twist in the wind." Gerald shook his head ruefully. "You mean the maple leaves that fall early or the pine tree that never has leaves?"

"That's for you to find out."

Gerald reached forward and put his arms around her, and she surrendered herself to his kiss. It was not the kind of kiss that she enjoyed although she could not have explained why. There was something almost passive in Gerald's kisses, and he was always the first one to break them off. Jori had a wild impulse to throw her arms around his neck and grind her mouth against his and put herself against him, but she knew this would confuse him.

When Gerald drew back, he said, "I'll be looking forward to the ball at the Hanfords."

"Don't buy any new clothes. You always outshine me. I've got a new dress, and I want to be the prettiest of the two of us."

"You haven't answered me about the date of our marriage. I'd like an answer."

"Don't be impatient." She patted his arm

and said, "Don't get out. I can make it." She jumped out of the buggy and gave him a brilliant smile. "Remember, try not to dress more spectacularly than I do, Gerald."

"All right," he said, taking her literally. "I'll just wear one of my old suits."

Jori watched him as he drove off, and a sense of disappointment came to her. *I wish one time,* she thought, *he would do something totally unexpected — even shocking.* A shadow touched her eyes, but she turned aside thinking of Princess and what fun she would have with her new toy.

Leland Hayden had once remarked, "It's hard to decide which is the messiest, my daughter Carleen's room or the way she dresses." Indeed, Carleen Hayden, at the age of ten, was in a constant state of disarray. She cared not at all for clothes and was perfectly content to wear some old clothes that her brother Mark had worn as a teenager. Since she spent every available moment outside, the party dresses and fine clothes that her sister Jori insisted on buying for her were mostly unused.

Carleen sat at a table while the pencil in her left hand moved over the paper before her. She wrote as she did everything else — with great enthusiasm. This made for rather sloppy handwriting, which was a matter of despair for her tutor, Mrs. Elmus Satterfield. Mrs. Satterfield sat beside Carleen watching her pupil's progress with something like despair. She was a tall, angular woman with sharp features, especially her nose. It had a red point on it constantly, hot weather or cold, and her eyes were sharp as ice picks. She seemed to have only one dress, which she wore every time she came to the Hayden mansion to give Carleen her lessons. The dress was dark gray with a high neck and long sleeves. The bodice fit loosely as did the skirt that came down to her ankles, and the entire dress was free from any decoration. Her hair was approximately the color of old burlap sacks that had been left out in the weather too long, and she kept it bound tightly up in a huge bun in the back. Her only ornament was a bosom watch that she looked at from time to time where it was pinned on her flat chest.

Occasionally Mrs. Satterfield looked around the room with an air of obvious displeasure. Carleen's room was full but not of bedroom furniture. Every available space was taken up with "trophies," including bird nests that covered the top of her bureau, a cage with a canary that twittered almost constantly, and a glass tank with turtles over by the window. Carleen had fished them out of the river and fed them with worms dug out of the garden. Hanging from the ceiling were several hornets' nests. Just beside the door on a table was a stuffed fox, his eyes looking bright and eager. Her birds' egg collection filled the drawers of the chest on which the fox kept eternal vigilance. Other trophies included various unusual plants stuffed into glass bottles and any sort of vessel that Carleen could find. The bed itself was the only piece of furniture in the room that was not covered with part of Carleen's collection.

As Carleen leaned over, her hand moving rapidly, Mrs. Satterfield saw her tongue emerge from the left side of her mouth. "Pull your tongue back in your mouth, girl!" she said sharply.

Carleen blinked and gave the woman a resentful look. Her hair, as red as hair can possibly be, she hated — though she liked her green eyes. Actually, this made a fine combination of coloring. She had gotten the red hair from her mother, and she spent some time each day bemoaning the fact that she didn't have black hair like her sister Jori.

"I don't know why I have to know all this old stuff, Mrs. Satterfield."

"A young lady needs to know a great deal

about the world in which she lives." Mrs. Satterfield leaned over and put the tip of her bony fingertip on the paper. "And this is not correct. The American Revolution was not fought in 1666. It was 1776."

A grimace twisted Carleen's lips to one side. "Well, what difference does it make? Who cares what dead people did? I'm interested in people that are alive." She turned to Mrs. Satterfield and said, "Why can't I learn something that I need to know?"

"And what do you propose that might be since you don't think history is a needful subject?"

"Well," Carleen said thoughtfully and put the end of the pencil in her mouth. "My sister's getting married. She'll be having babies. It would help me to know something about that. How do babies get born?"

The ordinary shade of Elmus Satterfield's face was something like the color of an aged biscuit. Now it turned scarlet. "That's — that's not for me to say. And take that pencil out of your mouth. Where are your other pencils?"

"Over there in that box on the table."

Mrs. Satterfield rose from the chair and moved over to the wall. She had to move a dried frog from the top of the box, and she did this simply by brushing it to one side. She opened the box and reached in, turning to say, "And your pencils are never sharp."

Suddenly a piercing scream broke from Mrs. Satterfield's throat. It seemed to increase in pitch so that it filled the room. As she screamed, she fell backward waving her hands wildly in an erratic fashion.

"What's the matter?" Carleen yelped, getting to her feet.

Mrs. Satterfield could not answer. Her mouth was opening and closing, but all that came out was unintelligible garbage. "The box!" she cried.

Carleen walked over to the box and grinned. She reached in and pulled out a small green snake no more than twelve inches long. It was an attractive green color, almost the color of Carleen's eyes. "It's just an old garter snake," she said. "It wouldn't hurt anybody."

But Mrs. Satterfield was not in the least interested in hearing that. She was moving rapidly toward the door when it abruptly opened and a tall, strongly built woman entered. She was wearing a crisp black dress, and her left hand was somehow crippled so that it made a closed fist. She had a wealth of light brown hair and a pair of striking gray eyes, well shaped and set far apart. Her features were pleasant, but now she was staring at Mrs. Satterfield with consternation. "What in the world are you screaming about, Mrs. Satterfield?"

"A snake! She had a snake in that box!"

"It's just an old garter snake, Aunt Kate," Carleen protested. "It wouldn't hurt anybody. See?"

Kate Johnson, age thirty-five, was Leland Hayden's sister-in-law. She had come to take over the raising of his children when her sister Loreen had died. She had come as a combination nanny and housekeeper and family member, and she was the most competent woman that any of the Haydens had ever seen.

"You shouldn't keep snakes in the house. I told you that. Now, get rid of him."

"But it's cold out there. I'm going to turn him loose next spring."

"Put him in the attic. It's warm up there."

Mrs. Satterfield interrupted. Her face had lost its red color and now was back to the biscuit color. "I refuse to stay in this house any longer and do anything with this young person." She waved her hand toward Carleen. "You may tell Mr. Hayden I will not be back." Grabbing her hat and coat from pegs, she sailed out the door. Carleen and Kate listened as her footsteps sounded down the stairway. Kate turned and shrugged. "Your father's going to have a fit."

"Don't tell him, Aunt Kate."

"Well, now, that's silly. Don't you think he'll notice that your teacher is gone?"

"He's never here in the daytime when she comes. We'll just play like she's here. I'm not learning anything from her anyway."

"I have no doubt you're right, but he has to know. Never put off bad news, Carleen." She looked around and shook her head. "This room is a mess. Aren't you embarrassed by it?"

"No," Carleen said in a practical way. "It's what I like in my room."

"Well, we're going to have to clean it up. I'll help you."

The two started making rather ineffectual efforts to clean the room. This primarily involved moving items from one place to another, and finally Kate laughed. "I swan, Carleen, you might as well sleep in the attic and use this place for your trophies."

"Aunt Kate, tell me some more about when you lived in Texas."

Kate Johnson had been brought up, along with her sister Loreen, in Lexington, Kentucky. But within a year after Loreen had married Leland Hayden, James Johnson had moved his family to Texas. Loreen had known none of the hardships that Kate endured on the wild frontier. It was these stories of frontier life that Carleen loved to hear Kate speak of.

"You've heard all about that," Kate said.

"No, you always think of something else. Did you ever see a bear?"

"Of course. I saw a lot of bears. Shot one once. Bear fat's good for drawing wounds."

"Did you ever see an outlaw?"

"I saw one."

"Tell me about it."

"Well, there was a family called Robbins. They were no good. The oldest brother Earl killed a man."

"Did he kill him with a knife?"

"No. Killed him with a shotgun. I don't remember what the argument was about."

"What'd he look like?"

"Oh, all the Robbins were good-looking people. He was a tall man, about six two, I guess. Had the blackest hair you ever saw and eyes to match. He had good teeth, too, I remember. A good-looking man."

"Was you in love with him?"

"In love with him! I reckon not! Why would I fall in love with an outlaw?" Memories stirred in Kate's eyes, and she said, "He came to my house once. I didn't really know him, but he knew our family. He was on the run from the law. I was all alone in the house, and he came in and made me cook him a meal."

"What else did he do?"

Kate suddenly laughed, and a sparkle came to her eyes. "When he got ready to go, he made me put all the food in a sack. Then he kissed me and gave me a gold coin."

"He kissed you! Really?"

"He really did."

"What'd you do with the gold coin?"

"Why, I still have it."

"Aunt Kate, I want to see it!"

"Why?"

"Because it's a treasure. Come on, show it to me."

Kate got up with a laugh. When she laughed she was a very attractive woman indeed. She usually kept her crippled hand behind her back, or at her side when strangers were there, but with Carleen she did not. "Come on then, I'll show it to you if I can find it."

The two went to Kate's room, which was at the end of the hall on the second floor. When they moved inside Carleen said, "You sure keep your room nice."

"Let it be a lesson to you." Going over to a chest, she opened the bottom drawer and moved things around, finally arising with a small box. Closing the drawer, she came over and stood before Carleen. "Should be in here." She opened the box and said, "There's a collar button that my father wore. It's made out of gold, too. Ah, here it is."

Carleen reached out and took the coin. She held it almost reverently as if it had some sort of spiritual significance. Her eyes were wide as she whispered, "I wisht I could meet an outlaw!"

Kate laughed, "You're not likely to in Little Rock."

"What are you going to do with it?"

Kate laughed. "Give it to you in my will if you're good. Now, let's go down and help Ellie get dinner on the table."

"I don't see why we can't go ahead and start. No telling when Father will be here." The speaker was Mark Hayden. He sat lounged back in his chair, toying with the fork beside his plate. Mark was just under six feet with a rather slender build. He had the same black hair as his sister Jori, and his eyes were a warm brown. He was dressed in the latest fashion, a pair of sleek brown wool pants, a white shirt with a red ascot around his neck, a caramel-colored vest and jacket.

The jacket reached to his knees, had a rather large lapel that came down to mid-stomach where three buttons were placed, and then cut back to his sides.

Jori was glaring at Carleen. "You didn't wash your hands. Look at them."

"They don't need it."

"You've been out digging worms for those turtles of yours. Go wash them instantly."

Grumbling, Carleen got up and left the room. When she was gone Jori turned to Kate. "Aunt Kate, can't you do anything with her?"

"No, but time will take care of that. She won't be digging worms in another year or two."

Carleen finally returned and plopped herself into a chair. Almost immediately Ellie, the housemaid, came and said, "Your father's here."

As soon as she had spoken, Leland Hayden stepped through the door. He was fifty but looked younger. He was no more than medium height and had brown hair and warm brown eyes. Taking a seat, he murmured, "Well, you shouldn't have waited for me."

Kate, who was more observant than the children, saw that her brother-in-law was pale and agitated, but she did not remark on it. She bowed her head as Leland asked a brief blessing, and Carleen said at once, "Mrs. Satterfield has left, Papa. She's not coming back."

Leland looked up from the spoonful of soup. Putting down the spoon he said, "Left? Why'd she leave?"

"It was nothing really."

"Carleen had a snake in her room in a box with her pencils," Kate said calmly. "Mrs. Satterfield reached in and got a snake instead of a pencil."

Carleen grinned broadly. "You should have heard her yelp, Papa. It was funny."

"It was not funny!" Jori said severely. "It was impolite. You did it on purpose."

"No, I didn't. I forgot about that old snake. Besides, it was only a garter snake. It wouldn't hurt anybody."

"Well, now we'll have to go to the trouble of finding another teacher," Jori said. Suddenly a thought struck her, and she said, "Oh, Papa, I went over to see the mare that Clyde has for sale. She's a wonderful animal. I think we ought to buy her. Clyde only wants fifteen hundred dollars for her."

Mark at once said petulantly, "Well, if you can have a horse that costs that much, I ought to be able to make a trip to England with Tom Seaton. You know, Father, it's a graduation present."

"You're not going to graduate," Carleen spoke up at once. "You failed your last two classes."

Mark shot a hard glance at Carleen and said, "None of your business. Besides, I can make it up when I get back."

Kate had said nothing up until now, but she had been watching Leland's face closely. "What's the matter, Leland?" she asked quietly.

Leland looked up and met Kate's eyes. She was the only one in the household who had the discernment to see that he was not himself. He had come to appreciate his sister-in-law. He had been deeply in love with his wife Loreen, and losing her had been like losing a limb. The children had been small, and it had been, as far as Leland was concerned, a blessing of God that Kate had been available. She had taken over running the household and was the one that Leland usually talked things over with when there was a decision to be made.

"I'd been hoping I wouldn't have to tell any of you this, but I'm afraid I'm going to have to." All of them suddenly grew serious and stared at their father. He was not given to moods and was usually happy and cheerful, but if they had been observant, they would have noted for some weeks that he had been less than happy.

"What's the matter, Papa?" Jori said. "Are you sick?"

"Oh, I'm well enough," Leland said. He put his fork down and braced his hands against the top of the table and for a moment tried to collect his thoughts. They were all aware that he was keeping something from them, and finally he said, "I had a meeting with the bank today. It was about the loan I applied for. I mentioned it to you."

"What's the matter? We've never had trouble getting money before," Jori said.

"Well, these are different times, daughter. I made a bad decision last year. I didn't see this depression coming, and I plunged into some stocks that looked good at the time. But they haven't been good. I should have been pulling back and selling." He looked up and made his apology as briefly as he could. "I had no idea such hard times were coming. Nobody did."

"But we'll be all right if the bank gives us the loan, won't we?" Mark asked.

"Not exactly, Mark. Even if we get the loan, we're going to have to cut back on our expenses."

"I can do without a teacher," Carleen

piped up at once.

Kate said quietly, "It's bad, isn't it, Leland?" She knew her brother-in-law well and was as aware of his weaknesses as of his strengths. He was one of the kindest men she had ever known, yet his worst fault, in her opinion, was that he could not discipline his children. Mark and Jori were spoiled to the bone, and it was too late to do anything about it.

"Yes, it is bad, Kate. I don't — I don't know what we're going to do."

"Well, the Lord will see us through it," she said calmly. She had a deep faith in God that she had not been able to communicate to the rest of the family.

"I wish I had your faith," Leland said in a defeated voice.

Kate looked at him and said, "Everyone has a measure of faith. That's what the Bible says. All you need is a bit of faith as big as a mustard seed."

Her words did not seem to cheer Leland Hayden up. He waited until the children had left the table and finally turned and said, "Kate, if Loreen hadn't died, things would have been different. She had more judgment than I ever had. I could never say no to the children."

"No, you never could," Kate said. She

came over and put her good hand on Leland's shoulder, her eyes filled with pity.
"But I think that the time is here when
you're going to have to say no to a lot of
things, brother!"

CHAPTER TWO

As soon as Luther Phelps entered the room, Leland's heart sank. He had been hoping desperately that Phelps would enter the room with a smile on his face, but the tall banker's countenance was without expression. Bankers like Luther had a way of masking their emotions. They were usually good poker players for this very reason. As Phelps sat down, Leland tried to convince himself that there was nothing wrong, but the banker's first words dashed all that hope.

"Leland, I feel terrible having to say this," Phelps said. His voice was even, but there was regret on his features. "But the committee has refused to approve your loan."

Phelps' words seemed to shatter Leland Hayden. He ducked his head and stared down at his hands that were clasped tightly together in his lap. "There's — there's no hope they'd change their mind?"

"I'm afraid not. You understand times are

tough right now — as tough as I've ever seen them. So many businesses have defaulted on their loans that the committee is scared. I'm a little bit scared myself. It's possible the bank itself might go down."

Leland looked up startled. "Not really! That couldn't happen, could it?"

"It's happened before. Banks aren't divine institutions, you know." Phelps had a bitter light in his eyes, and his lips were drawn together in a white line. "I don't know whether these depressions are an act of God or the foolishness of men, but I suspect the latter."

"I don't — I don't really know what I'm going to do, Luther."

"My advice is to sell out for what you can get, Leland. I've been hoping that you could salvage enough to start a new venture."

"I suppose I'm not the first stockbroker to come to you."

"No, nor the tenth either. It's hit everybody hard. But you'll be all right. You're a good sound businessman. It was just a combination of things — and no one could have foreseen this happening."

"I should have." Leland's voice was low as he shrugged his shoulders suddenly and got to his feet. He was unaccustomed to dealing with failure. His family had been well-to-do. He had stepped into a fine business that had prospered, and now it was all gone — or most of it anyway.

"Well, I know you tried your best, Luther."

"Let's stay in touch. Something will turn up. A good man like you will find a place."

"Yes, of course."

The two men shook hands and as Hayden left the bank, he somehow felt that his thinking had slowed down. He tried desperately to picture a world in which he had lost his place. Things would go on as always, but he himself — what would he do?

As he entered his carriage and picked up the lines, he thought of going home to face his family. A sudden wild impulse came to him to simply leave, to flee the scene of the accident, more or less, but a man could not do this. He tightened his jaw, gritted his teeth, and spoke to the horse, "Get up, Maude," and as the bay moved forward, he tried to frame the speech that he would have to make. It didn't matter much what words he put it in; it amounted to three words: "I'm a failure."

Carleen came dashing into Jori's room. "How was the ball, sister? Did you dance every dance?"

Jori was stripping off the dress that she

had worn to the governor's ball at the mansion. Her maid had built a fire, so the room was fairly warm. "Yes, I danced every dance." She began taking off her undergarments and answering the questions that Carleen fired at her. Finally she was somewhat shocked, as she slipped her nightgown over her head, to hear Carleen ask, "When am I going to get a bosom? I'm flat as a picket fence."

"You shouldn't ask such questions."

"Well, how am I going to know anything if nobody tells me? I'm afraid I'll grow up with a figure like old Mrs. Satterfield."

"No you won't. You'll be fine. You're just in between now. Don't try to hurry things so much." Jori moved over to the fire, backed up to it, and put her hands behind her, soaking up the warmth.

"How do you know which man to marry? You've had three men after you to marry them. Four if you count Roger. So, how do you know which one to take?"

Jori suddenly laughed. "Well, in the romances the woman just *knows*. She's walking along, and she sees this handsome fellow and then — *zing!* — like a bolt of lightning it just comes to her: *That's the man I'm going to marry.*"

"Is that the way it happened when you

saw Gerald?"

The question irritated Jori. She picked up her hairbrush and began brushing her hair. "That kind of thing is just in romances."

"Then how *do* you know?"

Jori found herself unable to answer the question. In truth she had had four proposals, and two of them were absolutely unthinkable. The young man before Gerald had been exciting and a lot of fun, but he had been almost penniless. She'd had a good time with Charles Johnson, but she'd always known she would never marry him.

"You think it over, and you put all his good qualities down on a piece of paper and his bad on another piece of paper. Then you add them all up."

Carleen stared at her petulantly. "That sounds like a business deal."

"Well, I'm afraid it is a little bit like that. Don't believe everything you read in the romances."

Carleen had her next question ready. "Are we going to be poor, Jori?" She had been thinking a great deal, obviously, about what her father had said about cutting back. "I may have to go to work in a factory."

"We're not going to be poor."

"If we are," Carleen said, "you won't be able to buy new dresses and horses."

"Don't worry about it. It may —"

At that instant there was a knock on the door. It opened, and Kate said, "You girls come down. Your father wants to talk to us."

"I'm ready for bed," Jori protested.

"Put on a robe and come on down."

Jori frowned, but put on her robe, tied the belt, and slipped on some warm house slippers. She left, and as she stepped out into the hall, she saw Carleen pulling at Kate's arm. "Are we going to be poor, Aunt Kate?"

"I don't rightly know."

"Would it scare you to be poor?"

"No," Kate said and smiled slightly. "I've been poor before."

The three hurried downstairs, and went at once to the study. Leland and Mark were talking together, and somehow Jori felt a chill. Fear was not something that came to her often, but her father's face was somehow . . . broken. She did not know any other way to put it. She waited for him to speak, and when Kate closed the door and stepped inside, he cleared his throat and said, "The bank refused the loan."

"What does that mean, Papa?" Jori asked quickly.

"It means we're going to have to sell everything we can."

"But not this house surely?"

39

"Yes. We can't afford to stay here."

"But it's worth a lot of money," Mark protested. "If we sell it, we'll have money."

"It's mortgaged, Mark, so after the mortgage is paid off, we won't get much."

A silence fell across the room, and finally Jori cleared her throat. "I'm sure Gerald's father will lend us some money. After all, I'm practically in the family."

Kate suddenly made a snorting noise. "His family is so stuck up they can't see past their noses. You'll be lucky if that young man doesn't break your engagement."

"He'll never do that! He loves me!"

Carleen did not miss the expression on Aunt Kate's face. She knew disbelief when she saw it. She moved over and stood close to her father, looking up at him. "I can get a job, Papa."

"Oh, I don't think it'll come to that, but it's going to be different." For a time Leland struggled trying to explain how they were going to have to cut back. "It would mean selling this house and finding a cheaper place. We'll have to sell all of the things that —"

"What about the horses?" Jori asked at once.

"They'll have to go I'm afraid, Jori. The place we rent won't have any accommodations for horses." Sadness touched his eyes. "It's going to be very hard."

Staring at his father, Mark said critically, "There must be something we can do."

"I wish there were, son, but I can't think what it would be."

Kate said firmly, "We'll survive. We'll have to let all the servants go."

Jori suddenly had a feeling such as she had never had before. It was as if she'd stepped on a trapdoor that had opened without warning. Servants had always been a part of her life — maids, drivers for the carriage, gardeners, cooks. They had been part of the universe that she moved in. She tried to think for a moment what it would be like having no servants, living in a small apartment somewhere, and it frightened her. She was a girl who was not easily frightened, but then she had never faced a situation like this. She half listened as her father and Kate set out the program they were going to have to follow, and the more she listened, the more she grew despondent and dreaded the future that was to come.

February had come, and Kate had watched her brother-in-law struggle through the process of changing one life for another. For herself it was not all that difficult, for she had known a grinding poverty and hardship in Texas. But she knew that Leland and the children were stunned by the changes. She and Carleen had been the only ones to show any signs of cheer during the past two months. Both Mark and Jori had grown bitter, and Leland moved like a zombie through the days.

Kate had come into the study with a tray and moved to place it on a table beside Leland. "I brought you some of those cookies you like so well, Leland, and some coffee."

"I'm not very hungry."

"Leland, you've got to eat. You've lost weight. I'm worried about you." And indeed Kate was worried. She had not forgotten the hard times in Texas, and as she studied the wan features of her brother-in-law she suddenly remembered how some settlers had just given up when hard times had come. More than one of them had simply given in, and hopelessness had killed them.

Now, as she kept her gaze on Leland's face, a nameless fear ran along her nerves. "Things are never as bad as they seem," she said cheerfully. "God's not going to forget us, Leland."

"Kate, I don't know what to do," Leland muttered. Misery colored his tone, and he seemed drained physically as well as emotionally. "I've tried everything, Kate, but nothing has worked. But we're going to have to do something."

"Have you tried praying?" Kate asked quietly.

"Well . . . no. I haven't done that, but I've never been much of a praying man. I wish I were."

"It's never too late to start," Kate said. "God speaks to us in our troubles. As a matter of fact, I think God whispers to us in our good times and shouts to us when we have problems."

Leland picked up a cookie, took a bite, and chewed it, then turned and looked at Kate with desperation written all over him. "Mark and Jori are miserable. Carleen doesn't seem to know how bad it's going to be."

"I think maybe we spoiled Mark and Jori. Maybe God is giving you a chance to try a different way with them."

"We're all going to have a different way!" Despair caught at him, and he said, "It's a terrible time for us, Kate. I guess I don't know what time it is in our lives."

Kate put her hand over his. "If you want to know what time it is, brother, don't look at your watch."

"Why — what should I look at?"

"Look at the obituaries in the newspapers — or if that fails, look in the mirror."

Leland stared at her, then laughed ruefully, saying, "That's exactly what I don't want to do, Kate." He got to his feet, tossed the cookie down on the plate, then wheeled and moved out of the room as if fleeing Kate's presence.

Kate picked up the cookie, looked at it, and then bit a piece off. She murmured softly, "Well, Lord, You've got a big job here, but then You're a big God. . . ."

Jori had hinted to Gerald about the bad financial situation her family was in. He had listened but had not seemed to realize how serious it was. He had merely shrugged his shoulders and said, "Well, sometimes things are good and sometimes bad in the world of business. Times are hard now, but things will get better."

Jori had waited for him to speak of this, and when she told him that her father was selling the house and they were moving to another place, he was astonished.

"Why, I didn't know things were that bad, Jori."

"I've tried to tell you, Gerald. It's worse than anything I can imagine. I'm going to have to sell my horses and my jewelry."

At this point Jori half expected Gerald to offer to help with the problems of her family. She saw something in his eyes, and hope came to her strongly. But then Gerald said weakly, "I'm sure it will all work out."

At that instant Jori knew that she would never marry this man, but she did not expect the decision to be made by Gerald's family. That was the way it happened, however. The next time she saw Gerald was when he came to her home. He seemed embarrassed and so awkward that finally Jori asked, "What's wrong with you, Gerald? You're upset."

"Well . . ." Gerald cleared his throat and seemed to be searching for words. "It's my family. We were talking last night about our marriage . . ."

Jori waited for him to finish, but he seemed to have run out of steam. "What did they say?" she asked, and even at that moment she knew from the uncertainty in Gerald's face what he would say.

"Well, they said . . . ah, that it might be best if we put it off — just for a time, you know."

Jori stared at Gerald Carter, and at that moment she was stirred by two emotions. Anger ran through her as she realized that she was being rejected because her family had lost everything. This told her a great deal about the Carters, and she was suddenly aware that she had been blind to their snobbishness before — as long as she was not the target of it.

The other emotion was, strangely enough, a feeling of relief. *I might have married him and found out what kind of a man he is when it was too late.*

Without another word Jori pulled the engagement ring from her finger. She extended it to him. "Tell your family they can stop worrying, Gerald," she said almost dryly. "I'm releasing you."

Gerald Carter was startled — but there was no mistaking the relief that washed across his face. "Oh, you keep the ring, Jori," he said quickly.

"All right, I will," Jori said shortly. She dropped the ring in her pocket and felt a grim satisfaction in knowing that she would sell it at once. She looked at this man whom she had nearly married and thought about how close to disaster she had come. "Good-bye, Gerald. We won't be meeting again."

He tried to speak, but something in her face stopped him. He muttered, "Well, good-bye, Jori, and . . . I wish you the best."

As Gerald left as hastily as he could, Jori pulled the ring out, stared at it for a long moment, thinking how filled with joy she'd been when Gerald had given it to her. Now it was just something to be turned into cash. Looking up at the door, she whispered, "Thanks for the great and wonderful love you gave me, Gerald. I'll never forget it." Burning tears came to her eyes, and with a quick violent gesture she threw the ring at the wall. It struck and fell to the carpet. Jori laughed harshly, then went over and picked it up. "Off to market you go, ring — and so much for romantic dreams of courtship and eternal love in marriage!"

The family was gathered together in the kitchen eating a simple supper that Kate had made. The servants had all been dismissed, so the family had to do their work. Of all of them, Jori missed Caleb House most. Their love of horses had been a strong bond, and when she'd said the last good-bye to him, she'd felt like crying. "You're the gloomiest man I've ever known," she'd said tightly, "but I'm going to miss your predictions of doom."

Caleb had suddenly grinned, a rare thing for him. The grin had spread all over his face. There had been no room for both the grin and his eyes, so his eyes seemed to vanish. "I don't really believe all that bad stuff

I said," he nodded. Taking her hand, he said, "You're going to make it, Jori. You're tough like me." He had turned and left, but his words and the grin had stayed with her.

As soon as Kate had asked the blessing Jori said loudly, "I'm not marrying Gerald."

Leland was surprised. He put his fork down and stared at Jori. "What do you mean you're not marrying him?"

"His family decided that we didn't have enough money."

Leland flushed. "You can't tell me, Jori, that they would do a thing like that because —"

"Yes, Papa, I can."

"I could have told you that," Kate said. "Good for you! The man had no more backbone than a jellyfish!"

"I'm glad, sister," Carleen said at once. "I never liked him much anyway."

Mark was staring at his sister. "You could sue him for breach of promise."

"No, but I got this out of him." She reached into her pocket and pulled out the solitary diamond. She handed it to her father and said, "Sell that and get what you can for it."

Leland took the engagement ring, stared at it. It was just another minor disaster, and he shook his head sadly. "I'll see what I can do," he said, slipping it into his pocket.

Kate got up, went over and put her good hand on Jori's shoulder. "That was a close call. You'd have been miserable married to a jellyfish." She stroked Jori's shoulder in a loving gesture. "That ring was the best part of him, anyway. Now you can wait until God sends you a good man."

Jori's lips drew tight, and she said rebelliously, "God will have a long wait, Aunt Kate. Men! I'm finished with the breed!"

Carleen piped up at once, "But how will you have babies if you don't have a husband?"

Jori laughed shortly as she rose from the table and gave them all a defiant look. "I'll adopt orphans!" she declared, and stalked out of the dining room.

Jori threw herself into the business of disassembling the life that they all had known. Everything not absolutely essential had to be sold. A place to live had to be found, but most of all they had to have a *way* to live. Her dreams had been so bad that she'd slept little. Most of them had been filled with fantastic scenes so terrible that she woke up in a cold sweat. She didn't speak of this to anyone but dreaded going to bed with every nerve crying out.

"It looks like we're going to have about ten thousand dollars left after everything is sold and the bills are all paid." Jori was sitting at her father's desk, going over the bills. She looked up and shook her head. "That's all we'll have, Papa."

"That's not much, is it, daughter?"

"No, it's not," Jori said. "It's not enough capital to loan out and live on the interest."

"But if we use the capital, we'll have nothing when it's gone."

Jori Hayden was a strong-minded young woman. She had taken a double blow and taken it well. The loss of the family fortune was the worst, but being rejected by Gerald and his family, though less painful, had still been unpleasant.

"We'll have to go into business," Jori said, "using this as a start."

"But, Jori, I don't know any other business except being a stockbroker." Bitterness tinged his voice as he added, "And I was a total failure at that."

Jori went over and put her arms around her father. She felt a great pity for him, for he was really a man who did not know how to handle trouble. Neither did she, but as she put her arms around him, she knew that she was stronger than him.

"We'll have to learn," she said firmly.

"There's something out there we can do, and we'll find it, Papa!" She spoke with all the force she could summon, but doubt tugged at her even as she spoke, dragging her down like an anchor.

CHAPTER THREE

Jori looked up wearily from the scattered papers on the table in front of her. The sound of a voice flowed in from the front street, and she rose and went to the window. The frost had coated the pane, so she lifted the window and looked down onto the yard beneath. A young boy bundled up in a coat far too large for him and with a wool stocking cap pulled down to his eyes looked up at her. He was pulling a wagon and had come to the front door singing his song:

Peanuts!
Two bags for five!

They brush your teeth,
They curl your hair;
They make you feel
Like a millionaire!

Peanuts!
Two bags for five!

For a moment Jori stood watching until the door opened as she expected it would and Carleen came out, took two bags from the boy, gave him some coins then disappeared. The boy, whistling an off-key tune, pulled his wagon around and trudged along down the driveway, singing his peanut song.

Jori moved heavily back to the desk, sat down, and stared at the papers. Slowly she moved them around, making notations in a tablet. She had taken over the business of selling what could be sold and had thrown herself into the work so completely that she went to bed tired each night. Still, as she sat there, the thought of poverty touched her and laid a frost on her nerves. She had never known want, and the idea was frightening to her.

She stayed at the job, doggedly trying to sort out those things she simply could not bear to put up for sale and listing those that she could. At times she felt like an equilibrist, striving desperately to keep her balance on a high wire. Once she heard a carriage stop outside but didn't leave the desk. Shortly afterward the sound of horse hooves came faintly leaving the driveway and heading for the main road. Following this she heard footsteps coming up the steps and looked up as the door opened. "What is it, Kate?"

"It's not good news." Kate stepped inside, shut the door, and came over to stand beside Jori. "That was the police."

"The police! What did they want?"

"It's Mark. He's in jail."

Jori stared at her aunt, disbelief in her eyes. "What do you mean in jail? What's he done?"

"It's not serious — or so they said. The charge is drunk and disorderly, but someone has to go down and pay the fine, and I'd rather it wasn't Leland."

Jori leaned back in her chair and closed her eyes. "Well, that's just what we needed," she said bitterly, "a drunk in the family."

"Mark's not a drunk. A drunk is someone who gets drunk all the time. Mark's unhappy as we all are. Don't worry about it," she said. "I'll go pay the fine."

"How much will it be?"

"I don't know, but I'll pay it. How are you doing with the list?"

"I think I'd like to just put the whole thing up for sale," Jori said bitterly, "rather than sell it all piecemeal."

"Don't be foolish." Kate gave Jori a hug, adding, "You're doing a fine job. I'll go down and get Mark out."

Mark emerged from the inner bowels of the Little Rock Police Station looking like it had been a rough night. His right ear was red and swollen, and he had evidently thrown up on his clothes. He looked all in all perfectly miserable. "Here he is, ma'am," the officer grinned. "A little the worse for wear, but he'll live."

"Thank you, officer. Come along, Mark. I've already paid your fine."

Mark had a hangdog expression. He said nothing, however, and when they were outside he became suddenly defiant. "I guess I'll never hear the last of this. A Hayden in jail!"

"I don't think you'll be hearing much about it."

"It wasn't my fault. I was just having a drink and this fellow —"

"You drive," Kate interrupted as they stepped in the carriage.

She waited until Mark had spoken to the horses and they had begun their journey homeward before she turned to face him, "Mark, you're acting like a baby."

"I don't want to hear any sermons,

Aunt Kate."

"I don't care what you want. Listen to me. You've never had any hard times, and now you're having some. You're not handling it well."

Mark ducked his head. "I know it," he muttered, "but what am I going to do? I'm not fit for *anything,* Aunt Kate!"

"Well, whatever is ahead of you won't be handed to you on a silver platter. We're all going to have a different kind of life, but that doesn't mean it has to be bad."

Mark Hayden stared at his aunt. She had a steadiness about her, a calmness, that he envied. She alone of the family had known no anxiety or fear at all of what lay ahead. He started to say something but realized that whatever he said wouldn't mean anything. "What did Father say about all this?"

"He doesn't know about it, and I don't think he needs to unless you want to tell him yourself."

"I'll do that. It would get back to him anyhow."

"It's always best to face up to the truth. You've got to get home and clean up. Your father's bringing a guest home for supper."

Mark stared at her in disbelief. "A guest for supper? What do you mean? I don't think any of us are really in the mood for having jolly parties for guests."

"I don't know who he is," Kate said calmly, "but I want you to go home and clean yourself up and try to be a little bit more positive, encourage your sisters. You're a man, Mark — so act like one!"

Albert Blanchard was in his midfifties, approximately the same age as Leland. The two of them had been in college together, but it was obvious that Blanchard's life had taken a different road. He was weathered, his face was deeply lined. His hands, they all saw, were hard with calluses. He was wearing a snuff brown suit and heavy boots that had not been polished in recent memory. He had a bushy beard that covered the lower part of his face, and his eyes were black and lively. He had a husky voice, and from time to time he would break into a slight stutter.

Leland had introduced him as simply an old friend from his college days, and all of them were wondering why Leland had chosen to bring him home. It was the first guest they had had since the blow had fallen. Kate had plunged in at once and made a good supper. It consisted of thick fried pork chops, red potatoes, creamed peas and onions, fresh baked bread, and a variety of cheeses and fruit for dessert.

They were having dinner in the smaller and less formal of the two dining rooms. After they had had their dessert, Leland leaned back and said, "I haven't heard from Albert in a long time, but I got a letter from him a few months ago. In the letter he told me about a venture I might be interested in. I wasn't interested at the time, but now I think I'd like for you to hear about it. Maybe you'd like to tell them about it, Al."

Al Blanchard brushed his whiskers back to take another sip of the strong coffee. He set his cup down and looked around the table. "Well, I don't know whether it's something that will appeal to you or not, but here's what it is. I guess maybe you don't know about Santa Fe. It's a trading center just this side of California. Up until now Spain has owned it, and, I'm tellin' you folks, she was plumb cutthroat in her taxation! The only way to get any goods there was to go through Vera Cruz, and then the merchandise had to be toted two thousand miles away on pack mules. Well, the cost of all that transportation, the tax, and Spanish merchants there brought the price of goods up somethin' fearful. A piece of calico that costs a few cents a yard in Boston sells there for three dollars a yard."

Mark leaned forward, his face alight with interest. "Why, that's an unheard of margin of profit."

"I reckon so," Blanchard nodded. "But it's so. I took one load myself. It's a hard tough trip, but I made some money on it."

"How far is it?"

"About eight hundred miles from Missouri, but maybe you heard about the revolution down in Mexico."

"I read a little about that," Kate said. "The Mexicans won their independence, didn't they?"

"They sure enough did, ma'am, and that's changed things pretty sharp. Santa Fe's wide open now. They ain't got no other way to get goods except to have the Spanish haul them in from San Francisco, and the Spanish are downright lazy. They won't be doin' much haulin'. So, like I told Leland, it's the right time to jump in and make some money."

"I don't know exactly how to get there," Jori said uncertainly.

"Well, look, I got a map right here. It ain't the best, but you can all come and take a look at it." They all got up and gathered around the map that Blanchard took from his inner pocket and unfolded. "Right here," he said, "is Franklin, Missouri, right in the western border. You see this river here? That's the Kansas River. The trail follows that until it gets to the Arkansas River, and then it hooks around and goes all the way to La Junta. Then you turn north and run along the Sangre de Cristo Mountains right into Santa Fe. Santa Fe is right on the Rio Grande River, don't you see."

"That river goes all the way to Texas."

"Yep, it shore does, but it ain't quite as safe goin' up from Texas. You have to cross through territories jist crawlin' with the Comanche and Cherokee and Shawnee. Best to stay away from those red devils if you can."

Jori listened as Blanchard spoke glowingly of the profit to be made, but finally she said, "But, Mr. Blanchard, we don't know anything about freighting."

"I didn't reckon as how you did, Miss Jori, but I thought you might hire a good man to take the train through."

"Why don't you do it, Mr. Blanchard?" Kate said. "You've made the trip."

"Takes a young man and a tough one. I might have done it in my younger days, Miss Johnson, but I'm past that now."

Leland suddenly said, "We always were pretty honest with each other in the old days, Al. I'm going to tell you now that we're pretty desperate." He laughed self-consciously and said, "I've got to find something to do. So far nothing has turned up. I feel a little bit like a man in the middle of a bridge that doesn't have any ends and all I can do is look down at the water."

"Why, it ain't that bad, Leland," Al Blanchard said warmly. "You're a young man. You can start all over again. I've had to do it twice. Lost my shirt in two ventures. But if I can do it, you can too."

"How much would it cost to get a train to Santa Fe?"

"Well, it depends on a lot of things. You've got to buy wagons and lots of mules or oxen. Then you got to buy the trade goods, and then at the other end of the line you have to pay the mule skinners off. It will take a bunch of them."

"How big should the train be?"

"I'd say maybe four big wagons, maybe twenty men countin' the mule skinners. Somebody to take care of the herd and cook. Oh, and you got to have about fifty mules."

"That seems like a lot for just a few wagons."

"Don't hurt to have more in case you get jumped by the Pawnee. They raid up north sometimes. Takes pretty tough men. I'm just

61

guessing, but I'd say somewhere between fifteen and twenty thousand dollars to do it."

Leland did not speak, but his eyes met Jori's. Both of them knew they would not have that much money even after everything was sold. "I want to thank you for sharing this with us. You're sure you're not going to get involved with it?"

"No, I got another venture or two."

"But you'd be willing to give us advice," Kate said, "in case we decide to do it?"

"Why, I'm mighty free with my talk, Miss Johnson," Blanchard smiled. "I have to throw this in though. It's a risky business. It's dangerous and it's hard, but the rewards are great."

Blanchard did not stay long after supper, and after he left the family sat around talking for a time.

"I don't see how we can do it, Papa," Jori said. "In the first place, we don't have enough money. And in the second place, if we did have enough money, it would take it all to make the trip. What would the rest of us do?" Jori paused. "We'd have to live, and that trip would take several months."

Kate sat quietly listening, and finally she heard her brother-in-law say, "Well, I didn't tell you about this, but I have a job offer with the Carter office."

"What kind of an offer?" Jori demanded. She had not forgiven the Carter family for advising Gerald to cast her off.

"Well, I'd be a clerk, more or less, a junior clerk at first."

"I won't let you do that!" Jori exclaimed. "We'll find something."

"Well, we can think about it for a little while, but Al says if we're going to do it, we'll have to get started by April. And that's not much time. It seems impossible to me."

The rest, more or less, agreed with him, all except Kate. She said nothing but spent the night seeking God in prayer.

Kate was late for breakfast. When she came down there was a light in her eyes, and she said, "I want to tell you about a dream I had last night." The rest of them were seated, but she stood looking at them with her eyes bright. "I dreamed of wagons with canvas tops, just the kind that Mr. Blanchard was talking about. They were pulled by mules."

"You think that means we're supposed to go into this?" Mark asked. He shook his head doubtfully. "I think we need more than that."

"There's more to the dream," Kate said.

"I dreamed that there were people walking alongside the wagons, and when I got closer, I saw that it was us. It was our family. We were all filed alongside the wagons headed to some place."

"It was just a dream," Mark mumbled.

"No, it wasn't. As I was watching us go along the trail with the wagons, I heard a voice. It said, 'Get thee out of thy country, and from thy kindred, and from thy father's house, unto a land that I will show thee.' "

"That sounds familiar," Leland said, shaking his head. "I can't place it."

"It's from the twelfth Chapter of Genesis," Kate said. "It's in the first verse. God said that when He called Abraham out of his home into a new country."

"Wait a minute," Jori said. "You're not suggesting that all of us go join that wagon train, are you, Aunt Kate?"

"Yes. That's what I'm saying. I believe it's what God wants us to do."

"Why, we can't do that," Mark exclaimed. "We don't know a thing about wagon trains!"

"We can do it," Carleen said, her face alive with excitement. "We can all go!" Her eyes were dancing, and she got up and stood next to Aunt Kate. "It'd be just like the frontier that you told me about."

"It will be pretty rough, honey."

The argument went back and forth with only Kate and Carleen in favor. Finally Leland stared at his sister-in-law. "Are you telling me we need to move to Santa Fe?"

"Why not? If we stay here, we'll soon run out of money," Kate said. "Besides, if Al Blanchard is right, we can make enough money to live there comfortably. Once we make the trip, we can send somebody back and make another trip, and there's bound to be something to haul from Santa Fe back on the return journey."

"But we're city people!" Leland protested.

"So was Abraham — from the city Ur of the Chaldees."

Mark threw up his hands. "It's crazy!"

Finally Leland said, "I don't know what to say."

"The least you can do, Leland, is to ask Al Blanchard what he thinks about it."

"All right. We'll do that, but I can tell you right now he'll think we're as crazy as I do."

Al Blanchard listened as Leland explained their proposal. He lifted his eyebrows with surprise, but he was not in shock. "Why, I never thought about you takin' your family, Leland."

"I never thought of it either, but we've got

to do something," Leland said. His face was tense, and he faced his friend squarely. "Can it be done, Al?"

"Well, shore, with the right man I believe you could make it."

"What's the country like around Santa Fe, Al?" Jori asked.

"Why, ma'am, it's the finest country you ever seen. Air is clear as any you'll ever breathe."

"But it's in the backwoods!" Mark protested.

"Well, it's not Little Rock, but if you establish a freight line, you can move back here and run it from this end or else you could move to San Francisco. That's citified enough for you."

The talk went on for a long time, and finally Al shook his head. "One thing is shore. Whether you make it or not depends on the man who runs the train, the wagon master."

"Do you know anyone you could recommend, Al?" Leland asked.

Blanchard shrugged his shoulders and seemed to be running through something in his mind. Finally he said, "Well, if I was gonna go into this myself, I reckon the man I'd want for my wagon master would be Rocklin."

"Rocklin? Who is he?"

"Well, he's all sorts of a fella." Blanchard shrugged and turned to face Jori, who had asked the question. "The thing about him is he knows the country better than any man in the West, I reckon, and he's tough. He's done some mule skinnin' himself, and he knows how to boss men. But you can't get him."

"Why not?" Jori asked. "Would he be too expensive?"

"No, it ain't that, ma'am. See the thing is, he's in jail in Fort Smith."

"Is he an outlaw?" Carleen cried at once, her eyes brightening.

"Well," Blanchard grinned and faced the young girl, "that ain't quite been settled yet, missy. Rocklin's kind of on the edge of a razor. If he falls off on the left side, he might be an outlaw. If he falls off the other side, he won't be. He's been kind of waverin' between the two, don't you see? But the thing is, he ain't never killed nobody that didn't deserve it."

Jori straightened up and stared at Blanchard with incomprehension. "He's a killer?"

"I reckon you see things different here, ma'am. You've lived in a civilized place all your life, but Rocklin, like lots of other fellas, has lived among the Indians and the worst men you can even think of. He's had a rough life, ma'am, and he's had to fight to save his own skin."

"I think we need a tough man," Kate put in. "But if he's in jail, he couldn't lead the train."

"Oh, he ain't charged with anything serious, Miss Johnson. He's just in the city jail there in Fort Smith. It ain't like he's in the federal pen or nothin'."

"What's he in jail for?"

"There was some liquor involved and a fight, and a man got shot. I ain't sayin' he didn't deserve it, but he had some influential friends. If you go see Sheriff Oswalt and explain it all, I think he'd be willin' to put Rocklin on probation."

That was the essence of Blanchard's visit. He had offered to write a letter to the man called Rocklin if someone decided to go look into the matter, and just before he left, he cautioned them. "I'm warnin' you, the Staked Plains ain't like Little Rock."

As soon as Blanchard was gone, Jori said, "My head's swimming. I don't know how to think."

"Well, I do," Kate said. "I still believe God wants us to go."

"You may be right, Kate," Leland said.

"It's a big thing, and it's so — so unorganized."

Kate suddenly laughed. "You think like a stockbroker, that everything has to be organized."

"Well, someone has to make plans."

"Of course they do, and that's what we're doing. But it's not going to be like a trip to Central Park," Kate said. She thought for a moment and said, "You know, I imagine when Moses struck the rock and the water poured out; some folks were complaining because he didn't use a fancier stick."

"What's that supposed to mean, Aunt Kate?" Mark asked with irritation.

"It means we're gonna have to use any kind of stick we can get to keep this family together, and this is the one that I see is in front of us."

The talk went on for over an hour, and finally Leland shook his head. "Remember the preacher last week preached on Moses, how that he prayed for his people when they were in battle. He held his hands up, and as long as he held them up, Joshua and the soldiers won. But when his arms grew tired and he dropped them, the army of Israel failed. Well," he said in a weary voice, "I'm like Moses, only it's my thoughts that are so tired that I can't seem to hold them up."

At that instant Jori Hayden knew she had to step to her father's aid. Mark was too unstable. She was the oldest child and the strongest in many ways. She said strongly, "I think Aunt Kate's right. We've got to do this. I'll go to Fort Smith at once and talk to the sheriff there about getting this man Rocklin."

"But he's an outlaw, or an almost outlaw," Mark protested.

"I'd use Blackbeard if I had to to make a new life for ourselves, Mark," Jori said. "I'm leaving first thing in the morning!"

CHAPTER FOUR

The narrow-gauged, wood-burning engine that had pulled the four cars from Little Rock to Fort Smith had passed out of the flatlands into mountain country. Jori ignored the cinders that came in from the window that some of the passengers opened despite the cold and enjoyed the green forest of firs and pines that covered the sides of the Ozarks.

The train pulled into Fort Smith emitting a shrill banshee scream, and when Jori saw Fort Smith itself she was disappointed. The town was a rough collection of false wooden fronts, and a wide central street had been churned to a sea of brown mud by late rains. Getting up from her seat, Jori moved stiffly down the aisle, thinking grimly *How could anything good come out of this mud-hole?* The conductor, a bulky, red-faced individual with a pair of piercing blue eyes, reached up to take her hand, grunting,

"Watch your step, miss." She took his hand, placed her foot on the steel portable step, and gave him a brief smile of thanks as she stepped down.

A quick look revealed a shabby building that had once been painted a brilliant turkey red, but time had weathered it to a faded brown. She waited until her suitcase was tossed off by a tall brakeman, then looked around to find someone to carry it, but there was no one. Only two people had gotten off the train, an elderly woman who was greeted by a younger couple and a short, rotund soldier wearing a rumpled private's uniform. He gave her a careless glance, then headed for town.

"Can I help you, miss?"

Jori turned to see a tall individual who was bundled up in a heavy overcoat. His Adam's apple was the most prominent feature, and he had a rather foolish grin.

"Can you tell me how to find the sheriff's office?"

"Why shore, ma'am. Go on down to that big street there, and you take the second turn. Ain't no trouble to find. Anybody can tell you. You in trouble that you need a sheriff?"

Jori smiled at the man's curiosity. "Not really," she said. "Thank you very much."

Stepping inside the station, she found herself facing a small man with a face turned blue by the cold who greeted her at once. "Help you, miss?"

"I'd like to leave my luggage here, please."

"I'll take that for you." The agent took Jori's bag, but before putting it away, he cocked his head to one side then asked, "Staying long in town, are you?"

"Not too long," Jori smiled, wondering if everyone in Fort Smith examined newcomers. Stepping outside, she followed the wide cinder path that led to the main street. The two lines of false front stores and shops were flung out apparently without thought, for they did not align themselves with the main street. As she moved forward she found herself depressed by the town. The people she passed, both men and women, were roughly dressed, and most men, it seemed, chewed tobacco.

As the train bellowed shrilly and left the town behind, Jori made her way down to the boardwalk that lined the edges of the streets. She passed by a hardware store, a blacksmith shop, and a milliner's with delicate hats in the window, which surprised her. *What woman living in this mudhole would buy fancy hats?*

As she drew even with one of the saloons,

a sudden explosion startled her. A man sitting in a chair tilted back against a storefront had just fired down the alleyway at some sort of target that she could not see. Twisting his head, he grinned at her and lifted the rifle. "Howdy, ma'am. You're new in town, I reckon?"

Does everybody want to know your personal business in Fort Smith? Jori thought with some irritation. The man turned his head slightly and loosed a flow of amber tobacco juice. Some of it hit the ground, some ran down his beard which was already crusted.

"I'm looking for the sheriff's office."

"Why, you want me to take you down there, sweetheart?"

"No, thank you. If you could just tell me how to find it."

"Go right down that there street and take the next turn to the right. If you're stayin' in town, they're havin' a dance tonight. Maybe me and you can do some fancy dancin'."

"Thank you, no. I won't be here that long."

Jori continued down the street until she reached the intersection. She turned right and at once saw a sign across the street: JAIL AND SHERIFF'S OFFICE.

"Hey, there, honey, come on up! You look

like you need a real man!"

Startled, Jori looked up to see two barred windows, both of them outlining men who were staring down at her. They called down with crude remarks, and she hurriedly entered the office.

"Well, ma'am, you caught me off guard."

The speaker was a rotund individual but appeared hard as a rock. He was sitting in a chair with one bare foot up on the desk and a pair of huge shears in one hand. He held the foot steady with the other hand and took a cut. The toenail sailed off, and the individual grunted with satisfaction. "Pardon me, ma'am. Didn't expect no visitors. I'm Sheriff Oswalt." He stuffed his foot into a boot and came to his feet. His eyes were an unusual shade of gray, and he had a huge sweeping mustache that almost hid his mouth. "Can I help you, ma'am?"

"My name is Jori Hayden. I need to speak to one of your prisoners, Sheriff Oswalt."

"Well, now, which one would that be, Miss Hayden?"

"His name is Rocklin."

"Oh, yeah, Chad. You be wantin' to see him?" For a moment he struggled, and Jori was certain that he was attempting to keep himself from asking, *Why would you want to see him?* He managed to overcome the temptation, and suddenly Jori decided it would be best to talk to him first.

"Do you have a few moments, sheriff?"

"Why, certain I do, ma'am. Here, take this cheer." Oswalt came around the desk, moving quite quickly for such a big man. With one hand he swept a calico cat off of the cane-bottom chair saying, "Git, Ginger!" then dragged it around in front of his desk. He waited until she was seated then went back and took his seat behind the desk. "Exactly whut is it you'd like to talk about? Is it official business?"

"Oh, yes. I live in Little Rock with my family. . . ."

As Jori told the story — at least all that she thought the sheriff might want to hear — she noticed that he had a habit of twisting his mouth to one side as if he were trying to shake off a fly. There was no fly, so she assumed it was purely nerves. Finally she ended by saying, ". . . so you see our friend Mr. Blanchard believes that your prisoner would be the best man to lead a wagon train to Santa Fe."

"Wal, now, you know he's been arrested and waitin' trial?"

"I don't know much about the details, sheriff. Is it serious?"

Oswalt rocked back and forth in his seat,

and his mouth twitched rapidly. "Wal, yes — and no. It was an argument over some whiskey that somehow got sold to some Indians. That's against the law around here, don't you see? I ain't been able to get the right of it yet. As far as I know Chad ain't never been in the business of sellin' liquor to nobody, but he was there. There was a shootin', and they's about half a dozen different stories. A fellow was shot up and died — and there's gonna be a trial of everybody that was mixed up with it."

"Would it be possible at all for Rocklin to be released in my custody?"

Oswalt shook his head thoughtfully, then took out a cigar from his inner pocket. He bit the end off, spit it on the floor, then struck a kitchen match on the desk leaving another track on the scarred surface. He held the tip of the cigar in the glowing flame until it was puffing nicely then finally he said, "I reckon that might be done. I think myself Rocklin was just in the wrong place at the wrong time. But Judge Chatham, he's liable to think different."

"But do you have the authority to turn him loose?"

"I guess I can do that. The other fellers might holler some." A faint humor stirred in Oswalt's eyes. "Don't reckon as how you'd want to take the other three, too? Save the taxpayers the cost of a trial."

Jori smiled. The sheriff seemed an amiable enough man. "No, but I would very much like to have you release the prisoner to my father. He's a very respectable businessman in Little Rock. You could check with the governor there. They're good friends."

"Wal, now, I'll tell you what, Miss Hayden. I'll let you talk to Rocklin, and if he agrees, I'll take your word for it and we can work out the details." He got up suddenly from his chair, saying cheerfully, "We got a room down here where you can talk private like."

Jori followed Sheriff Oswalt down the hall saturated with the odor of old cabbage and rank bodies. He opened a door that had a hasp and a padlock on the outside. "I'll have to lock you in when I bring him, you understand?"

"Of course, sheriff."

Jori entered and found that the furnishings consisted of two battered chairs and one table even more dilapidated. She sat down cautiously in the chair and waited. One small window admitted a pale shaft of light that touched a battered cuspidor, which had been overused it seemed to her.

She waited nervously arranging in her mind the speech that she would make to Rocklin. It was a task that she had not looked forward to, but something that had to be done. *I must be crazy coming here like this. How can we put our trust in a man we know nothing about — except that he's in jail.* Finally she heard steps coming down the corridor, then the sheriff opened the door and said, "Here he is, ma'am. Chad, this here is Miss Hayden. Miss Hayden, this is Rocklin. Like I say, I'll have to lock the door."

"You sure I'll be safe with her, Billy?"

Chad Rocklin was not what Jori had expected. She was prepared to see someone more brutal, but Rocklin appeared pleasant enough. He was a tall man, over six feet she guessed. His face was wedge shaped and topped by thick tawny hair roughly cut. His eyes, deep set and wide spaced, were a startling shade of light blue. He had a straight English nose, a cleft chin, and she noted a scar along his left jawbone going down into his shirt collar. He wore buckskins, dirty and shrunk until they fitted his lean body almost like a second skin, and he wore moccasins such as she had never seen before.

His eyes were fixed on her, and he had a slight smile on his broad lips. For some reason this made Jori nervous — and this angered her. She had expected to dominate the man, but she could tell this was not going to happen.

"You behave yourself now, Chad, you hear me?"

"You know, Billy, I think it'd be better if you gave me one of those good cigars of yours. It'd calm my nerves down, and I wouldn't be as likely to attack this young woman."

Oswalt suddenly laughed, reached into his pocket, and came out with a cigar and three matches. "If I thought givin' you a cigar would make a respectable citizen out of you, I'd of given you one a long time ago, Chad. Miss Hayden, you just holler when you're ready to leave."

The door closed behind the sheriff, and Jori heard the lock go into the hasp. She found it difficult to think of a way to talk to the man, and finally blurted out, "I need to talk with you." It sounded inane, and she saw Rocklin stare at her curiously, then move over to the window where he stood looking out without saying a word. He seemed to have forgotten Jori, and she tried to think of some way to speak of her mission.

"I miss birds in this place."

"I'm sure. Rocklin, I would like to —"

"I saw a bird die once." Rocklin's voice was soft as a summer breeze and had a hint of the South in it.

The sentence seemed senseless and had absolutely nothing to do with what was in Jori's mind. "What's unusual about that? Lots of birds die," she said with asperity.

Rocklin turned to face her. He leaned his back against the wall and crossed his arms. She noticed that his hands were square and very strong looking. "It was on the Missouri in the headwaters. I had been trapping beaver, and I looked up and saw this bird straight over my head not over fifteen feet up, flying as hard as you please. I was about to look back at the trap I was baiting when suddenly he just fell out of the sky."

Jori was bewildered. "What killed him?"

"Nothing," Rocklin said quietly with a look of wonder in his cornflower blue eyes. "I went over and picked him up. There wasn't a mark on him. He just died." He took the cigar that Billy had given him, bit the end off, spit it out the window then lit it. She watched him, wondering if the story had some meaning. When the cigar was glowing, he suddenly blew a series of perfect smoke rings. "Aren't those rings pretty now? It took me a long time to learn how to make smoke rings."

"Well, yes, I'm sure they're very nice, but —"

"About that bird. It occurred to me that he didn't have an idea when he woke up that morning that he was going to be dead that night. He didn't know he was about to leave this earth." Suddenly he removed the cigar, held it lightly, looked at it for a long moment, then he turned to face her. "Kind of like it is for us. When we wake up in the morning, as far as we know, it's our last day on earth. We're the same way as that bird, don't you think?"

At that moment Jori had to rethink her position or at least the way that she would speak to this man. She expected a dirty, rough-looking mule skinner with blunt features and a rough speech, but one like that would never have made the observation that Rocklin had just made.

"I suppose you're right," she said, "but we can't go back to bed and cover up, can we?"

"No, you're right. I sure thought about that bird a lot though. What do you want to see me about, Miss Hayden?"

Now that Jori was confronted by the man's direct gaze, she spoke very carefully. "My father wants to take a wagon train loaded with trade goods to Santa Fe. We have a friend whose name is Albert Blanchard."

"Al Blanchard? Why, he's a friend of mine."

"I know. He recommended you to lead the train across to Santa Fe, and I've come down to see if we could hire you to do that."

Rocklin laughed shortly, took a puff on the cigar, and blew another smoke ring. "Maybe you didn't notice this is a jail. There's a lock on the door. Billy out there is a good fellow, but he'd shoot me if I tried to get away."

"I've talked to the sheriff about this. He's willing to release you in my father's custody if you're willing to take the job."

"Billy said that?"

"Yes, he did." Jori was very confident now. "About the money. I'm sure —"

"Miss Hayden," Rocklin interrupted her, "I want you to know that I appreciate the offer, but I'll have to turn you down."

"But why? It would get you out of this place."

"It would never work," Rocklin shrugged. He leaned back against the wall and studied her thoughtfully. "I don't think you folks have any idea what kind of a thing you're proposing."

"Mr. Blanchard told us it would be a hard

trip, but we're ready to take the chance."

"*We're* ready? What do you mean *we're* ready to take the chance?"

"Why, my family and I. We're going along." Jori thought for one moment of telling him about their financial problems, but she was too embarrassed. "We thought we might buy a place and live in Santa Fe."

Rocklin shook his head. "Well, Miss Hayden, I'll tell you right now. I might get the train through, but no man with sense would take you and your family along."

"But we're ready to take the chance."

"Well, I'm not. In the first place, I won't work for a woman." He saw her face grow stubborn and added quickly, "I don't think you understand exactly what a wagon master is. Most people don't. He's like the captain of a ship, Miss Hayden. His word's the law. For instance," he said. He paused and took another puff on the cigar and blew two more smoke rings. "What would you do if we were halfway to Santa Fe and I told you to do somethin' you didn't want to do?"

"Why, we'd discuss it."

"No. I'd make you do it the same way I'd make a man do it."

Jori felt a flash of anger. She stared at him with rebellion in the set of her lips. He was watching her carefully, and she noted that he made an idle shape standing there. His lips had a rolling half smile, as if he knew the rules of a game that she didn't. "I'm a reasonable woman," she snapped, stung by his attitude.

"I don't mean to be insulting, but you don't know what you're talking about. You're not an outdoor woman, and I take it your family's the same. When you're on a trek like you propose, there has to be decisions made sometimes in an instant with no time for debate. The boss has to do some unreasonable things. Nope, thanks for the offer, but you'd better get yourself another man, Miss Hayden. But anyhow, I got me a good cigar out of your visit. I enjoyed talking with you. Talk to Blanchard. He knows lots of men that might do that job for you."

Jori could not answer she was so stunned. "You mean you'd rather stay in jail?"

"Reckon so. It beats being dead." Suddenly Rocklin moved to the door, rapped on it hard with his fist, and hollered, "Billy — we're all done."

Jori heard the lock rattle in the hasp so quickly she thought that the sheriff must have been outside listening. "Better put me back in my room. Me and Miss Hayden have finished our talk."

Oswalt gave the pair a curious look, then

nodded. "Miss Hayden, you go down to my office. I'll take Chad back up to his cell."

Jori waited until the two had vanished then got up and walked stiffly down the corridor. She moved through the door, and when she got into the sheriff's office, she stood there waiting until he came back. "I take it Chad turned you down."

"Yes. I don't understand it. I don't want to insult your jail, sheriff, but it seems to me like a man would do almost anything to get out of here."

"Most men would, but Chad Rocklin now, he's as stubborn as a blue-nosed mule. I reckon you'd better get yourself another fellow, Miss Hayden."

"Well, I thank you for letting me see him, sheriff. The train doesn't leave until morning for Little Rock. I'll need a place to stay."

"Hotel's right down the street. You tell the clerk that I sent you down. He'll give you a good price and look out for you. Sorry it didn't work out, Miss Hayden."

"Thank you, sheriff."

The room was framed with rough lumber, and there was a single window with a shade discolored by sun and rain. The bed was an old one of good make, but the mattress and quilt were almost unspeakable. The floor had been painted once but now was worn to a leprous gray.

Jori had eaten in the restaurant and then had made her way back quickly to the room. She had received several crude invitations from rough-looking men on the way and was relieved to get back in the room. There was no key for the door so she shoved the single, straight-backed chair under the knob.

It was still early, but there was nothing to do and no heat in the room, so she decided to go to bed. Pouring the icy water in the pitcher into a basin, she found she could not bear the cold water, so she hastily undressed and put on the heavy nightgown that she had brought. She also put on a pair of heavy socks and slipped under the covers, shaking almost violently with the cold. She thought of the warmth of her own bedroom with longing, and tried to go to sleep.

There were other guests in adjoining rooms, and the walls were so thin she could hear the profane talk of two men. She lay awake for a long time until finally a quiet came to the hotel. Her mind was on the mission that had brought her here, and she was disgusted that she had failed. She was a stubborn woman, accustomed to having her own way, and failure of any kind stirred a deep resentment. Her anger was concentrated on Chad Rocklin. She remembered his words about women and how he would point-blank refuse to work for one. She doubled up her fist and whispered, "He must be a fool! Only a stupid man would choose to stay in that place rather than get out and make some money!"

For more than an hour Jori tossed and turned, trying to think of some way out of her dilemma. Perhaps Blanchard did know someone else, but he had been so positive that Rocklin would be exactly the right man for the job. Finally she lay still, and her mind worked rapidly. An idea came to her, and eagerly she seized on it. She was an imaginative girl, quick-witted and strong-willed, and as she developed the scheme in her mind, she began to smile. Finally she laughed and said aloud, "We'll see in the morning who wins this argument, Mr. Chad Rocklin!"

"Well, you're back, Miss Hayden."

"Yes, sheriff. I wanted to ask your help." Jori had eaten a poorly cooked breakfast at the restaurant and had waited impatiently until the sheriff's office had opened at eight o'clock. She had been watching, and she saw that he was surprised as she plunged

88

into her scheme. She had to behave a little differently from her ordinary ways, but Jori Hayden would have been a good actress. She tried to make herself as helpless as possible as she said, "Sheriff, I didn't tell you everything. My family and I are in serious trouble. . . ." She kept her voice soft on a pleading note, and looked up at him, holding her eyes wide open so that he could see how troubled she seemed to be. She told about how the financial panic had caught them and how this was the only way that they could possibly survive. Finally she said, "I know Rocklin said no, but I believe I thought of a way that you could influence him to change his mind."

"Why, he ain't an easy man to influence. What are you thinking?"

"If you could just make it clear to him somehow," Jori whispered confidentially, "that if he doesn't help me, he's going to be in this jail for a *very* long time. Isn't there some sort of . . . well, some sort of way that you could do that?"

Billy Oswalt was a man who loved his humor, and suddenly this seemed like a good joke to play on Chad Rocklin. Rocklin, as a matter of fact, had evaded Oswalt several times, and now the sheriff saw a way to get some of his own back.

"You know, I think I might be able to do that. We'll try anyhow. You set right here, and I'll go get him."

The sheriff disappeared, but soon returned with the prisoner. Rocklin looked at her hard and nodded. "Good morning, Miss Hayden."

"Rocklin," the sheriff said abruptly, "Miss Hayden here has told me the deal she's offered you. I don't mind sayin' I think you're a fool for turnin' her down."

"You're probably right, Billy, but that's my decision."

"Have you thought that you might be in this jail of mine for a year?"

"Why, the trial won't take that long."

"It might. You know how Judge Chatham is. He can be pretty hard tailed. He kept Mike Sidell in here coolin' his heels for that long. I expect he might do the same for you if he gets his back up."

"Why would he get his back up?" Suddenly Rocklin turned and his eyes gleamed as he studied Jori, then his eyes came back to the sheriff. "I see. The deal is, I either go help this woman or you keep me here in your jail for a year."

"Well, the judge and me are pretty close, and you are a dangerous character."

Silence filled the room, and Jori was holding her breath. "I hate to see a lady mis-treated, Chad," Oswalt said righteously. "Besides, you don't have no business in here. Get out of Fort Smith, get out of the territory and go do somethin' different."

"So it's take the job or stay here and rot. Is that right?"

"Your choice," the sheriff grinned.

"Well, Billy," Rocklin said with a slight smile, "you got the best of the argument."

"Good! I'll get your stuff. You take him out of here, Miss Hayden. But you remember, Chad, you're in this young lady's custody. If you give her any trouble, I'll have you picked up and brought back."

"Thank you so much, sheriff, for your help," Jori said warmly. She stood waiting while the sheriff collected what seemed like an armory. There were two pistols in holsters attached to a belt and two rather strange-looking rifles that she had never seen the likes of before. Rocklin took them and said, "I guess I'm ready to go now. Thanks for your hospitality, sheriff."

"You behave yourself now."

"I'll do my best. Tell your wife I enjoyed her good cookin'."

As soon as they were outside, Jori said, "The train's leaving here in less than two hours, Rocklin. We can settle your wages and duties when we get to our house."

"I've got to take my horse. I won't go without him. I'll go back in jail first."

"How could we take a horse?"

"They always have a car for stock going back toward Little Rock. I can ride with him and take care of him."

"Very well. But let's go arrange for the tickets now."

The train had pulled out of Fort Smith at ten o'clock. Jori had waited while Rocklin had put his horse in the car along with his gear. She felt somehow uncertain and nervous about everything, not just about Rocklin but about the whole plan.

Finally as the train made its way through the mountains headed back to the south, Rocklin came in and sat down across from her. "I thought I might find out a little bit about my boss," he said.

Jori was startled. "Find out what?"

"Well, how old are you?"

"What difference does that make?"

"None." Rocklin was smiling as if enjoying a joke of some kind. "Are you married?"

"No."

"How come?"

Jori sat up straighter. "That's none of your business, and it's not pertinent to our relationship."

"You want to ask me about myself? I'm not married. Don't expect to be."

"I don't care in the least about your matrimonial adventures, and I thank you not to ask any more personal questions."

"Just as you say." Rocklin suddenly leaned back, pushed his hat forward, and said, "Wake me when we get to Little Rock."

Jori stared at him for he seemed to be totally relaxed. She somehow knew this man was going to be trouble, but she also knew that her life and those of her family would be in his hands. She sat upright, looking out the window as the scenery flowed by, wondering how she and her family would get along being under this man's total control.

CHAPTER FIVE

Jori waited impatiently while Rocklin examined the big stallion that he called Red. They had arrived in Little Rock in the middle of the night, and Jori was exhausted, her eyes gritty from lack of sleep. She watched as Rocklin went over the horse, patting him and speaking to him softly.

"Can we go now?" she asked impatiently.

"I guess so. How far is it to your home?"

"About thirty minutes, but I'm not sure we can get a cab to take us."

Indeed, this proved to be the case for some time. Finally the station master agreed to have his assistant take them home in his buggy. "I'll have to charge four dollars for that," he had said, and Jori had quickly agreed to it. Fifteen minutes later the two of them were seated in the buggy's backseat. The big stallion Red was tied to the back, and Rocklin's guns were under their feet.

"Pretty night," Rocklin observed. They had not said a word for ten minutes until finally he broke the silence.

Jori shook her head. "I'm so tired I don't even care."

"That's no way to live. You need to look up. See those pretty stars up there?"

Jori looked up involuntarily. Indeed, it was a beautiful night. The weather was cold, and in the open carriage they caught the full chill of the wind. They followed the winding road that led beside the Arkansas River toward the area where the Hayden ancestors had built their house. From time to time the driver turned around to glance at them, but when they remained silent he lost interest.

"You'll probably see a lot of this river."

Rocklin's remark interested Jori. "What do you mean?" she asked.

"The trail to Santa Fe follows alongside the north bank of the Arkansas for a long ways."

"This same river?"

"Same one. Not quite as wide as it is here."

Jori wanted to ask more questions, but she was still apprehensive, wondering if they had done the right thing by hiring this man. She thought, *We haven't hired him yet. He may not be the man to take us.*

Twenty minutes later the driver pulled the buggy to a halt, and Rocklin jumped down. He held up his hand, Jori took it, came to the ground and quickly withdrew her hand. She turned to the driver and paid the fare, saying, "Thank you very much."

"You're welcome."

Jori turned toward the house while Rocklin removed his gear from the floor of the buggy, then her luggage. He moved around to his horse, then waited for her to speak.

"We'll have to wake them up," Jori said. "Everybody's asleep at this hour." She walked up the steps and found the door was unlocked. "There's no sense getting everyone up, but I don't know where you'll sleep."

"Doesn't matter," Rocklin said, shrugging his shoulders. "You have a stable, I guess."

"Oh yes. It's in the back."

"I'll make me a bed in the straw. See you in the morning, Miss Hayden."

He turned and was gone before she could speak. She watched him as he led the horse around the house. She was dissatisfied with the arrangement, but it was too late to wake people up.

Going inside, she groped her way up the stairs, and when she got to her room she closed the door softly. It took all her energy to undress and put on her nightgown. When she got into the bed, the last thought she had was, *Well, we're this far at least. . . .*

"Where did you put him, Jori?" Leland asked. He had come downstairs early to find that Jori had already risen. He listened closely as she told him about getting the sheriff's permission to bring Rocklin with them on probation. Before she had time to finish, Mark and Carleen came down the stairs followed by Kate.

"Where is he?" Carleen said, her eyes dancing. "Is he an outlaw?"

"Don't be foolish!" Jori said irritably. "We got here late. I didn't want to get you all up, so he slept in the stable."

"Well, he's probably hungry," Leland said. "Someone go get him, and he can have breakfast with us."

"I'll go," Carleen said. Before anyone could speak she darted out the door and was gone. Leland grinned ruefully. "I think she's already fallen for our wagon master."

"What's he like, Jori?" Mark asked.

"He's got an outdoor look."

"Well, that's a good thing," Mark grinned, "since the trail to Santa Fe is outdoors. Tell me something more than that."

"No. I'm going to help Aunt Kate fix breakfast."

"I guess we'll all help. Mark, you set the table," Leland said. "I'll fix the coffee."

Carleen slipped inside the barn and looked around and saw no one, but a whinny came to her, and she ran down the aisle that contained the stalls on each side. In one of them was a big red horse looking down at her. Her eyes grew big, and she said, "What's your name?"

"His name is Red."

Carleen whirled to see a man rise up out of the stall on the other side. He had straw in his hair, and for a moment she was frightened. But then she said, "I'll bet you're our wagon master."

"You think so? Maybe I'm a burglar."

"No, you're not a burglar. Burglars don't have horses. You say his name is Red?"

"That's right. What's your name?"

"I'm Carleen."

"Carleen Hayden, I expect."

"Yes. I know your name. It's Rocklin. I heard my sister and my father talking about it."

She watched as the big man came out. He brushed the straw off of his shoulders, and she asked suddenly, "Where's your gun?

Don't you wear a gun?"

"Sometimes I do. I don't think I'll need one today."

Carleen studied him carefully, her eyes big. "How many people have you killed?" she demanded suddenly.

Rocklin suddenly grinned. His teeth looked very white to her against his bronze skin. "Not too many. I killed more of them than they did of me."

"That's foolish!"

"I expect it is. What are you doing down here?"

"I came down to get you for breakfast. They're fixing it."

"I reckon I need to shave first. You know where I can get some water?"

"There's a pump outside. Can I watch you?"

"I charge fifty cents for spectators."

"You're teasing me."

"That's right, Miss Carleen, I am. Come on. You can watch me shave if you like."

"Good, and then we'll go on up to the house and eat breakfast."

"Here they come," Mark said. He was peering out the window of the front door as the two figures appeared. "He's a big one, and he looks pretty tough."

Leland came over to look out. "I guess he is." He opened the door, and as Carleen came skidding in, she said, "He's not wearing his gun, but he's got one."

Ignoring Carleen, Leland put out his hand. "I'm Leland Hayden. This is my son Mark, and you're Rocklin."

"Yes, sir, I am."

"My sister-in-law and my daughter are cooking breakfast. I expect you're hungry."

"I pretty well stay that way, Mr. Hayden."

"Well, come along. It ought to be about ready."

Mark asked as they turned to go in, "What time did you get in?"

"Middle of the night sometime. It was a pretty tiring trip."

"He's got a big red horse whose name is Red. Will you let me ride him, Rocklin?"

"Mr. Rocklin," Leland said at once.

"Mr. Rocklin, will you let me ride him?"

"Maybe you can ride with me. Red's kind of particular. He throws nearly everybody off."

"Even you?"

"Even me, sometimes."

As they entered the dining room, the first person Rocklin saw was Jori Hayden. She was putting a pan of biscuits on the table, and she flushed slightly when she saw him.

"Good morning, Miss Hayden. I hope you slept well."

"Well — yes, I did."

At that moment Kate came out the door and Leland said at once, "This is my sister-in-law, Katherine Johnson."

"Just call me Kate. I don't believe I heard your first name," Kate said.

"Chad."

"Well, sit down, everybody. The food's all ready."

"You sit here by me, Mr. Rocklin," Carleen said.

Rocklin moved over to the chair and waited until the two women had the food on the table and then the men all sat down. Leland said, "We're used to saying a blessing over the food."

"A good habit," Rocklin said pleasantly.

They all bowed their heads, and Leland asked a quick blessing. As soon as it was over, Carleen started bombarding Rocklin with questions, usually calling him just Rocklin and being corrected by her father.

The breakfast was scrambled eggs, grits, fried potatoes, and biscuits.

"Best meal I've had in a long time, Miss Kate. You're a good cook."

"Anybody can scramble eggs," Kate said.

"Not everybody can make biscuits,

though."

The meal went pleasantly enough, but Jori said hardly a word. Finally, as they were sipping coffee, toward the end of the meal, Mark said, "Rocklin, have you ever led a train to Santa Fe?"

"No, I never have."

A stunned look crossed Mark's face. He turned to his father. "How can we hire a man who's never led a single train?"

"Al Blanchard recommended you, but he didn't say you had never led a train."

"Oh, I've been on several of them, usually as a scout. Did a bit of mule skinning, but I've never actually been the wagon master."

Kate said, "Tell us about yourself. Mr. Blanchard wouldn't have recommended you unless he believed in you."

Rocklin sipped his coffee and held up the cup. "Mighty tiny cup. I'm used to big mugs. It'll take a lot of these to fill me up."

At once Kate got up, took his cup and went out into the kitchen. She came back with a big mug and said, "How's this?"

"That's just about right." He sipped the coffee and said, "I guess you do need to know a little about me. Al didn't tell you much?"

"Not much except you've been in the West all your life."

"My parents were farmers. They were killed in a Comanche raid when I was twelve years old."

Jori looked up, shock on her face. "How awful," she whispered. "What happened to you? Who kept you?"

"Well, the Comanches did for four years."

"The Comanches! You were a captive?"

"I was practically a Comanche. You either get that way or die."

"Then you probably learned how to speak their language."

"Had to do that, Mr. Hayden. Picked up a spattering of all the languages of the tribes, the Kiowa, the Pawnee."

"Did you escape?"

"Yes, I did. We were on a raiding party, and I slipped away. After that I bumped around, did a lot of things. Drove a wagon, as I said. Trapped beaver in the mountains for a year. Soldiered in the dragoons for awhile. Mostly I just traveled around the West. It's about all I know."

They all sat there entranced as Rocklin spoke of his experience in the West. It was a new world to them, one they did not know, and it was rather frightening.

"Well, what do you think about our venture, Mr. Rocklin?" Leland said with some hesitation. "Al told me it would be a rough trip."

Rocklin sat loosely in his chair, a limber man with incredibly blue eyes. "I've already told your daughter I think you're making a big mistake."

"In what way?" Kate said. She leaned forward, and her eyes were intent on the big man who sat idly in the chair toying with his coffee cup.

"Well, it's too rough for women, I think. Hard enough on men."

"But can it be done?" Leland demanded. "I don't know if she told you, but we're in real difficulty here. We've got to do something."

"Your troubles here might look pretty small if we were halfway there and got surrounded by Pawnees. But, in answer to your question, it can be done if you're ready to pay the price. But it'll be hard — real hard."

"Which way do we go?" Jori asked impatiently. She had made up her mind and wanted to hear no more talk of the hardships. "I have a map here, but we can't make much sense out of it."

"Let me see the map. I don't put much stock in them. Some maps were drawn by people, evidently, that never went along the way or saw the place."

They moved into the dining room where Jori unfolded the map that she had obtained. They all gathered around with Rocklin standing over it. He said, "Here's the way the trail runs. As I told Miss Hayden, we follow the Arkansas River a long way. Most of those that made the trip leave from Franklin, Missouri, right here."

"Why, that's a long way from here," Leland said. "Is that necessary?"

"If you go on the Santa Fe Trail it is." He began to trace the journey on the map with his finger.

Finally Jori leaned forward and said, "Why can't we go across here? From Fort Smith you can go straight across to Santa Fe. It's almost a straight line."

Rocklin suddenly grinned. It made him look even younger. "Yes, ma'am, it does, and it goes right through the Llano Estacado. Right here. You see on the map?"

"What's wrong with going through that, Rocklin?" Carleen demanded. She had squeezed in between her father and her brother and was looking up with inquisitive eyes.

"Well, Miss Carleen, the Llano Estacado means 'the Staked Plains' and it's pretty much of a desert."

"But why don't people use it?"

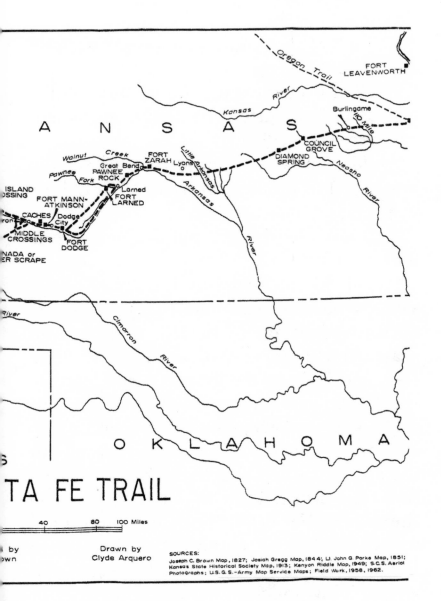

FORT
LEAVENWORTH

Oregon Trail

Kansas River

A N S A S

Burlingame

110 Mile

Walnut Creek

COUNCIL
GROVE

DIAMOND
SPRING

Pawnee Fork

Great Bend

FORT
ZARAH

Lyons

Little Arkansas

Neosho River

ISLAND
CROSSING

PAWNEE
ROCK

Larned

FORT MANN-
ATKINSON

FORT
LARNED

Arkansas

CACHES

Dodge
City

ron

MIDDLE
CROSSINGS

FORT
DODGE

River

NADA or
ER SCRAPE

River

Cimarron River

O K L A H O M A

TA FE TRAIL

40   80   100 Miles

by
own

Drawn by
Clyde Arquero

SOURCES:
Joseph C. Brown Map, 1827; Josiah Gregg Map, 1844; Lt. John G. Parke Map, 1851;
Kansas State Historical Society Map, 1913; Kenyon Riddle Map, 1949; S.C.S. Aerial
Photographs; U.S.G.S.–Army Map Service Maps; Field Work, 1958, 1962.

"Because of the Comanches and the Kiowa and the Pawnee. It's their country."

Leland shook his head. "You mean they don't attack trains on the Santa Fe Trail?"

"Sometimes, but it's not so likely."

"Which way would you take?" Leland demanded.

"Well, if it was just me, I'd go through the Staked Plains, but it'll be dangerous whichever way you go."

Rocklin spoke for some time about the journey, and finally Jori asked, "How long will it take to get there?"

"It'll take about three months. You have to time your trip by the grass."

"What do you mean by the grass?" Kate said. "What does that have to do with this?"

"Your stock has to be fed. If there's no grass, they'll starve. So, you need to leave early spring when the grass is turning green. But before you leave you've got to get your wagons, your stock, your drivers, and whatever freight it is you're going to haul out there. And I'll tell you right now, not many first-class drivers want to risk their hides on the Santa Fe Trail. They'd rather haul freight back East without the dangers of Indians." He suddenly looked at Leland and asked, "How much money do you have?"

Rocklin's abrupt question disturbed them

all, but Leland said, "Not enough, I suppose. We might could raise ten thousand dollars."

"Well, you'll need it all and then some."

"What do we do first?" Jori asked, hating to feel helpless.

"Someone has to buy the wagons and the livestock and hire the skinners."

"We don't know how to do any of that," Mark said. Despair was on his face. "I think we're crazy to try it."

"No, we're not crazy," Kate said suddenly. "God is going to be with us."

Her words brought Rocklin's head around. "You really believe that, ma'am?"

"I surely do. Are you a man of God?"

"I'm sorry to say I'm not."

"Well, I'll pray that you will be. God gave me a vision of us going on this trip, and I believe it. He'll take care of us."

"But we don't know how to buy anything," Leland said. "Rocklin, you'll have to buy the wagons and the livestock. If you'll tell me what we'll need that'll sell best in Santa Fe, I can take care of that."

Jori suddenly said, "I'll go with Rocklin to buy the wagons and the stock and handle the money."

"You'll have to tell me what to buy," Leland said.

"Well, a wagon will hold about five thousand pounds. You don't want to haul heavy items. They wouldn't sell in Santa Fe anyhow."

"Well, what would they buy?"

"Cloth and other staples, as lightweight as possible. They like cloth, and some special foods that are lightweight. I'll help you with that."

The enormity of the undertaking seemed to have stunned them all. Kate looked around the table and suddenly laughed. "All of us look a little bit green."

"It's a big thing," Mark said biting his lip. "I'm still not sure we ought to do it."

"I think we don't have any choice," Jori said abruptly.

Kate said, "You know, when you leave a place it's best to leave it quick and be done with it."

Rocklin suddenly smiled. He liked this woman very much. If a woman had to go on a wagon train, he knew this was the kind that would make it. She showed the signs of rough living, and he knew that she would last better than the others.

"I reckon you're right about that. I have a friend that had dogs that had to have bobbed tails. He told me one time he heard of a fellow that used to cut off their tails an inch at a time which would be misery for the dogs for a long time. No, better just get it all done at once."

Jori said, "When do we start, Rocklin?" Now that it was settled she was ready to go, and she did her best to put her doubts behind her.

"We're ready for sunup in the morning," Rocklin said cheerfully.

He rose suddenly, saying, "I know you folks will want to talk this over a lot. It's not too late to back out. No shame in that. It'll be tougher than any of you think." He turned and grinned. "How would you like to ride my big red horse, Miss Carleen?"

"Yeah!" Carleen yelled. She jumped up and dashed out of the house followed by Rocklin.

As soon as the door closed, Leland sat down and looked rather pale. "I don't mind telling you I'm a little bit shaky about all this."

Jori knew that she would have to be strong. "It'll be fine, Papa," she said. "Don't you worry about it. Rocklin and I will start getting the wagons and the livestock. We'll need to be out of this place pretty soon anyhow."

"And we've got to go all the way to Missouri just to start," Mark said. He rubbed his chin, and there was a doubtful look in his eye. "I wish we were there."

Kate said nothing. She was looking at this family of hers. She knew they were soft and had never had to endure any hardship. Memories of her own childhood and early girlhood when things were harder than these soft city dwellers could imagine came to her. *Well, Lord,* she prayed silently, *You'll just have to toughen them up because they'll need it before we get to Santa Fe.*

CHAPTER SIX

A small delicate bird with black and white ladder-back stripes made a syncopated sound as Jori leaned up against the rails of the corral. Ordinarily she was delighted to find a new species of bird, but she gave this one a bleak look then pressed her forehead against the top rail of the corral. *I've never been so tired in my whole life.* The thought seemed to move slowly through her mind. It made her suddenly believe that her whole thought process was like a river of mud moving no more than a few feet a day.

As she leaned her forehead against the roughness of the post, she tried to think of how many days she had been doing something like this with Rocklin. It came to her that when the two of them had started out to locate mules and wagons the weather had been cold, but the days that rolled by turned into weeks and now the promise of spring was in the air. It was hot now, and the dust from the corral seemed to settle on her, coating her hair, making her eyes gritty, and even getting into her mouth. She suddenly turned her head to one side and spit in as ladylike a fashion as such an act was possible. Lifting her head wearily, she saw Rocklin walking around a large mule held by a man in the dirtiest clothes that Jori had ever seen. *How can he be interested in another mule? We must have looked at every mule in Arkansas!* But Rocklin never seemed happy unless he had examined every point of the animals that they had seen.

Finally she saw him nod, begin speaking, and knew that he was negotiating the price for the four mules he had picked out. This debate, she knew, might go on for some time, so turning, she walked over toward the buggy, opened the top of the keg full of water, and dipped into it with a tin cup. She drank thirstily though the water was tepid and had a bitter taste to it. "We've got to find some better way than this to carry water," she muttered, then put the cup back, covered the water keg, and climbed up in the seat. She was so tired she dozed off almost at once, and when the buggy suddenly swayed, she turned quickly to find Rocklin had taken his seat beside her. The fine dust from the corral coated his face, but he seemed not to notice it. "We got four fine animals," he nodded with satisfaction.

"How many more do we have to have?"

"I reckon this will just about do it." He made no move to pick up the lines but sat there, a loose-bodied man with the marks of hard work on his tan hands and face. She once had seen him remove his shirt, and his body was white, making his hands and face look like a pair of gloves and a mask. A fly buzzed around his head, and he brushed it away absently. "I reckon you've seen enough mules to do you, haven't you, Miss Hayden?"

"Oh, for heaven sake, call me Jori!" she said. There was irritation in her voice, and she pulled her shoulders up and asked irritably, "Are we going back home now?"

"Just one more stop to make."

"Where's that? To look at more mules?"

"No. I heard about a good mule skinner that lives down the road a piece. Williamson said he was a dandy, and we're short at least one skinner."

"What about the wagons?"

"They'll be waiting for us in Little Rock. Al Blanchard made a good deal. I trust his judgment anytime."

"All right. Let's go as quick as we can."

He suddenly grinned at her and said,

"You're doing better than I figured."

"You didn't think I could do it?"

"Well, you've never done anything like it, have you?"

That was true enough, Jori thought, but she hated to admit it. "You don't have to worry about me on the trail if that's what you're thinking."

Rocklin did not argue. He never did, Jori had noticed. He seemed fresh, and, although they had missed much sleep in their travels to find the animals and assemble a crew, he almost never seemed to be weary. Now he picked up the lines and said, "Williamson will deliver the mules to Little Rock. That was part of the deal. We don't have time to babysit them, but they're fine animals."

He picked up the lines, slapped them on the team, and left at once at a fast trot. As they moved along at a brisk pace, Jori swayed back and forth, determined not to let him know that she was so tired she was almost sick. "How do you like this kind of a life, Jori?"

"I don't like it at all. It's something I have to do."

He did not look at her but was watching a hawk sailing high in the sky. "There's the fellow I admire. He's got all the room in the world to move around in. Doesn't have to

116

worry about paying rent, anything like that. He's got it made."

She did not reply and was dozing when he surprised her by saying, "Carleen tells me you were going to get married."

"That's right."

"What happened?"

"It's a personal thing." She was suddenly irritated. "Don't you understand that, Rocklin? Some things are none of your business."

"I'm just plumb nosy, I guess. Men are nosy creatures." He grinned slyly and added innocently. "They get it from their mothers, I reckon."

Rocklin had a way of irritating Jori although it was nothing she could put her finger on. He seemed amused at her efforts to learn about mules and about everything else that had been completely out of her sphere.

"What about you? Were you ever married?"

"Oh, that's personal," he said soberly.

"Yes, it is. What about this mule skinner?"

"His name is Lonnie Fortier. He comes from New Orleans, but he's been around here for a few years."

She asked no more questions, and half an hour later as they pulled off onto a side road, Rocklin said, "That's the house if I got my instructions right."

The house was little more than a shack. Smoke was curling up from a crooked stove pipe, and the yard was littered with tin cans and trash of every description. Rocklin pulled the team up and was about to get out of the wagon when two men suddenly came out.

"What do you want?" the taller of the two asked.

"Lookin' for Lonnie Fortier. My name's Rocklin."

"He's dead," the taller man said. "I'm Dixon Bragg, and this is my brother Duke. This is our place now. He was our cousin."

"What did you want with him?" the smaller man named Duke said.

"Wanted to hire him to do some mule skinnin'."

"Well, he's past all that," Duke said. "You can move on if that's all you want."

The smaller man was staring at Jori. He was a sly-looking man with shifty eyes. "How are you doin', sweetheart?"

Jori did not answer, and the large man named Dixon laughed. "That's a pretty fancy woman you got there. She yours?"

"I'm not anybody's," Jori said and was instantly sorry that she had spoken.

Duke started to say something else, but

suddenly a movement behind him caused him to whirl. "Get back in that house!" he yelled.

Rocklin straightened up and saw a young boy break from the house and start running desperately. The two men instantly leaped forward and grabbed him. The larger of them slapped the young fellow in the face. It was a meaty sound and knocked the boy's hat off.

Only it was not a lad, Rocklin saw. Long black hair suddenly spilled out, and he caught a glimpse of a thin face filled with determination and fright. She fought silently, and Dixon held his hand back to slap her again.

"Hold it right there, Bragg," Rocklin demanded.

Bragg kept hold of the girl's arm. He whirled and said, "Git on your way!"

"Didn't you hear me? I told you to let that girl go."

Dixon merely cursed him, and without warning Rocklin suddenly pulled a pistol from his left side and, without appearing to aim, fired it. Dixon let out a shrill scream, and his leg suddenly collapsed.

The other Bragg started to go for his gun that he wore on his side, but Chad fired before he could. The shot plucked his hat off. "The next time I'll shoot your eye out, Bragg." He got down and walked over toward the two.

"You shot me in the leg!" Dixon yelled. "I'll kill you for that!"

"Shut up," Chad said, "or I'll finish the job." He turned to the girl. "What's going on here? Who are you?"

"I'm Callie Fortier. Lonnie Fortier was my pa."

"She's our cousin," Dixon Bragg said. He had gotten to his feet and looked down balefully at the wound in his leg. It was merely a flesh wound, but hatred flared in his eyes. "She stays here with us."

"He is no blood kin to me — no!" There was a foreign flavor to the girl's speech, Rocklin noted.

"Where's your mother?" he asked.

"She's dead. They came and took this place and say it's theirs. They — they try to bother me." She cast a look at the Braggs and said, "Let me go with you. I can't stay with them."

"Sure. Get your things," Chad Rocklin said. He kept his gun down at his side.

"You can't take that girl," Duke Bragg said.

"You open your mouth one more time and I'll put you down, Bragg."

Bragg opened his mouth to speak, but something he saw in the tall man's face stopped him. He looked down at his gun that lay in the dust, and at once Rocklin reached over and picked it up. He took the gun away from the other Bragg and tossed them into the back of the buggy. He turned then and waited. "I'll throw the guns out when I'm a mile away from this place."

"I'll kill you, you can bet on it," Duke Bragg grated.

Even as he spoke, the young woman came out. She had a bundle in her right hand. "Get in the buggy," he said. He waited until the girl had scrambled into the backseat then got in himself. The Braggs suddenly started shouting at him, and Rocklin laughed and fired twice. The dust blew up at the feet of the two, and they yelled and backed off. Rocklin laughed and struck the horses, who started out with a violent jerk.

The voices of the Braggs cursing them followed them and then faded in the distance. "What happened to your father?"

"He died. He had a bad heart, him. These men, they take his things. They say they are his cousins. They try to use me for a bad woman."

"My name's Chad Rocklin. This is Miss Jori Hayden. Your name's Callie?"

"Oui."

"Are you French?"

"My father, he was French. My mother, she was not."

"Where can we take you?"

"What do you do?" the girl said. She had a straightforward way about her, and Chad Rocklin liked the way she had fought.

"We're taking a mule train through to Santa Fe."

"Mules? My father was a mule skinner."

"That's why we came, to get him to work for us."

"Take me with you. I can drive as good as my father."

"Couldn't have a woman mule skinner."

"But you take other animals, many extras. I have heard my father talk about the trains that go. They carry many mules and horses. I can take care of them."

"Don't you have any other family?" Rocklin said. He turned around and studied the young woman. "How old are you?"

"I have seventeen years, me." She had gray eyes, well shaped and wide spaced. The man's shirt she wore did not conceal the womanly lines of her figure.

"Please," she said. Her voice caught, and there was a trace of fear in her eyes, "take me with you. I have nothing here."

"We can't bring her on the train," Jori said suddenly. She turned and saw that the woman was watching her carefully.

"I can care for horses. I can cook. Please, take me."

"You can go," Rocklin said. "We'll find something for you, Callie."

Jori became furious. "We'll talk about it," she said.

Abruptly Rocklin turned to her, and she saw that there was a steely aspect. He stopped smiling. "No, we won't talk about it. I've told you what we'll do."

Jori felt her face flame. She started to answer, and she saw that Rocklin was waiting for her to do that. Suddenly she remembered that he had warned her that there would be times when his word would be law. *That was on the trail,* she thought, *not here.* Still, he was waiting for her to reply.

She swallowed hard, and suddenly he said, "What would you do, Jori, leave her here for those men?" She could not answer, and he said, "You're a woman. You ought to have more gentleness in you."

Jori Hayden suddenly found she had nothing else to say. She clamped her jaw shut, and there was silence in the buggy.

The girl said not a word, but finally Rocklin turned and said to her quietly, "We're going to Franklin, Missouri. The train will be put together there. I'll have to try you out to see if you can handle stock."

"Merci, Mr. Rocklin. You won't be sorry. I'm a hard worker, me."

"I had a friend once, a trapper. He talked like you. He was from Baton Rouge."

"He was probably Cajun."

"That what you are?"

"Yes."

"Well, we'll see how it works out. I'll look out for you the best I can, but it'll be tough."

Callie Fortier said in a quiet, steady voice, "I am used to that, me."

They reached Little Rock at sundown and went at once to the house. It was growing dark by the time Rocklin pulled the buggy up, and Jori did not wait for him to help her down. She jumped to the ground and moved quickly into the house.

"I make trouble for you," Callie said.

"No you don't, Callie. Miss Hayden just doesn't know much about mules and wagons and things like that." He hesitated, not certain how much to tell her. "It's like this. They've had a lot of money and now they have only enough to take a train through to Santa Fe. They've hired me to get it there." He went on to explain the situation and finally stepped to the ground. She stepped out and he saw that she was somewhat less than average height but was active and moved very quickly. "I'll find you some place to stay. I don't know where it'll be. It'll take several days to get all the mules together and check all the wagons. Come along. I've been camping out in the barn. There's plenty of room. I'll get you some blankets. We'll probably be here for another couple of days."

"Thank you for taking me. Miss Hayden, she does not like me."

"She's just a little used to having her own way." Suddenly Rocklin laughed softly. "That'll probably change on the trail to Santa Fe."

Inside the house the family had gathered around Jori, talking, and she explained quickly that they had found enough mules.

"The mule skinners are here. A rougher-looking crowd I never saw," Leland said.

"I expect they have to be," Jori said shortly, "to drive mules. I've seen enough of them to know that they're the most stubborn creatures on earth."

"The wagons are here, too. Al Blanchard found them for us. I never saw wagons like them, but he says they're just the thing. Conestoga wagons they're called."

"How'd you get along with Rocklin?" Mark grinned. "I thought once or twice you might shoot each other."

"It was all business," she said, then added awkwardly, "he picked up another member for the crew."

"Another mule skinner?" Kate asked. "Is he different from the rest?"

"It's not a he. It's a she. She's not a mule skinner." She began to tell the story of how Callie Fortier had been added to the party. She told the story in great detail, and Mark took a deep breath.

"You mean he just pulled his gun and shot the man?"

"Yes, in the leg. He shot the other man's hat off, but he could have killed them both. I thought for a minute he meant to."

"Well," Leland said, "Rocklin was telling me how that a woman had never been down the Santa Fe Trail." He grinned suddenly and laughed in a way they had not heard from him in some time. "And now we've got a whole wagonload of females."

"Rocklin thinks that'll be trouble," Jori said shortly. "We'll have to show him we can do it, won't we, Carleen?" She smiled as Carleen nodded.

"I won't be no trouble," she said.

"Well, I'm going to bed," Jori said. "I'm

worn out chasing after mules. I hope," she said devoutly, "there are no mules in heaven!"

The mule skinners were sitting around a fire that they had made, and when Rocklin came up to them, he nodded briefly and spoke as they greeted him. "This is Callie Fortier," he said. "She's going to help with the loose stock."

"Another woman?"

The speaker was Grat Herendeen. He was by far the toughest of the mule skinners, a huge man, six feet two and weighing two twenty. He got up and stood staring at the young woman. His hair was stiff, and he had hazel eyes and blunt features. "Bad luck to have a woman on the trail."

"Not your worry, Grat. You drive the mules. I'll take care of everything else. Come along, Callie. I'll get you fixed up."

He led her off. He had found a room that had been used for supplies and he opened the door and said, "You can sleep in here. I'm sorry there's no bed. We'll get something to eat and some blankets. You'll need 'em on the trail anyway."

Callie put her bundle down, then looked up at him. "I thank you for saving me from those men."

"Sure. Listen, if any of these men bother you, just tell me."

"I have a gun." She reached down and fumbled with the strings on the blanket. She unrolled it and picked up a holstered gun, a small one. "If they bother me, I will shoot them."

She was so serious that Rocklin had to grin. "No, I need them to drive the mules. Just tell me if they bother you."

Suddenly Callie looked at him, and a thought came to her. She smiled slightly, and her lips curled upward at the corners in a delightful fashion. "Well, what if *you* bother me?"

"You can shoot me, I guess. But shoot me in the foot not the head. Come along."

Callie studied him then laughed. "I will not shoot you, I think."

"Good. Come along. We'll see if we can find something to eat."

Callie Fortier belted the gun around her waist. He winked and said, "Remember, if you got to shoot anybody, don't kill 'em. Just shoot 'em in the leg or somethin' like that."

"Yes. I will do that, Mr. Rocklin."

"I reckon you can call me Chad."

"Chad. That is a funny name."

"I'm a funny fellow. Come along. We'll get

128

something to eat." He turned and did not see the smile that came to her. She followed quickly after him, staying close as they left the barn.

■ ■ ■ ■

PART TWO:
THE WAGON MASTER

■ ■ ■ ■

CHAPTER SEVEN

Reluctantly Jori emerged from the fitful sleep that had been her lot. Usually she slept very well, but the night had produced nothing but abrupt awakenings and long periods of lying in the bed staring at the ceiling.

The sound of rough, coarse voices came to her, and interwoven with the voices was the sound of mules braying — an ugly cacophonous sound that Jori knew she would learn to hate on the road to Santa Fe. She loved horses but could find nothing in the ugly mules to admire. The days and weeks she had spent with Rocklin looking them over had not increased her appreciation for the breed. She had asked Rocklin once why they couldn't use horses, and he had replied, "For one thing, they don't hold up as well as mules. For another thing, they cost more. And for a third thing, Indians like them a lot better than mules."

A thin, faint line representing the dawn

touched the window to her left, and, reluctant to move, Jori lay there thinking, *This is the last night I will ever spend in my room.* She thought of it as *my* room because it was the only room she had ever known. She had been born in this house, and memories came back of her childhood when this very room had been filled with her toys and girlhood treasures. Now she looked around and traced the furniture that had grown so familiar to her, and the sadness that came to her was almost physical. Again the sounds of men's rough laughter came, and she tried to shut it out of her mind. Leaving her home was like a little death to her, and though she had tried to hide her feelings from her family, when she was alone, especially in bed at night, the thoughts of severing herself from the only life she had ever known seemed indeed like a sort of doom. She had always known that she would leave this room but only for another one. She would move from this room into another fine house with a husband. There was nothing frightening about that, for this room would be there if she wanted to come back for a visit. But there was something dreadful, terminal, and utterly final about what was going on in her life and in the life of her family.

Time passed, and the pale sunshine filtering through her windows grew brighter. But Jori's mood darkened even as the room brightened. She suddenly felt as if she wanted to strike out, to hit something, but there was nothing to fight. She was caught up in a river, an inexorable carrying away, that was taking her to a destination that seemed dark and hopeless. She was shocked when she felt tears swim in her eyes and run down the sides of her temples. She was not a crying young woman, for there had been little to weep over in her life up until this time. There was enough now to bring tears, and she let them flow freely until, suddenly, the pounding of footsteps outside in the hall and then the opening of the door in a violent motion shocked her and ran along her nerves. She sat up abruptly as Carleen came sailing into the room calling out, "Get up — get up, Jori!"

"Don't you ever knock, Carleen!" Jori exclaimed. She shook her head at Carleen's costume. She wore a pair of men's blue jeans, the smallest that could be bought and which Kate had altered to fit her. She wore a red and white checkered shirt, and her hair was pulled back in pigtails. "What do you want?" she asked with irritation.

"It's time to go. We're getting ready. Come

on, Jori." Carleen came closer and leaned forward and stared at Jori. "What are you crying about?" she said.

"I'm not crying!"

"Yes, you are. There are tears running all over your face. I don't believe it. There's nothing to cry about."

Jori threw the covers back and swung her feet over the side of the bed. "Go away and knock next time you come in a door."

Carleen shook her head. "We won't have no doors to come through, not until we get to Santa Fe. We're gonna camp out. It's gonna be great." She stepped closer and stared with disbelief at her sister. She had been excited and getting underfoot ever since the final preparations for the beginning of the great journey were underway. She had paid little attention to Jori, and now she said, "I don't know what you're crying about."

"Don't you tell anybody I was crying, Carleen!"

Carleen shrugged. "I won't, but I still don't know why you're squawlin'. It's gonna be just great!"

"Go on now while I get dressed."

"All right, but hurry up."

Carleen dashed out the door leaving it wide open, and Jori got up and shut it. She dressed quickly in the early morning light, not bothering to light the lamp. She was wearing a light green dress, high waisted in the fashion of the day. The sleeves were long and came down to her wrists with a pair of turned-down cuffs. She slipped into her flat, low-cut leather shoes, then took one last look around the room. She would come back later for the clothes she was going to take, but this was good-bye to her life. Straightening up, she moved over and poured water out of the pitcher into the basin. She washed her face quickly, looked into the small mirror, and then turned and left her room.

As Kate cooked breakfast, she was reminded of her earlier life when she did most of the cooking for a large family. In these later years she had done only specialty cooking, making things that she desired herself. Now, however, the memories came back of harvesttimes when she had cooked for twenty men at a neighborhood farm for little money. She thought of the cabin raisings where she had joined the other women, cooking for the workers who laid the logs, and realized that she had missed something of that time.

She looked up as Jori entered and saw at

once the young woman's face was stiff and unnatural. *She's grieving and sad to leave home.* Ignoring the thought, Kate smiled and said, "You came just in time to help with breakfast." She saw Jori's eyes go over the mountain of scrambled eggs and the platters full of biscuits piled high like small mountains and the bacon laid out on platters.

"What in the world is all this food for!" Jori exclaimed.

"It's for the mule skinners and the men on the train." Kate flipped over six pieces of bacon with a spatula expertly, and they sizzled on the frying pan, sending up the strong odor of meat cooking. "We couldn't take all the groceries with us, so I thought we might as well fix a breakfast."

Leland entered from the door and said nervously, "Is the breakfast about ready?"

"All ready," Kate nodded. "Everybody lend a hand, and we'll take it out and feed them."

Mark and Leland helped Kate and Jori take the meal outside. A table was set up, and the men were sitting around smoking and laughing as Kate made the preparations. She lifted her voice and said, "All right, you men, line up here and get your breakfast."

Kate watched as the men shuffled over and thought again of her earlier days. She had been accustomed to rough men then, but for the past years, since she had been Leland's housekeeper and had watched over his children, that memory had faded. It came back strongly now along with the smells of tobacco, leather, and even alcohol from the mule skinners. "Pick up a plate and bring it to me." Grat Herendeen was the first man, a huge man with his bull whip coiled and over his shoulder seeming almost a part of him. He grinned at her as she filled his plate with the eggs and motioned toward the bacon. "Help yourself, Grat."

"Smells mighty good, Miss Kate," Herendeen said. He moved down and picked up a cup that Jori had filled from the large coffee pot. He winked at her and said, "Going to be a nice trip. Not used to having ladies along on freighting trains." He waited for her to respond, but she didn't, and he moved on.

They loaded their plates, and finally the last man in line came to stand before Kate.

"Good morning," Kate said. She had not met this man before. He was no more than average height but trim and strong looking. His curly brown hair escaped from the cap he was wearing, and he had warm brown eyes. She put an extra portion of eggs on his plate and said, "Help yourself to the bacon and the biscuits."

"It looks mighty good, ma'am." He hesitated and then stood before her, holding his plate in one hand and his cup in the other. "Are you born again by the blood of the Lamb, ma'am?"

Kate was surprised but suddenly she laughed. "Yes, I am."

"Well, I reckon I knowed that before I asked. I could tell you're a handmaiden of the Lord."

"My name's Kate Johnson."

"I'm glad to know you, ma'am. My name's Brown — Good News Brown."

"Good News? That's not your real name."

"Yes, ma'am, it is. My ma was a real Christian, ma'am, and she wanted to give me a name to let people know where I stood with God. So, she took part of that Scripture out. She'd been readin' the story of the birth of the Savior in Luke the day after I was born, so she told me. You know, she read that verse that says when the angels said to the shepherds, 'Fear not: for, behold, I bring you good tidings of great joy.' My ma always said that sounded like the angels are saying I've got good news for you. So she named me Good News. Fellows mostly call me News. That's all right."

"Are you a preacher?" Kate asked.

"Me? No, ma'am. Just a voice in the wilderness."

Kate found herself liking the man. He did not have the roughness about him that some of the other men had. "Maybe we can have services on the trail."

"I reckon I'd like that a lot, ma'am."

"You'd better watch out for this fella, Miss Kate."

Kate turned quickly to see one of the mule skinners that she had already met standing there. His name was Stuffy McGinnis. He was a short, spare, young man, wiry and tough, with the biggest mustache she had ever seen. She had already discovered he was a happy-go-lucky fellow and loved to play practical jokes. He was grinning at her now with fun dancing in his eyes. "I guess it's my Christian duty to warn you about Good News here."

"Is that right, Stuffy? What's he done?"

"Oh, he's the downfall of women, Miss Kate, I'm sorry to announce to you. It's just terrible the way he leads young women into the ways of unrighteousness."

"Stuffy, you couldn't tell the truth if your life depended on it."

"Oh, he'll deny it," Stuffy said, nodding

wisely and winking at Kate. "But everybody knows that he's a terrible fellow where women are concerned."

Kate suddenly faced McGinnis squarely. "Are you born again yourself, Stuffy?"

McGinnis opened his mouth, started to speak, then suddenly found it necessary to clear his throat. "Well, not exactly."

Good News was delighted. He laughed and clapped Stuffy on the shoulder. "No, he ain't born again, but he's gonna be before this here trip is over." He winked and said, "You and me'll gang up on him, Miss Kate. We'll get him saved, baptized, sanctified, and filled with the Holy Ghost before we get to Santa Fe."

"I'll be glad to cooperate with you on that, Good News."

Stuffy was suddenly nervous, a most unusual thing for him. "I don't reckon as how I need any help," he said stiffly. He turned and walked away.

"You're forgetting your eggs, Stuffy," Good News called out. But then he turned and shook his head, his eyes warm. "Never knew Stuffy to turn down seconds, but good to have a fellow believer on the trail, Miss Kate."

"I'll look forward to having some meetings and talking about the Lord," Kate smiled. She watched as Good News turned away and noticed that he walked over to where Stuffy was, sat down and began talking earnestly with him. *That's a good man,* she thought. *We'll probably need more like him on this journey.*

Brodie Donahue finished his plate and drained the last of his coffee. He was a tall man with wide shoulders, a solid neck, and black hair and eyes. He was fine looking, clean shaven, and better dressed than most of the mule skinners. He turned to Charlie Reuschel and said, "Look at that filly, ain't she a pippin?"

Charlie turned to look at the young woman who was standing alone at the table staring off into space. "A fine-lookin' gal."

"She's a daisy, ain't she? Better go make myself available."

"You heard what Rocklin said about the women," Charlie Reuschel said. He was no more than average height but very strongly built. He wore a hat always, for he was bald. He had light blue eyes and was the best shot of any of the men in the train. It seemed he could not miss with a rifle or a pistol.

"Ah, that's just talk."

"I don't reckon Rocklin's one for just talk. You better behave yourself."

Indeed, Rocklin had given a talk to all of the men on the train. It had been a short talk in which he had informed them that they were to keep themselves on their best manners where the women on the train were concerned. He had ended by saying, "I'm not much of a one for rules, but anybody that breaks this one I'll come down on him pretty hard."

Donahue had paid little attention to the speech. He was a rough fellow and could handle himself in most any kind of fight. He knew that Chad Rocklin was a pretty tough man, or he would not have been chosen to lead this train. Donahue, however, was not one to worry about things like that.

He got to his feet, brushed his black hair back, and shoved his hat back on his head. "A man that won't take a chance of a whippin' to get next to a good-lookin' one like that don't amount to dried spit, Charlie." He left and went over at once to where Jori was standing. "Ma'am, my name's Brodie Donahue. Don't think we've met."

Jori turned and looked up into the face of the tall young man. "I'm Jori Anne Hayden."

"Right pleased to know you. Guess you're lookin' forward to this trip."

"No, I'm not."

"Well, that's speakin' right out," Brodie said with surprise. "You don't like Santa Fe?"

"I've never seen it."

"I haven't either, but I always like to see new things." He glanced over at the wagons and said, "Anything I can help you with, you just say."

"As a matter of fact, there is one thing. I want to take a desk that my grandfather made. Would you help me get it into the wagon?"

"Sure enough, Miss Jori."

Brodie followed Jori into the house and up the stairs. He was impressed with the ornate furniture and the wealth that the house bespoke. He followed her down the hall and into a room. She motioned toward a rather small, rosewood desk barely large enough to sit at. "My grandfather made that."

"Mighty fine workmanship." He walked over, picked it up easily, and said, "Anything else?"

"No. Just that."

As Jori turned and walked out of the house, Brodie followed her, admiring her figure. *She's a little bit snooty,* he thought, *but get out on the trail and she'll break down, I expect.*

Jori stopped in front of the Conestoga wagon that she would be traveling in. "Just put it in wherever you can find room."

"Sure enough, miss."

The wagons were loaded, but Brodie was lifting the desk to put it in the back of the wagon when Rocklin suddenly appeared. "Take that back in the house, Brodie."

Brodie turned, surprise washing across his face. "But the lady said she wanted to take it."

"I am going to take it. It belonged to my grandfather."

Rocklin stood to one side, loose jointed and looking hard and capable. "I'm sorry, Jori, but we can't take anything else. We've talked about this before."

Jori looked around and saw that her father and brother were watching. Beyond them, Kate had approached. Some of the mule skinners also had perked up and were grinning. She saw two of them grab Herendeen, lean over, and whisper something to Jake Fingers, and Fingers laughed quietly.

Jori Anne Hayden was accustomed to having her own way. It had molded her and made her, and now she felt a sudden urge to demonstrate the independence that had always been a part of her character. "This was one of our family pieces, the only one that I'm taking. I'm taking it with me, Rocklin."

Rocklin did not hesitate. "Every pound counts. I've tried to point that out. We're going across some bad rivers, and we'll probably have to unload some of the wagons. We'll probably even have to leave some of the gear."

Grat Herendeen suddenly moved closer. "Aw, let her take the desk, Chad. Don't weigh much."

Every eye suddenly focused on Rocklin, at least among the mule skinners. It was a challenge lightly made but unmistakable. Grat was that kind of a man. He had to be first. Beside his bulk Rocklin looked almost small. He was as tall as Herendeen, but Herendeen's bulk was impressive.

"There's not room for the desk, Grat." He turned to Jori and said briefly, "Sorry, miss, it can't go."

"And I say it will!" Jori cried, suddenly weak with anger.

Suddenly Leland Hayden was there. He was a soft-spoken man who had had an easy life. It had not been easy for him to throw himself into a wild venture such as this, but he understood clearly that Grat Herendeen had thrown down a challenge. He understood also that there must be no question as to who was the captain of this wagon train.

"We'll leave it with the Nelsons, Jori." He came over and put his hand on her shoulder and added softly, "We'll come back and get it some day. I promise."

Jori suddenly understood that there was no appeal to this. "All right, if that's the way it has to be."

Brodie had watched this little drama very carefully. He was standing next to Good News Brown and said, "If I'd had my say, I'd let her take the desk."

"It ain't your say," Good News replied shortly. He watched Rocklin and shook his head. "He's a pretty tough nut, ain't he, Brodie?"

The wagons were finally loaded, which had taken some doing. Eddie Plank, a big overflowing man with brown eyes and brown hair, was in charge of most of this operation. He was capable though slow moving, but when the wagons were finally loaded, he nodded with satisfaction. "Reckon it's all on. We're ready to go."

Rocklin nodded and moved over toward his horse. Mark stopped him and said, "You were pretty rude to my sister." He was still upset by the scene.

"No, that's wasn't rude." Chad suddenly smiled. "You'll know it when I get rude, Mark."

"It wouldn't hurt to take one piece of furniture."

"She put me in a bad spot. I had to make a choice."

Mark started to argue, but Rocklin interrupted him. "Are you going to pull your weight on this trip?"

Mark flushed. He had already been drinking, and the smell of liquor was on him. He was soft physically and spoiled, but he had nothing to measure himself by. He had always been given what he wanted, and his friends had surrendered to his wishes. Now, looking into the tough face of Chad Rocklin, he felt a sudden spurt of anger. "I can handle my end of it!"

"You can't handle the trail if you're drunk."

Mark Hayden's face flushed. "Mind your own business," he muttered, then turned and stalked away stiffly. He was aware that his father was watching him, and he stopped to say, "We should have got another man for the wagon master."

"I don't think so," Leland said. "I think you need to pay attention to him. You don't need to be drinking, especially in the morning."

"A drink never hurt anybody, Father."

Leland Hayden watched his son go, and a sudden fear touched him. "I haven't done much to make a man out of him," he said softly to himself. "Maybe this trip will help."

Pedro Marichal, the head drover, had watched the confrontation between Rocklin and the Hayden woman. Pedro was a tall, lean man with dark eyes and black hair beginning to be sprinkled with gray. He was aware of the girl Callie who was seated on her mare beside him. "What did you think of that, Callie?"

"He was mean to her."

"She's spoiled. You can tell by looking."

As Pedro studied her, he recalled how Rocklin had asked him to try her out to see if she would be able to help with the remuda. It was a tough job keeping the spare mules and horses together, and Pedro had been doubtful. He had tried her out and been pleased to discover that Callie Fortier was better than most young men her age.

Now he suddenly asked, "How'd you learn to ride and handle animals?"

"My father was a mule skinner."

"This trail's gonna be hard," he warned.

"I don't care, Pedro."

He smiled. She was wearing men's clothing that did not altogether conceal her trim, young figure. "What are you going to do when some of the men make up to you?"

It was the same question that Rocklin had brought up, and Callie smiled at Pedro. "I'll shoot 'em in the foot."

Pedro abruptly laughed. "That's a good idea. You do that."

The train started out, and Jori was surprised to see the mule skinners riding on the back of the horse closest to the wagons, although Charlie Reuschel walked beside his team. She was also surprised to see that the only animals with lines really attached to guide them were the off-leaders, the front horse on the left-hand side of each team. She did not understand that, but she determined to ask someone.

She rode in the front seat of the wagon for two hours and discovered exactly how hard a seat could be. It was a simple board with no padding and no back. Once she looked with envy at the girl Callie who was riding a horse at the back of the line of wagons. She was laughing and talking with Pedro, and the thought came, *I wish I could ride a horse.* The pace was slow enough, so she leaped down and started walking alongside the wagon. Carleen piled out after her, and they had not gone more than a hundred yards when Rocklin came by on his big red horse.

"You decide to walk all the way to Santa Fe, Carleen?"

Carleen looked up at the man on the big horse and grinned. "My bottom got sore. Didn't yours, Jori?"

Jori flushed. "Don't talk like that."

"Like what?" Carleen said.

"Never mind."

"If you'd rather ride, Jori, I'll have Callie cut out a horse for you."

Instantly Jori nodded. "I'd like it a lot better."

"Come along. We'll pick you out a good one." Rocklin swung out of the saddle so that he could walk alongside Jori. "Wagon seats do get pretty hard."

Jori did not answer. It aggravated her to have to take a favor from this man, but, *after all,* she thought, *these are our horses.*

"Callie, will you put a saddle on that sorrel over there?"

"Yes, sir."

Ten minutes later the horse was saddled, and Callie had handed the lines to Rocklin. She had mounted and ridden back to help with the stock. "This is a good horse. I don't reckon he has a name."

"How are you gonna ride in that dress?" Carleen had suddenly appeared and was staring at Jori curiously.

"That is a problem, I reckon," Rocklin said. "We don't have a sidesaddle in the train."

"I don't need one." Jori made an instant decision. She lifted her foot up, put it in the stirrup and grasping the saddle horn pulled herself into the saddle. She plumped down with both feet dangling from the left side of the horse and glared at Rocklin, daring him to laugh.

"Well, that's one way, I reckon, but I'd sure hate to ride all the way to Santa Fe like that."

"I want to ride with you," Carleen said.

"Come on up then."

Rocklin suddenly reached out, picked Carleen up, and put her on the back of the horse behind the saddle. He watched as Jori rode off and shook his head. "Well, it seems like I find more ways to irritate that woman. It's going be a long trip if things don't change."

CHAPTER EIGHT

As Jori looked back at the wagons, it occurred to her that they well deserved the nickname of "prairie schooner." They were huge wagons made in Pennsylvania, heavy and lumbering, all pulled by eight mules. Some called them Conestogas; others called them Pittsburghs. She pulled the sorrel up and waited, watching as they swayed heavily as the wheels dropped into different tracks. They had high prows and sterns and enormous wheels with iron tires six inches wide. She had heard Rocklin explain that most wagons had wheels no more than three inches, but it was his considered opinion that the wider wheels were less likely to burrow down into the soft ground. She had talked one evening after supper to Addie Joss, the only black man on the train. He was a quiet man with a ready smile and handy in every way, especially as a blacksmith. He had told her that the wagons were built like ships and as watertight as possible. "We're gonna be crossin' some pretty big rivers," Addie had nodded, "but these are good wagons made out of white oak, hickory, bois d'arc — all of it well seasoned."

Shifting her weight uncomfortably, Jori longed for a sidesaddle. They were not as comfortable as the saddles that men used, but it would be better than perching sideways. The sorrel snorted, bent his head, and bit at the new spring grass that light rains had brought out. The sounds had become familiar to her — men's voices, the mule skinners' whips popping like gunshots over the heads of the mules, the stay chains and the traces jingling musically, and, from time to time, the raucous braying of the mules.

Despite herself, she thought there was a grace about the Conestogas. The covers were white, following the bows that arched over the wagons, which in turn followed the curve of the prow and the sterns. It occurred to her again that they looked more than ever like ships that sailed the rolling plains of the prairie instead of the blue seas and oceans.

One wagon had passed them on the day they had left Arkansas for Franklin. It was painted red and blue with the white sails giving it a patriotic flavor. But their wagons had been simply oiled and were designed strictly for utility. Eddie Plank had informed her that each wagon contained anywhere from twenty-five hundred to three thousand pounds of cargo. In addition to the trading goods there were extra spokes, extra chains, all sorts of tools, and cooking gear needed so that there was not a spare inch left unused. Uncomfortably, Jori thought of the encounter she had had over her grandfather's desk. She hated to be wrong. Noticeably, the relationship between her and Rocklin had not modified.

The sound of hoofbeats caught her attention, and she looked up to see Rocklin, who had ridden on ahead, coming back at a fast gallop. He rode well, she admitted, but then all of the men did. He stopped to say a word to her father who was in the first wagon and then came alongside her. He was smiling. "Good news. We'll be in Franklin before dark." He turned his horse, which immediately fell into step with her mare. "I guess you'll be ready for a change."

"Be nice to sleep in a bed or even to sit in a chair."

Rocklin merely smiled at her. She noticed that he never stopped searching the horizon, his eyes moving from point to point. "What are you looking for?" she asked curiously.

Rocklin started and then gave a half laugh. "Indians."

"Indians? Are they here?"

"Just the tame ones. The hostiles won't be a problem until we cross the Arkansas."

He seemed comfortable enough with silence, this tall man with the restless eyes. She studied his tawny hair and wondered about the scar that began near his ear and followed his jawbone all the way down into his neck. "How'd you get that scar, Rocklin?"

"Foolishness."

His brief enigmatic reply amused her. "Probably an interesting story."

"Not one for ladies." He suddenly turned to face her, and she met his eyes. He had the bluest eyes she had ever seen, almost the color of the cornflowers that grew in the woods throughout Arkansas. He held her glance, then said, "Been pretty rough on you. You're not used to such things."

"It has been hard." Indeed, the admission did not cover the trouble. She had been bitten by mosquitoes and troubled by a strange sort of black fly that delighted in crawling in her nose and ears. Rocklin had included a tent in the gear despite the extra weight. It was large enough for the women, and Addie Joss put it up for them every night at the end of the day. There were no cots or beds, simply blankets, but Jori had been so tired each night that she had fallen asleep as if struck by a mighty blow.

"Does it get any worse on down the trail?"

"Worse? Why, I figure it's pretty easy. No storms, no hostiles, plenty to eat, good water. This is about as good as it gets, Jori."

A voice sounded, and Rocklin looked and saw that Callie was hailing him. "I'd better go check on that. Maybe there'll be a restaurant in Franklin, though there wasn't the last time I was there." He turned his horse and said, "Come on, Red," and the big horse shot out at a dead run. Jori watched as he dashed back toward the remuda, saw him speaking with Callie and noted that the young woman was waving her arms about in an excited fashion. She turned her horse around and dashed away with Rocklin after her.

"I wonder what that was about?" Jori envied the young woman's freedom. Her clothes were certainly more practical. Wearing a dress across the prairie was not the most comfortable thing in the world. All the petticoats except one she had dispensed with, and the shoes that she had started out with were totally inadequate. She made up her mind that one thing she would buy in

Franklin was a pair of shoes, even if they had to be the clodhoppers that some of the men wore.

"Pitiful excuse for a town, isn't it?" Mark muttered. He was surly as he slumped on the seat of the wagon, a small one Leland had included for the women to ride in. Kate ran her eyes over the paintless buildings that seemed to have little form and noted that the most important thing about Franklin were the animals. There were mules and oxen and horses everywhere.

"Well, it's not St. Louis or Little Rock, Mark, but it's probably the closest thing to a town we'll see for nearly a thousand miles."

Mark did not speak. He was weary, and the one supply that he had brought with him from Little Rock was liquor. His eyes were red rimmed even now.

Kate was tempted to speak to Mark, but she knew that this was not the time. She loved the boy as if he were her own. He had a sweet nature usually, except when he was crossed. He was spoiled, of course, as was Jori, but she had hope for both of them. It was her prayer that this trip, even the hardship, would do something for them that they needed.

The wagons pulled up just outside the edge of town, and Rocklin disappeared. He came back quickly and said, "No hotel, so we'll camp as usual."

The mule skinners did not seem to find that unusual. They at once began making preparations, and the campfires soon put out acrid smoke that rose to the late afternoon sky. "I think I'll go to that store and see if I can pick up a few things. It'll be our last chance," Kate said. She started to get down when suddenly she found Good News there. He put his hand out, and, as always, she hid her crippled hand behind her. He took her free hand and handed her to the ground.

"Goin' shoppin', I reckon?"

"Yes. I do need a few things."

"You mind a little company?"

"Why no. Come right along."

The two walked over to the store, and Jori soon joined them. Inside the store, which was the largest building in town, Rocklin and Jesse Burkett, who was probably the quietest man on the train, were going over a list.

"Look at this, Aunt Kate," Jori said. She carried the cash, and she handed the list over to Kate.

Kate studied the list carefully. It included

flour, coffee, sugar, bacon, and meal. "No frills there," Kate smiled. "Let's get some dried fruit," she suggested. "Maybe I can make some pies."

"That'd be mighty good," Rocklin said.

Buying a few things was a pleasant enough break, and Kate heard Jori ask the store-keeper, "Do you have such a thing as a sidesaddle?"

"A what?" The clerk was a short, roly-poly man with round eyes and round face. Everything about him seemed to be round, even his mouth when he opened it. "No, ma'am, I ain't got nothin' like that. Plenty of saddles."

"No, thank you."

Jori moved away and Kate said, "Why don't you ride astride like a man?"

"You know I can't. Not in a dress. In the first place, it'd chafe me raw."

"Well, with two women as smart as we are, we should be able to make some kind of an outfit. I've been thinking about it. Let's find some good material, and we'll make you something you can ride in."

By the time Jori awoke, the sun was shining in through the gap in the front of the tent. Kate and Carleen were gone, and the sound of activity outside the tent was evident.

Throwing back the covers, Jori stood for a moment irresolutely then glanced down at her clothing that lay neatly folded on a camp stool. She picked up the white blouse, slipped it on and buttoned it up, then reached down and picked up the skirt that she and Kate had labored on by a lantern light until late. The material was a royal blue and much heavier than the dresses she usually wore. She held it up by the waist and smiled, thinking how simple it all had been, for Kate was an expert seamstress. She lowered the skirt, stepped into it, noting it came down just to her ankles. Basically they had made a full skirt, slit it in the front and the back, and then sewed up the separate side so that, in effect, she had a divided skirt. She fastened a black leather belt around her waist, slipped on her shoes, and then turned around quickly, feeling the freedom. It felt rather strange, but the thought that she would be able to ride astride pleased her. Quickly she ran a comb and brush through her hair and put on the small white hat with the wide brim that kept her face from the full force of the sun and exited from the tent.

The first person she saw was Addie Joss squatting before a fire, pushing some bacon around with a fork. "Good morning, Addie.

How are you today?"

"Just fine, ma'am. I've about got your breakfast ready."

"Where did everybody go?"

Addie had a tin plate by his side. He put four strips of bacon on it and then as he broke two eggs into the skillet, he remarked, "They done gone over to town to do a little shoppin', I guess. Got only bacon and eggs for breakfast. Maybe I could make biscuits later."

"That's fine, Addie."

"The coffee's ready, Miss Jori."

Jori got her tin cup, filled it with coffee, and then sat down on a box of trade goods. She took the plate from Addie and began to eat, finding that she, as always, was hungry. The outdoor air did something to her appetite. "Are you glad to be going to Santa Fe, Addie?"

"Don't make no never mind to me, ma'am, as long as it ain't Mississippi."

Not for the first time Jori wondered about the man. "What's wrong with Mississippi?" she asked, taking a bite of bacon.

"It ain't good for black folks in Mississippi."

"Were you a slave there, Addie?"

"Yes, ma'am, I was."

"Did you run away?"

Addie nodded and considered her for a moment. He was a handsome man with pure black skin and high cheekbones. "Yes, ma'am, I did, but I reckon there's a reward out for me there so I'll be pleased if you don't tell nobody."

"Of course not. Things will be better for you, do you think, in Santa Fe?"

"Any place would be better where a man's free."

Jori ate her breakfast, thinking about the problem of slavery. Her family had once owned two slaves, but her father had disliked the institution and sold them. Because they were not farm people, they did not require a large amount of labor and found that they could get along much better by hiring their help.

When she finished her breakfast, Jori thanked Addie then said, "I think I'll go into town myself."

"Yes, ma'am." A light of humor touched his eyes, and he said, "Some of the hands got pretty rambunctious last night."

"What do you mean?"

"They went to the saloon and acted up. Got into a fight with some other men. They're in jail until Mr. Rocklin pays their fine."

Jori was irritated. "Who was it?"

164

"Well, ma'am, your brother. He was one of them. Wiley Pratt and Charlie Reuschel, they was in on it. A couple more."

"Well, I'd better go get them out."

"Mr. Rocklin is plumb riled up about it," Addie Joss grinned. "He threatened to beat 'em with a bull whip, but I don't reckon he will. He needs 'em to drive the wagons."

As Jori left, she thought of Mark and anger came over her. "He's disgracing the whole family," she muttered. "I'm going to have a talk with him."

Rocklin was examining the hoof of one of the mules, but he put it down and looked up as Jori walked rapidly toward him. "Morning, Jori," he said.

"What's this I hear about some men being arrested?"

"That's about the size of it. They took on too much liquor last night and got into a fight. There's not much law around here, but there's a judge and a sheriff. We'll have to pay their fines or else go off and leave 'em."

"You know we can't do that," Jori said.

"Reckon that's right enough. You want me to do it?"

"We'll both go."

"All right." Rocklin gave her a quick look

and said, "New dress?"

"It's — it's a new skirt." She looked at him defiantly. "It's a riding skirt. I can ride astride now."

"Well, that's sensible. Don't know why more women don't do that. Looks nice, too."

Despite herself, Jori felt pleased by his compliment, but she said shortly, "I didn't buy it for looks but for comfort. Come on, let's go get them out of jail."

They said very little on the way, Rocklin doing most of the talking about the supplies that they had to buy before they left Franklin. They reached the jail, which was an unpainted frame building with a sign *Sherif's Office.*

"They can't even spell in this place. Look how they spelled sheriff," she said.

"I reckon education's no requirement for being a lawman here," Rocklin grinned. He opened the door and stepped back, and when she entered he followed her. A man was sitting behind a desk with a plate of scrambled eggs in front of him. He put his fork down and nodded.

"Howdy. What can I do for you?"

"I'm Rocklin. This is Miss Hayden. We've come to pay the fines for our men."

"I'm Sheriff Smith." Smith was a tall, sad-

166

looking individual who surprisingly wore a suit and tie. He nodded and said, "That'll be ten dollars each, forty dollars total."

"They do any damage?" Rocklin said.

Jori fished the money out of the leather purse that she carried. "Just to themselves. They tangled with some pretty rough characters. I'd suggest you get 'em out of here before they get into more trouble."

"Well, that's our intention."

"I'll get 'em for you."

Sheriff Smith took the money, shoved it into a drawer, and then disappeared through a door. The two stood there listening as the voices came faintly, then the door opened and Smith came out followed by Mark Hayden and the three members of the train, Wiley Pratt, Stuffy McGinnis, and Charlie Reuschel. They all looked the worse for wear, and Mark avoided looking directly at Jori.

"I enjoyed havin' you boys with us," Sheriff Smith said cheerfully. "Come back anytime."

"Come on, Mark," Jori said as she wheeled around and walked outside. She waited until he was outside. "What do you mean by doing a thing like this? You're a disgrace, Mark!"

"Don't you start on me, sis," Mark said.

His lips were puffy where he had evidently taken a blow, and his ear was red.

Jori started to speak, but then Rocklin came out followed by the three others.

"I need to speak to you, Rocklin."

"Sure. You fellows get on back. We'll be leaving tomorrow. You'd better check your mules and your equipment."

The three left rather sheepishly, and Rocklin turned to wait with an inquiring look in his eye.

"I want you to put Mark to work."

"I don't need you to boss my life!" Mark snapped.

Jori ignored him. "Treat him just as you would any of the other men. Make him work." She turned and walked away, her head held high.

"I guess you heard the boss," Rocklin remarked.

"She's stuck up and spoiled. That's what's wrong with her."

"But she's the boss. Come on."

"Come where?"

"I'm gonna put you to work."

"I don't have to take orders from you."

"Then you stay here in Franklin while the train goes to Santa Fe." A hard light glinted in Rocklin's eyes, and Mark was taken aback.

"My father owns this train."

"And he made me the wagon boss. You know the rules. I put a man afoot if he doesn't keep the rules. Make up your mind, Mark. You going to pull your share of the load, or are you staying here and becomin' a full-time drunk?"

Mark's face flushed, but he knew he had no choice. He didn't say a word but clamped his lips together. "Come on then," Rocklin said. The two made the walk back toward where the train was camped. Rocklin spotted Pedro Marichal and Callie Fortier and went straight for them. "Pedro, I've got a new helper for you. Put him to work and be sure he pulls his share."

"Sí, señor."

Mark stood there feeling about as miserable as he had ever felt in his life. Pedro studied him carefully and said, "Can you ride?"

"Of course I can ride," Mark said stiffly.

"Take that bay and saddle him up." He lifted one eyebrow and grinned. "We've got a long way to go, boy, and not one mile of it's gonna be much fun."

CHAPTER NINE

As Mark Hayden slumped in the saddle, he was aware of a queer tinge that arose somehow within him. It was a stray current of something out of his far past, a half-warm regret and somehow aptly sentimental. For a moment he tried vainly to remember more clearly, but he had drunk so much of the raw whiskey that he had bought at Franklin and hidden in the wagon beneath a pile of goods that his thoughts were not working very well. A raucous sound overhead drew his eyes upward, and he watched as a cloud of blackbirds wheeled against the blue-gray sky, then by some common consent gathered themselves into one unit and headed to the south. The dust raised by the wagons was so fine it clogged his nostrils and made him blink his eyes. He wished for a rain, and when he looked overhead, he saw that the blue was fading and the whole sky was turning into a gunmetal gray.

From far up ahead came the sound of the cracking of the mule skinners' whips, and their voices were coarse on the noon air. Mark slumped even more bonelessly in the saddle, wishing that he were back in civilization again. The sound of a rifle made a round-shaped echo, striking over the land's great stillness, and at the same time the raw liquor in Mark's stomach seemed about to erupt. The memory of home laid a strictness around his mouth, and reaching into his inner pocket he pulled the silver flask out, unscrewed the cap, and lifted it. The whiskey burned like lye as it went down, scraping against the tender lining of his throat.

Suddenly Mark became aware of a movement to his left. Wheeling quickly, he blinked and saw Callie Fortier sitting on her horse watching him carefully. He seemed to see derision in her eyes, and anger ran across his nerves. "What are you looking at?" he demanded.

"You!" Callie's face was shadowed by the broad-brimmed hat she wore, and her gray eyes were steady as she watched him.

"Well, go watch somebody else." Rebellion boiled over in him, and ignoring her, he took two more swallows of the whiskey. He capped the flask and put it away. "Now," he snapped, his voice slurring slightly, "I guess you'll run to Rocklin and tell him that I've been a bad boy!" He waited for her to answer, but she did not say a word. There was something about this girl that bothered him. He had seen disapproval in her eyes from the beginning, and when he had tried to be friendly she had been curt and answered in monosyllables.

"Go tell him then. What's he gonna do, fire me?" He turned his horse around and left, hanging onto the saddle as the horse made a rough trot across the prairie.

Callie watched him go and wondered what sort of man he was and what sort he would become.

"Not much of a hand, is he, Callie?"

Callie turned to see Pedro, the herd boss, who had ridden up beside her. He rode a magnificent bay stallion, and his eyes were such a dark brown that it was almost impossible to see the pupils.

"Not much, I think."

"He's spoiled," Pedro shrugged. "He'll get some of that knocked out of him pretty soon." He took a cigar out of his pocket, put it in his mouth, and held it there without lighting it. "You're doing well, Callie."

Callie turned to smile at him, and Pedro

held her eyes for a moment. He saw sadness there, and he knew enough of her history to understand that it was the loss of her father that had put it there. He had not spoken of this before, but he knew it because Rocklin had told him. "I'm very sorry about your father," he said quietly.

Callie looked at him quickly and saw the sincerity of the drover's face. "Thank you, Pedro. It was a hard loss."

Pedro shifted the cigar between his teeth, dropped his head, and seemed lost in thought. He was actually trying to think of something to say that would be a comfort to the girl. Pedro summoned a smile. "You'll get over it, señorita. You're young."

"Young isn't always good, no."

Pedro stared at the young woman and shrugged. "It's better than what comes later," he said shortly.

Leland Hayden looked up as Rocklin pulled his horse to a stop beside the wagon. "What's up ahead, Rocklin?" he asked.

"Good news. There's a fine campsite ahead. We'll get there in about three hours." Rocklin's eyes rested on the older man's face. He saw the weariness there, the sunburn that must have been painful, and the slight tremor of the hands that held the line of the horses. He shifted his gaze to Kate Johnson, and something passed between the two of them. He liked this woman very much. "She's got bottom," he had said to Good News Brown once. It was the highest compliment he could pay to a woman about her good sense.

"You're doing good, boss. You're gonna make it."

The words seemed to make Leland feel better. He straightened up and managed a grin. "I should have done this when I was a young man."

"No time like the present."

"I guess the worst of it lies ahead of us, doesn't it?"

Rocklin shrugged his shoulders in a habitual gesture. "Look at it this way, boss. Today we got plenty of water, the stock is holding up, no hostiles puttin' arrows into our livers." He grinned, and his teeth seemed very white against his bronze skin. "Just enjoy the day." Reaching down, he untied a sack around his saddle horn. "Brought supper," he said and handed the bag over.

Leland took it and handed it to Kate, who opened it and reached inside. She pulled out the limp body of a quail and exclaimed, "Quail! My favorite!"

"Mine too," Rocklin nodded. "I gutted them for you, but I hate to pick the feathers on the dratted things. Love to eat 'em though."

"I'll save you the fattest one, Chad."

Chad laughed suddenly, turned his horse around, and rode off at a gallop.

"That man's got more energy than anybody ought to have," Leland murmured.

"I'm glad he's with us."

"So am I." Leland held the lines loosely in his hands and suddenly laughed. "Imagine me driving mules across the world all the way to Santa Fe. We never know what's ahead of us, do we, Kate?"

"No, and that's probably a good thing. Rocklin's right. Just enjoy the day."

A shout from up ahead caught Leland's attention. He leaned over and looked up and saw that Stuffy McGinnis was engaged in some kind of an argument with Eddie Plank. "Those two are always arguing," he said. "I don't know why." His mind went back to his remark. "What do you think, Kate?"

"About this journey? I think it's good. I think God's in it."

Suddenly Leland grabbed the lines with his left hand, reached over and took her good hand. "You're good to have around, sister-in-law," he said. "I don't know what I would have done without you all these years."

"You would have managed."

"Maybe, but I'm glad you're along."

Chad Rocklin made it a point several times a day to go around and check all the wagons and then the mules and the riding stock. When he saw that the herd had fallen behind by half a mile, he touched Big Red with his heels. "Come on, boy," he said, "show what you got." He enjoyed the feel of the big horse's muscles moving smoothly underneath him and let him have his head.

He pulled up shortly to where Callie was trying to get some recalcitrant mules back to the main herd. Taking out his rope, he uncoiled it and began to pop them using it as a whip. He saw Callie smile at him, and the two of them got the mules back in the main herd and headed in the right direction.

"There may be something more stubborn and more stupid than a mule," Rocklin remarked, "but offhand I can't think of it."

"I like them," Callie said simply.

Chad laughed and turned to look at the girl. There was a light dust on her face, but the skin beneath was clear and smooth as anything he had ever seen. She had a fine ivory complexion, and there was a liveliness now in her gray eyes that made him wonder. "Never knew a woman that loved a mule. As a matter of fact, never saw a man that loved one either."

"I do."

"Why in the world would you like a mule?"

"Maybe because no one else does." She smiled at him, and he saw that her teeth were perfect, unusually white and very even. Her lips were soft, well shaped, and the corners of them turned up into smiles. "Everyone needs someone to like them, don't you think?"

"I reckon that's right, but mules are sorry creatures."

"They're tougher than horses," Callie said.

"Well, if it's toughness you want, I reckon you found it in a mule."

The two rode along talking idly. Suddenly Chad glanced around, his eyes narrowing. "Where's Mark?"

"I don't know."

"What do you mean, you don't know? He's supposed to be helping you."

"I haven't seen him all afternoon."

The curtness of Callie's reply was a tip-off to Rocklin. He reached out and grabbed her arm. This pulled her eyes around, and she said quickly, "Don't pull me, please."

"Sorry. I reckon I'm a little bit upset. Mark's supposed to help you. I take it he hasn't been doing it."

Reluctance made Callie's face stiffen, and she merely shrugged her shoulders. The whole picture suddenly became clear to Rocklin. He had not been watching Mark closely enough. Now his lips tightened, and he said, "You won't have to do all the work from now on, Callie." He suddenly kicked the big horse into a dead run, and Callie watched him ride off. She said nothing, but five minutes later when Pedro drifted close she told him what had happened. Pedro laughed, and his eyes gleamed. "I'd hate to be that Mark. He's gonna get his tail kicked!"

As soon as Rocklin rode up to Leland Hayden's wagon and saw the small brown mare that Mark had been riding, he pretty well understood what had happened. "Pull up, boss."

He waited until the wagon stopped and then stepped out of the saddle. Moving forward, he tied his horse to one of the wheels and as he did, Leland and Kate dismounted and came back to where he stood. "Is Mark in there?" Rocklin asked, his voice stiff and hard.

"He — he didn't feel well," Leland said. "I think he picked up some kind of cold."

Rocklin's glance went at once to Kate. He saw that she was saying nothing, but he saw something pass between the two.

Rocklin moved over to the wagon, threw back the canvas cover, and saw Mark lying flat on his back. Grabbing him by both ankles, he dragged him out. Mark gave a wild cry as he came out of the wagon; he hit the ground hard.

As Mark came to his feet, Rocklin took in the red rimmed eyes, and the smell of raw whiskey was unmistakable. "What do you mean putting your hands on me?" Mark said, his voice slurred.

Jori suddenly appeared, and her eyes were angry. "What are you doing, Rocklin? He's sick."

"No, he's not sick. He's drunk."

Jori started to speak, but Kate suddenly interrupted her. "Be quiet, Jori."

Jori turned with astonishment and saw that Kate's eyes were fixed on her, and her lips were tight with displeasure. Very rarely was it that Jori had heard her aunt speak like this, especially since she had become a grown woman. At that moment she understood that she was in a different world and that the old world would not work any longer. Clamping her lips together, Jori turned to Rocklin and saw that he was waiting for her to speak. When she did not, he turned and said, "Mark, you're a sorry excuse for a man. You haven't done an honest day's work since we left Little Rock, but you're going to from now on."

"I'm tired of riding herd on these stinking mules!"

"You won't have to anymore. You just lost your good job. Addie Joss will take your place."

"Good!"

"Nope, you'll be the wood finder."

The alcohol had dulled Mark's senses, and he could not make sense of that. "What?" he demanded.

"You see those boxes on the back of all the big wagons? They're wood boxes. There'll be times when we camp and there won't be any wood. That's why they need to be filled, and you'll be the filler. Every night when we camp if those boxes aren't full, you don't eat. I want those boxes filled."

"I won't do it!" Mark said angrily.

"If you don't, then you won't eat. Up to you."

Rocklin reached out, unhitched Mark's

horse, walked around and mounted his own and rode away without another word.

"He can't do that to me, can he?"

"He's the wagon master, son," Leland said heavily. He turned around and walked toward the head of the wagon.

Kate came over and said quietly, "You'll have to give in, Mark."

Mark said furiously, "Not me, Aunt Kate!"

Kate exchanged glances with Jori and shook her head slightly then turned. She got up into the seat and said, "Let's go."

"What will happen, Kate?" Leland asked.

"That's up to Mark."

For the next two hours after the incident, Mark trudged along staying just behind the light wagon. His legs were weak, and by the time he saw Rocklin had formed the wagons into a circle, he was having to reach for breath. He went over at once and sat down beside one of the wheels and pulled his hat down over his face and went to sleep.

He was awakened sometime later by the delicious smell of something cooking. Moving his hat brim back, he saw Kate, Jori, his father, and Carleen roasting small birds over a fire. The fat was dripping into the flames and sent up a delicious aroma that made his stomach hurt. He had eaten nothing all day, and now he desperately wanted some food, but his pride kept him where he was.

He sat there in total misery while the others talked and ate.

Finally he heard Rocklin say, "Better get some sleep. It's gonna rain tomorrow. Looks like a flood coming." He heard Rocklin's footsteps approaching and then knew the big man was standing right over him. "If I were you," Rocklin said mildly, "I'd fill those wood boxes. It's a long way to Santa Fe without something to eat, Mark."

Mark did not respond. He sat there angry through and through, then he heard softer footsteps and his aunt's voice. "You'll have to give in, Mark."

"Not me," Mark said and turned away from her.

The next day at breakfast Mark was ravenous. He waited for his father to intervene but saw that was not going to happen. Jori finally came over and said, "Mark, come and eat something. It won't hurt you to fill the boxes. You don't have to fill them all up."

"I won't do it, Jori. He can't make me."

He got to his feet and said nothing to anyone until, finally, the train started.

The rain started at the same time. It was only a soft drizzle at first, settling the dust, which made everything smell good; but soon it began to come down in a solid sheet. They had all brought slickers, and Mark went to the wagon where Kate fished his out in silence. He half expected her to offer him some food, but she did not.

All morning long Mark trudged beside the wagon. He broke his stride only once to forge ahead and go to the wagon driven by Charlie Reuschel. "Charlie, you got anything to eat?"

"Not for you," Charlie grinned down. The rain was running off of his hat. "The boss said you don't eat until you fill the wood boxes. Was I you, I think I'd get to work. A long way to Santa Fe on an empty belly."

At that moment something turned inside of Mark Hayden. He knew that the word was out, that the mule skinners all grinned at him, and some of them laughed outright and made fun of him.

"I've got to do something," he said. His pride was strong, and when they pulled up for camp, the rain was coming down steadily. He watched as Addie Joss and Rocklin put up a tarpaulin and Rocklin helped get a small fire going. It was hard with wet wood, but he had told Kate to cover up the wood that they were carrying, and there was enough for a small fire. Kate cooked supper, and Rocklin came over and said so quietly that no one could hear him, "Mark, we're all of us fools when we are young. You wouldn't believe some of the crazy things I did. When I look back, I see that I didn't make a thing off of it. You're gonna have to work, son. Why don't you come and get something to eat?"

Mark knew that he was whipped. It almost hurt him to have to speak, but he grunted solemnly, "All right. I'll get the wood."

"Well, that's fine. Better come and have some supper. It's right good. It might be the last hot meal we have for a time in this rain."

Mark watched as Rocklin walked over and said something to Kate and saw her begin to stir. He moved over as soon as Rocklin left. "Here, Mark, some of this stew ought to be good," Kate offered.

Mark took the bowl, and it was all that he could do to keep from crying out with pleasure as he ate. He could not meet Kate's eyes nor his father's, but finally he said, "I'll get the wood. I told Rocklin."

"That's fine, son," Leland said quickly.

Kate put her hand on his shoulder and said nothing, but when he met her eyes, he saw that she was pleased with him. "I've got some biscuits from this morning," she said.

"You can put some of the sorghum I've got left on them. It'll go down good."

Jori watched all this, and as soon as Rocklin left, she followed him. The rain had slacked off, but it was still falling in something more than a mist but less than the driving rain they had endured all day. "Rocklin," she said, and when he turned, she saw he was watching her cautiously. "How long would you have kept him from eating?"

"Don't know, Jori."

"He's my brother," Jori said with some reluctance, "and he's weak, but we all are. Don't you understand that?"

"Sure I do. But don't you understand if we make it to Santa Fe, we're going to have to give everything we've got. If I let down, I'm not just letting myself down, I'm letting every man and every woman in this train down. We've got to hang together. That's what it means to be in a thing like this."

Jori weighed his words and then said, "I don't understand you."

"Nothing much to understand."

"You would have let him starve?"

"Didn't think it would come to that, Jori. Most of us have a breaking point, and I figured Mark would find his before he starved. As a matter of fact, I can remember a few times when I was about his age and just as stubborn and just as proud. I had to almost be broke in two. Well, it didn't hurt me. It may even be good for Mark."

"You're too hard."

Rocklin put his gaze on her, and not for the first time was intensely aware of the clean-running physical lines of her figure and the lovely turnings of her throat. She had a mouth that was ripe and self-possessed, and her face was a mirror that changed as her feelings changed. He suddenly was aware that old hungers were stirring in him and knew such things were hopeless with this woman.

"I guess that's right. I've had to be." He watched her for a moment and then turned and disappeared into the darkness.

CHAPTER TEN

The rain had poured down steadily for two days with scarcely a break. At times it was almost impossible to see through the slanting lines of drops as they formed a curtain over the train. The darkness of the sky added to the gloom, and Jori was absolutely miserable as her horse plodded along beside their light wagon. The ground had turned to a mud that seemed to suck the hooves of the animals into it. Up and down the line the raucous curses of the mule skinners were punctuated by the cracking of their whips.

Occasionally the sun would break through, and the rain would modify until it became a mist that soaked clothing to the skin. The rays of the sun threw an amber corona of nearly futile light, twisting the shadows of the trees beside the road into tortured shapes. The lack of sleep and the miserable weather was enough to keep Jori irritated, and finally Carleen, who did not seem to mind the weather at all, said loudly, "I don't want to talk to you anymore, Jori," and had splashed off in the mud to find someone else. Jori had the impulse to call her back and apologize, but she felt too miserable for that.

At noon they stopped to rest the animals that were already exhausted by the half day's labor of pulling the heavily loaded wagons through the sea of mud. Jori got off her horse, and her feet sank in the mud halfway to her knees. She gave a disgusted cry and pulled her foot out, leaving the shoe in the mud. This meant that she had to get down and fish it out. She stood there on one foot undecided as to whether to put her foot back into the mud-filled shoe then gave up. With a sigh she shoved her foot in and managed to make her way over to Kate who was fishing in the back of the wagon for something in which to make a cold lunch.

"This is awful, Aunt Kate," she said. "I don't think it'll ever stop raining."

"It always has." Kate turned. Her hair was wet and hung down her back in strings. "I reckon Noah and his folks felt the same way, but from what I hear about the trail ahead, there'll be days when we'll be wishing we could have some of this water."

"I've got to change shoes. Look at these."

"If you've got any boots, you'd better put 'em on. You're going to need 'em."

Jori climbed into the wagon and had to move boxes and supplies until she finally found the box containing her extra shoes and a pair of knee-high boots that she had bought at some time in the past. She sat there amid the conglomeration of supplies and clothing, putting on dry socks and the boots. She scrambled outside and found Good News talking to Kate. "Howdy, Miss Jori. Think it's gonna rain?"

Jori gave him a disgusted shake of her head. Carefully she came to the ground and looked for a good path, but there was none. "Bring me my horse, will you, Good News?"

"Sure will." Good News brought the horse over, and Jori mounted him from the back of the wagon.

"I'll have dry feet until I get off," she said. She looked ahead and said, "I'm going to ask Rocklin how far we're going to go today." She moved away, and Good News stared after her. His eyes were thoughtful, and he shook his head.

"Trip like this is a little bit hard on ladies." He turned to Kate and smiled. His eyes were a warm brown, and admiration shaded his tone. "I don't ever hear a complaint out of you."

"Complaining doesn't do much good as far as I can tell." Kate had pulled out some biscuits and bacon that had been fried the last day. "How about a biscuit sandwich with bacon. Not too tasty."

"Go down mighty good, Miss Kate." He took the two biscuits Kate had sliced and stuffed with bacon and turned his head to one side. "Thank You, Lord, for these good bacon sandwiches." He bit into one, and the bacon crunched beneath his teeth. "Mighty good," he repeated.

Kate studied the slight smile on his face. "Have you found anyone to expose to the gospel?" she asked, knowing his fondness for speaking of his faith.

"Just the usual congregation. Most of them ain't too eager to hear about their sins, but I keep trying."

"I admire you," Kate said. "If every Christian were as outspoken as you, Good News, the kingdom of God on earth would be people. The family of God would be enlarged."

"Well, it seems like I don't do a lot of good, but I just keep trying. Right after I got saved I promised the Lord I'd be a voice for Him, even if it was a sorry one. So now when I put my left foot down, I wanna say

'Hallelujah!' and then, when I put my right foot down, I wanna say 'Praise the Lord.' " He took another bite of the sandwich then nodded. "I appreciate your words though. I do get a little bit discouraged."

"I'll tell you what I got on my mind for today. As soon as we camp, you and Joss put that tarpaulin up. I'm going to set up and make fried pies."

"Fried pies? Why they ain't nothin' but my favorite!" Good News exclaimed.

"I brought dried apples and peaches. Which is your favorite?"

Good News laughed. He liked this woman very much. Actually, he was rather shy with women. He was not a handsome man. He had little of this world's goods and was uneducated. Still, there was something about Kate Johnson that made him feel warm inside. "There ain't no such thing as a bad pie, ma'am. The worst fried pie I ever had in my life was real good."

Kate suddenly laughed. She had, indeed, a warm rich laugh that came from her heart, and she said, "Well, you'll be an easy man to please. You come by, and I'll make one of each for you."

"You can count on it, Miss Kate."

Kate rode in the wagon for the rest of the

day. Leland was silent, and she knew he was discouraged by the steady downpour and by the misery of the trip. From time to time she would make an encouraging remark, but he merely answered in monosyllables. Finally she gave up the attempt and sat there watching the mules as they struggled to pull the Conestogas through the mud.

The hours passed, and Rocklin went down the line shouting, "Make camp!" When Leland put their wagon into place and Kate stepped down, Rocklin came over. He had a small deer over the pommel of his saddle. "Fresh meat tonight. Pretty fat, too."

"Good. I'll dress the thing."

"No need of that, ma'am." Addie Joss had appeared, his smile lighting his face. "Give me that varmint, Mr. Rocklin."

"You can have my part of it. I'd rather shoot 'em or eat 'em rather than dress 'em." When Joss moved off to some distance and began dressing the deer, Kate asked, "Did you expect all this rain, Chad?"

"Sure didn't, but it's not unseasonable this time of year. April brings these spring rains. We'll be wishing we could have some of it when we cross the Arkansas and hit the desert country."

The two talked for awhile, and finally Kate said, "Well, I've got to start making

192

my pies."

Rocklin stared at her. "How are you going to make pies without an oven?"

"You wait and see. Don't eat too much of that deer. Fried pies are my specialty."

Rocklin visited every wagon and spoke with most of the men. He saw that they were in a bad humor, and that was understandable. Wiley Pratt, a short, muscular man, was outspoken. "I wish I had stayed back in St. Louis," he complained.

"Oh, Wiley, this is fun!" Stuffy McGinnis was grinning widely. He winked at Rocklin and continued to tease Pratt. "Look here. This is just like a vacation. We got plenty of rain and good food and a good chance of bein' scalped by Indians. What more could a fellow want?"

"I wish you'd shut up, Stuffy. I'm tired of listenin' to you!" He gave Rocklin a hard glance and said, "He's not kidding about those Indians though. I hate Indians. The only good one's a dead one."

Rocklin was accustomed to this attitude from many men. Wiley Pratt was speaking what many a frontiersman felt. His years with the Comanches had changed his attitude, but he knew it was useless to argue.

"Well, you boys enjoy those steaks."

"I don't know how we're gonna cook 'em," Pratt complained, "with it rainin' like this."

"You'll find a way."

"Eat 'em raw. That's what I say," Stuffy grinned. "It won't hurt you none, Wiley."

The darkness had fallen as Rocklin made his way back to the canopy that shaded the fire and the Hayden family. "It smells good," he said.

"Sit down here," Kate smiled. "I saved you a good, juicy steak."

Rocklin seated himself, crossed his legs, and took the tin plate. There was only the steak and bread, but hunger had sharpened him, and he ate it quickly. As he ate, Carleen sat beside him peppering him with questions. Rocklin had grown to expect this from the young woman. "What was it like when you were a boy?" she asked him.

"About like it is for you."

Carleen shook her head. Grease coated her mouth from the steak, and she didn't bother to wipe it off. "No, boys have it better than girls."

"How do you figure that?"

"They can do all kinds of stuff. All women can do is wear long dresses and cook."

"I think there's a little bit more to being a woman than that," Rocklin said, winking at

Kate, who was smiling at Carleen's remark. She persisted, however, asking him about his boyhood life, and as he finished his steak, he told her several stories. "You know, Carleen, once we had a mule on our place that was downright cantankerous. He didn't mind doin' light work, but whenever we tried to hitch him to a heavy plow he pitched a fit. Anytime he saw a heavy tool he would rear up and break away and run into the barn. One of my jobs when he did that was to go put a trace chain around his neck and have a bigger mule drag him outside. He was pure poison to hitch and hated heavy work worse than any man I ever saw. I think I was kind of like that mule."

"Sounds to me like you've done a lot of work," Leland muttered.

"Oh, I have all right, but I've got a lazy streak in me."

"Here," Kate interrupted. "Everybody can have one pie." She had put back two for Good News, but she did not mention that. "Which do you want, Rocklin, peach or apple?"

"I purely hate makin' decisions, Kate. You just give me whichever one's the closest." She handed him a pie, and he cautiously bit off the end. "This is the best peach fried pie I ever had. That was one of the things I missed living with the Indians. They weren't much on making pies."

"What did they eat?" Carleen demanded.

"Mostly puppy dogs. Nice fat juicy ones," Rocklin said with a straight face. He saw Jori staring at him and gave her a wink. "Puppy dog stew. That was my favorite."

"You didn't really eat puppy dogs!" shrieked Carleen.

"Sure did. Indians like puppy dogs the way you like that pie there." He looked over and saw that Leland was slumped with his back against the wagon wheel. He was wet and miserable, and Rocklin said, "It looks a little bad right now, boss, but the sun will be out pretty soon and it'll be better."

Mark spoke up for the first time and said, "I didn't think it'd be like this."

Rocklin shrugged his shoulders. "That's what I have to say about most things that happen. I remember once I was pinned down by a bunch of Kiowa Indians. They was out to get my scalp, and I remember thinkin', *When I got up this mornin' I didn't think it'd be like this.*"

Carleen laughed and said, "You made that up."

"Maybe I did. I know you like made-up stories."

"Can't we wait until this rain slacks off?"

Jori asked abruptly. "It is wearing the animals out and us, too."

"No, that won't do, Jori. If we stopped every time we had trouble, we'd never get to Santa Fe."

"I keep thinking about back home with warm beds and nice food cooked in a stove and sitting down at a table to eat it," Mark said. He pulled his sodden jacket closer around his shoulders and said, "I dreamed about that last night."

A silence fell across the group, and Rocklin said quickly, "You know, Mark, the best thing I can think of is not to look back. There's a story in the Bible about that."

"You mean about Lot's wife?" Kate smiled.

"Yes. That was one stubborn woman. Lot told her plainly not to look back. She did and turned into a big block of salt." He took another bite of the pie, savored it, and then looked across at Jori and grinned. "I wonder if she's still there."

Jori could not help but smile at his imagination. "You like to make the best of things, don't you?"

"Seems best," Rocklin said. He finished his pie and lifted the tin coffee cup and drank the last drop. "When I was in jail once there was a fellow there that was a piano player. Well, he loved that piano, but, of course, we didn't have one in the jail. So this fellow made him a keyboard out of a piece of wood and used some ink to paint the keyboard. He'd just sit there for hours with that thing on the table. I never will forget it."

"What was he doing?" Carleen demanded, her eyes big.

"Well, his fingers were going over that keyboard just like it was a real piano. Of course, it didn't make any noise. It was kind of spooky. He'd sit there for hours, and I guess there was music in his head, but he about drove me crazy. But," he reached over and pulled Carleen's pigtails, "he was doin' the best he could under the circumstances."

"And that's what we'll have to do," said Kate. "I declare you're a comfort, Chad. Here, I'll reward you with another pie."

"I want one, too," Carleen begged.

"You can have half of mine," Rocklin said. He broke the pie in two and gave her half. "It'll be better pretty soon."

Kate had made a stew after the steaks from Rocklin's deer had played out. The train had another hard two days, and she was crouched in front of the fire stirring it. She looked up and saw Good News come toward her. "Sit down and see what this stew tastes like."

Good News at once sat down beside the fire, took his hat off and placed it beside him. He took the spoon she gave him, tasted the stew, and said, "That's prime, Miss Kate."

"You don't have to call me Miss Kate. Just Kate's enough." She looked at him oddly and turned her head to one side. She was a healthy, strong-bodied woman and had long, composed lips that held back some hidden knowledge and a way of studying people that sometimes disturbed them. "Is your real name Good News?" she asked abruptly. "I can't imagine naming a baby that."

"Sure is. Like I told you, my mama wanted me to proclaim the gospel, and she figured that's a good way to get started."

"I imagine people look at you strangely when you tell them your name."

"Almost always," he agreed, "but then that gives me a chance to tell them about the Lord Jesus."

They sat there for awhile, and he spoke for a time about his experiences with his name. Suddenly he looked at her and asked directly, "Have you ever been married, Kate?"

"No, I never have. Have you?"

"No, I haven't. Of course it's not odd about me, but I just wonder about you. Why didn't you ever marry?"

Kate was silent for a moment, then she held up her maimed hand. "Most men want a whole woman."

Her answer and the gesture shocked Good News. He straightened up and shook his head and then said with disbelief, "Why, Kate, you're as handy a woman as I ever saw! That wouldn't mean a thing to a man with sense."

Kate did not answer him. It embarrassed her to talk about her infirmity, and she quickly changed the subject. "Tell me about which part of the Bible you like best."

"I guess I like the Psalms and the Gospels, and I like Revelation, too. My uncle had a dog once, and he named it Revelation. I asked him why, and he said it was because he didn't understand a thing about him. That's about where I stand. I like it though."

"One of my favorites is that part of Hebrews that talks about people who had great faith."

"That's one of my favorites, too."

She got up and went to the back of the wagon and pulled out a Bible and came back and opened it. Finding the place, she read the first verse of Hebrews 11: " 'Now faith is the substance of things hoped for, the evidence of things not seen.' "

She handed him the Bible and said, "What do you think that means, the evidence of things not seen?"

He took the Bible and held it but did not look down at it. He was silent for such a long time that Kate asked in a puzzled tone, "What's the matter?"

"Well, I love this Book but —"

"But what?"

"But I can't read." He looked up and there was pain in his eyes, and suddenly Kate Johnson saw that underneath the rough exterior of Good News Brown was a sensitive man. She knew that he was intelligent, and she had heard him play his fiddle and sing in a clear tenor voice. He was good with mules. She had heard Rocklin say as much, but now he had revealed a side of himself that she had not dreamed of.

"How did you miss out on learning to read?"

"My folks didn't put no stock in it, and it's too late now."

"Why, don't be foolish, Good News," Kate said sharply. "It's never too late! You're a smart man."

"Me? Nobody ever accused me of that!"

"Well, you are." She studied him for a moment and said, "There's a verse of Scripture that says nothing is impossible with God. Do you believe that?"

"Yes, I believe it. I believe everything this Book says."

"Well, I'm going to teach you how to read." She watched as Good News lifted his head and hope came into his eyes. "Do you really think I could learn, Kate?"

"I know you can."

"I'd give anything if I could read this Book."

"Well, you can do something for me."

"For you? What can I do for you?"

"You can teach me how to use that whip of yours," Kate Johnson smiled. "Who knows, I might have to use it on someone one of these days."

CHAPTER ELEVEN

Callie pulled her horse up and straightened in the saddle. The mules, for once, were fairly well behaved, but she knew them too well to trust them much. Her eyes went across the level plain. To her left was the river bottom about two miles away, and scattered trees to her right broke the monotony of the plains. Pedro had kept her informed of their progress, pointing out that they had crossed One Hundred and Ten Mile Creek, which was ninety-five miles from Franklin, and then Bridge Creek and Big John Spring. Council Grove lay just ahead, and she knew that, according to Pedro, they would reach there in two days. "Council Grove," he said, "is about a hundred and fifty miles from Franklin. We're just getting started."

Letting herself sway with the smooth gait of her mount, Callie glanced forward to where the wagons were sloshing through the muddy ground. She heard Stuffy McGinnis, the most amiable of all the skinners in her mind, singing:

I'll tell you how it is when
You first get on the road;
You have an awkward team and
A very heavy load.
You have to whip and holler, but
You swear upon the sky.
You're in for it then, boys,
Root hog or die.

A smile touched Callie's lips, for most of the songs that the mule drivers sang were obscene beyond belief, as was their language. She knew that Rocklin had laid the law down to them all that on this drive they would have to forget about their cussing.

"Let me ride with you, Callie."

Callie turned and looked down to see Carleen looking up at her, bright eyed and excited.

"All right. Put your foot in the stirrup." Callie kicked her foot out of the stirrup, helped the girl get on behind her, and then felt the girl's arms go around her waist. It gave her an odd feeling, for she was not accustomed to being hugged. "They're pretty, aren't they?"

"What's pretty, Carleen?"

"The wagons. Look at them. They look like ships, don't they?"

Indeed, Callie had had this idea herself. The Conestogas were enormous wagons with high prows and sterns. Rocklin had told her that the wagons were built with curves like a ship so that the goods stored inside would hold steady. He also informed her that they were practically waterproof and could float.

"The covers look like sails," Carleen said.

"They do a little bit."

"How old are you?" Carleen demanded.

Callie was accustomed to the girl's incessant questioning. "I am seventeen years old, me."

"Why do you say *me* at the end of your sentence?"

"It's the way Cajuns talk."

"Say me some French."

"What do you want me to say?"

"Anything. I just like to hear it."

Callie smiled and described the prairie scene in French. "How you like that, little one?"

"I'm not little. I'm ten and I'll soon be eleven, and I'm big for my age."

"I should say young one then."

"Seventeen. I wish I was seventeen."

"Enjoy yourself. This is a good time for you, cherie."

"What does *cherie* mean?"

"It means dear."

"You mean like with horns?"

Callie suddenly laughed. "No, I mean like you call your mama dear mama."

"My mama's dead."

"Well, your sister then."

"When I get to be seventeen, I'm going to get married. And I'm going to have two boys and one girl. The boys will be named Charles and Thomas, and the girl will be named Eloise."

"That would be nice. What about your husband?"

"He will be tall and carry a pistol, and if anyone messes with me, he'll shoot 'em."

Callie was vastly amused by the girl's vivid and fruitful imagination.

"Why do you always wear man's clothes?"

"They're more comfortable on the trail."

"Did you wear dresses when you were at home?"

"Not much. My papa, he was a mule skinner. I go with him, and dresses are not easy to wear."

The two were suddenly interrupted, for Grat Herendeen seemed to be waiting in the path before them. The big man said,

"Hello, Callie."

Callie nodded and did not speak. Her eyes were watchful. She had learned about men at a hard school, and she well understood the desire that showed clearly on the big man's face. "Why don't you get down and walk with me a spell? Kid, you can ride the horse."

"I'm working, Herendeen."

"You can call me Grat, Callie."

"You can call me Miss Fortier," Callie said.

Herendeen stepped closer. He reached up and got Callie by the arm. "Don't be that way," he said. "Be friendly to a man."

Callie tried to jerk her arm back, but his grip was immensely strong. She could smell the tobacco and thought she could trace the smell of liquor on his breath. "You'd better get back to your wagon," she said.

"I will after awhile. Just take a little walk. No harm meant."

"You let her go!"

Grat turned to look at Carleen, who was staring at him from behind Callie's back. "Kids should be quiet when grown-ups are talking," he said. He would have said more, but suddenly there was the sound of an approaching horse. Herendeen and Callie looked up quickly and saw Rocklin coming at a dead run. He pulled his stallion up, and the glance he laid on Herendeen was hard.

"You better get back to your wagon, Grat. Your right wheel is wobbling."

"I'll fix it later."

"You heard what I said. Get back to your wagon."

Callie suddenly straightened up. There was something charged in the air. Herendeen carried a pistol at his side, and his whip was coiled over his shoulder. She knew from experience that the whip could be as deadly as the pistol. She had seen men cut to pieces by them, and she breathed quicker, sensing the potential for disaster.

Herendeen stood there, a bulky, dangerous shape in the noon sunlight. He was a man who liked trouble as other men liked liquor or women. His brute strength had won him victories, and the thickness of his skull had protected him from defeats. He had a sly look as he turned his head to one side. "You savin' this girl for yourself, Rocklin?"

Callie's face grew warm, and her glance shifted to Rocklin. He did not look at her. His eyes were fixed on Grat Herendeen. "I'm not going to argue this matter, Grat. You either get back to your wagon or start walkin' back toward Franklin."

Herendeen's face suddenly flushed. The anger that lay beneath the surface of the big man was evident. "You wouldn't put me afoot."

"You bet I would. Just try me."

The impulse was there. Callie saw it and sensed it. She saw Herendeen's hand brush against the butt of the gun at his right side. As far as she could tell, Rocklin was, as always, loose and easy in the saddle, but she knew that was all an illusion. Her life had been hard, and she had seen men shot down before. If Herendeen made a wrong move, there would be death on the prairie.

Herendeen passed the moment by. "Just out for a walk," he said. "No harm in that." He turned and walked back toward the train. He rolled slightly, the bulk of his body pulling him. Only once did he look back, but there was danger in that look.

"You have made yourself an enemy, Chad," Callie said.

"Doesn't matter."

"He may try to shoot you."

"He'll have to get in line. What are you doing back there, Carleen?"

"I got tired of walking. I wanted to ride for a spell. Can I ride with you?"

"No, I've got work to do."

For a moment Callie studied the big man quietly without seeming to. He was like a machine, she decided, made for hard usage. He did not have the bulk of Grat Herendeen, but there was strength in his long body. His chest was deep rather than wide, and there was something of the quality of a mountain lion that she had seen once — smooth and easy but explosive at times.

Chad expelled his breath and pushed his hat back on his forehead. "You've been doing good, Callie. A good hand with mules. Not everybody can handle them critters."

"I've done it a long time."

"What will you do when we get to Santa Fe?"

"Work."

"What kind of work?"

"I'll find something."

"Don't you have any family at all?"

"Just an uncle and an aunt and some cousins outside of Baton Rouge. I'll never get to them."

"I guess you and me are both orphans. Maybe we'll start a club. The Rocklin and Fortier Orphans Association."

"I don't have any mama. I want to join, too," Carleen demanded.

"You don't qualify, punkin. You've got a daddy and a sister and a brother."

"I want to join anyway."

"You can be an honorary member then." He looked at Callie and turned his head to one side. "If Grat gives you anymore trouble, let me know."

Callie suddenly laughed. She touched the gun at her side and said, "I will shoot him."

Rocklin grinned broadly. "Well, like I said, I need him to drive mules. Just let me take care of him."

Kate and Jori had been watching the scene from where they sat on the seat of the wagon. Leland was riding Kate's mare, for he had grown tired of sitting on the hard seat. Kate waited until she saw Rocklin ride off and then shook her head. "He'll have trouble with Herendeen one day. He's a bad one."

"I wish he weren't here."

"Hard to find good mule drivers, and Chad says he's the best."

Jori was watching Carleen, who was riding behind Callie. "I didn't want to bring that girl with us."

"Callie? Why not?"

"It didn't seem like a good idea." She continued to watch the two and then said, "I tried to get Chad to leave her there, but he wouldn't."

211

"Was there a place to leave her?"

Reluctantly Jori told the story of how the girl had nowhere to go. "Chad was afraid to leave her there with those two men."

"Well, I see that as a good thing. He's hard, but he's got a soft spot." She looked up suddenly and said, "I hope it doesn't start raining. I'm sick to death of it."

The train swayed forward, and the rain did not come. Instead, the sun came out and shone brilliantly. Rocklin came by to say that Council Grove was only ten miles ahead and they would camp there that night. Carleen had come back and joined the two women on the seat. She was a constant spring of talk, her voice filling in any silence.

Suddenly Carleen jumped up and said, "Look at that!" Before the two women could even turn, she was out of the wagon and running toward a grove of trees.

"Come back here, Carleen!" Jori shouted, but the girl did not stop.

"What does she see?" Kate asked, straining her eyes. "I don't see a thing."

"We can't go off and leave her," Jori said with exasperation. She pulled the two mules to a halt and jumped out of the wagon. She saw her father on a mare headed toward the grove of trees and ran lightly. The ground was dried up so that her feet did not sink in.

"Carleen, where are you going?" Leland called out.

Jori reached where Carleen was kneeling down, and her heart leaped when she saw an unconscious man lying there. At first she thought he was dead. "Carleen, come here," she commanded. Her father swung out of the saddle and went over at once. The three of them then looked down at the man.

"He's not dead," Carleen said.

The man was young, Jori saw, and she caught the raw odor of alcohol. Beside him was an empty bottle, and over to his left was a canvas suitcase stuffed with gear.

"You go back to the wagon, Carleen," Leland said. "We've got to help him. I'll go get Rocklin."

Carleen sped off, and Jori stared down at the unconscious man. His lips were moving, and she leaned forward but could make no sense out of his words. "He's dead drunk," she said in disgust.

"What in the world would anybody be doing drunk out here in the middle of this terrible country?"

Jori looked around and saw no signs of a horse, a wagon, or any means of transportation. She looked back at the man and saw that he was very thin. His clothes were filthy, and he had not shaved in days, it appeared. He had several bruises on his thin face and a raw wound on his forehead.

Rocklin must have been close because he came almost at once. Swinging out of the saddle, he came over and looked down at the unconscious man and shook his head. "He's taken a beating." Without saying anything Rocklin walked around and looked at the ground. He walked in ever wider circles, and finally he came back and said, "He was with a wagon. They left him here, I guess, but his gear's still here."

"What'll we do with him?" Jori asked.

"I don't know."

At that moment Carleen came near and heard the question. "We can't leave him here," she said. "We have to take him with us."

Rocklin glanced at her and shook his head. "Well, we'll make camp here. By morning he should be sober enough to talk, and then we'll see."

Carleen was sitting beside the unconscious man. A bed had been made in the light wagon, and she had crawled in. She had always taken care of sick or wounded animals and birds, and to her this was just

214

another wounded creature. The man suddenly flung his arm out and then cried out in pain. Carleen reached out and pushed his hair back off his forehead. "It's OK," she said. "Don't be scared."

The man's eyes opened, and he stared at her. "Where is this?" he muttered. "Who are you?"

"I'm Carleen Hayden. What's your name?"

The battered man licked his lips, which were swollen. "Paul."

"Oh, like in the Bible." The man looked at her and then struggled to sit up but was groaning with pain.

"My Aunt Kate is cooking some broth for you. You'll feel better when you eat."

The man stared at her with incomprehension then slumped back whispering, "I wish I were dead!"

Carleen studied the man and then said, "Don't be scared, Paul. It'll be all right." She sat there for thirty minutes, and when he did not move, she got out of the wagon.

The others looked at her, and Mark asked, "Did he wake up?"

"Yes. His name is Paul."

"What else did he say?"

For a moment Carleen considered telling them what he had said about wanting to die, but then she shook her head. "Nothing. I'm going to take care of him."

Rocklin suddenly laughed. He found this amusing. He came over, ruffled her hair, and grinned. "Well, good to have a nursemaid around. You can take care of me when I get sick, punkin."

CHAPTER TWELVE

To just open his eyes was a struggle, and when he tried to move, his body protested violently. Paul Molitor groaned and opened his eyes to slits. He knew he was lying in a wagon, for he saw the canvas over him. The wagon was not moving, and he could hear voices close at hand. His head was splitting, and he had cuts inside his mouth that hurt. The smell of food cooking came to him, but he felt no sense of hunger. The liquor had taken his appetite away, as always.

A rustling at the rear of the wagon toward his feet drew his gaze to a young girl who crawled up beside him. She was dressed in pants rolled up at the cuff and a gray shirt. "You're awake," she said.

Molitor struggled to sit up and groaned involuntarily. "Where am I?"

"I told you. Don't you remember when you woke up?"

"No."

"I'm Carleen — Carleen Hayden." She crawled over some sacks and boxes to get at him. She was on her knees and bent over staring directly into his face. "You can't sleep forever. You've got to get up and eat."

"Where is this place?"

"It's a wagon, Paul. Come on, get up."

Molitor's head seemed to swim, but he was terribly thirsty. "You got any water?"

"Of course we got water. There's a whole river of it outside there. Get up, and I'll give you some."

Molitor moved slowly. He could smell himself, the dried vomit on his shirt, and he had not had a bath in recent memory. Weakness came to him then, and he was tempted simply to lean back and die, but the girl who called herself Carleen pulled at his shirt. "Come on," she said. "Get out of the wagon."

With the girl's encouragement and help, Paul scooted down over the boxes to the end of the wagon. The ground seemed faraway, and when he let himself down and stood up, a dizziness came to him.

"Come on and sit down. You can meet my folks."

The last thing Molitor wanted was to meet anyone, but he did begin to feel stirrings of hunger. He followed the girl over to where a woman was cooking something over a fire. To her right a younger woman and an older man were standing, their eyes fixed on him.

"Paul's thirsty," Carleen said. "Here, Paul, I'll get you some water."

The older man nodded and said, "Well, you finally woke up. My name is Leland Hayden. This is my daughter Jori and my sister-in-law Kate."

Molitor licked his lips and tried to think of a suitable reply, but none came to him. Carleen came back and handed him a cup full of water. He spilled a great deal of it but gulped at it thirstily. When he finally lowered it and gave it back to the girl, he said, "I'm Paul Molitor."

"You better sit down here, Molitor," Leland said. "You're not in too good a shape."

"I've got some broth brewin' here. It ought to do you good," Kate said. "Sit down and eat."

Molitor sat down, shakily, leaning back against the wheel of a wagon. He saw that one of his shoes was gone and could not remember where he had lost it. He took the bowl of soup that the woman handed him and took a spoonful. The hot broth hurt the cuts in his mouth and inside his lips, but he ate it hungrily.

"Thanks," he said. "That was very good."

He handed the bowl back to Kate and looked around. "I don't know where I am exactly."

"This train's going to Santa Fe. We just crossed Diamond Springs." Leland saw that the name meant nothing and said, "You're past Council Grove. We'll be to the Little Arkansas in a few days."

Jori spoke then. Her voice was crisp. "What were you doing out here in such poor condition?"

Molitor cleared his throat and tried to arrange his thoughts. He had been drunk for so long that it was difficult. "I left St. Louis awhile back headed for Franklin. When I got there I worked at a stable."

"Why'd you go to Franklin?" Leland asked curiously. "There's nothing much there except the businesses that fit out wagon trains."

"I heard there was a friend of mine there, but he was dead when I got there so I got a job in a stable. That was about three weeks ago. I met a man there named Fenton, a trader. He said he was going to take a train to Taos in New Mexico and he needed a cook."

"You're a cook?" Jori said. It was in her mind as it was in the minds of the others that he had a frail look about him, not likely to be a good bet for a wagon train cook.

"No, I'm not a cook and I told him. But the night before he left, I guess I drank too much and when I woke up I was in a wagon on the way."

"What happened? Why'd you leave the train?" Leland asked.

"I — I didn't. Fenton put me out."

"Why would he do that?" Jori demanded. "He just left you, you mean?"

They all saw that Molitor was searching for an answer. "I guess it was because I couldn't cook and I stayed drunk." He looked at Leland and cleared his throat. "I need to get back to St. Louis."

"Well, we can't leave you. There's no way for you to get there that I know of unless we meet a train headed east."

A silence fell over the group, and Kate said quickly, "You can travel with us, Paul. We're sure to meet a train headed back to Franklin. Until then you can make yourself useful."

Paul Molitor looked down at his hands that were thin and trembling. He already was dying for a drink and saw nothing in the future but a grim dark way.

"I don't guess I'm very useful," he said and dropped his head.

The others looked at him, and Leland said

as cheerfully as he could, "Well, you'll feel better after awhile."

A group of the mule skinners had gathered around a fire and were cooking steaks. Pedro Marichal had shot an antelope and sold it to them and brought it by. "I hate antelope," Wiley Pratt said. "It's like eatin' shoe leather." He shoved his hair back, and his hazel eyes were filled with disgust. "Shoe leather might be better."

Grat Herendeen dominated the group as usual. "Eat it and shut up, Wiley. I'm tired of your bellyachin'."

Wiley was a hot-tempered man, but he knew better than to cross Herendeen. Sullenly he took out his knife and cut off a piece of the tough meat and began chewing it.

Stuffy McGinnis was working on his own steak. "I'm gonna get me a job as a cook on a river boat when I go back," he announced.

"What makes you think you can cook?" Brodie Donahue squatted on the other side of the fire from Stuffy. Except for Herendeen he was the largest of the drovers. He had wide shoulders and a solid neck. His hair and eyes were black, and he was as tired as the rest of them.

"I'll learn how. Them river boats, now,

that's the life. I took a trip on one. There was fancy women, gamblin', liquor flowin' like the river itself. Yep, maybe I'll become a river boat gambler."

Jesse Burkett grunted and took a swallow of black coffee. He was a tall man, lanky, with brown hair and blue eyes. He had lost his wife and three children to cholera two years earlier and had not smiled since then. "You're not much of a gambler, Stuffy. Even I can beat you."

Eddie Plank, a big man with an overflowing stomach, was eating his steak as if it were the best thing in the world. "Better enjoy this. It may be scarce down the way."

Grat Herendeen had been quiet for the most part. Now he shook his shoulders in a dissatisfied manner. "We should have been further along the way than this. Rocklin's not much of a wagon master."

Brodie Donahue laughed shortly. "Better not let him hear you say that."

"He can hear it if he wants to," Herendeen said.

Brodie Donahue, alone among the mule skinners, had no fear of Grat Herendeen. His face was scarred with battles in the past, and although not as large as Herendeen, he was fast and almost as strong. "If you don't let Callie alone, you may find yourself sent back."

"Nobody's sending me back," Herendeen said. He stared across the fire at Brodie and gave him stare for stare. "Rocklin makes lots of rules about us stayin' away from the women," Herendeen grunted. "But I notice he stays pretty close to the old man's daughter and to Callie, too. I guess he thinks he's a ladies' man."

Jess Burkett shook his head. "He's a good man."

"He's pretty tough, too. I knew him in the mountains," Wiley Pratt said.

"Tough enough," Brodie said. "You'd better stay clear of him. Rocklin will cut you off at the knees, Grat."

"No, he's soft." Herendeen fell into a morose silence, and the rest of the men began talking about what lay ahead.

"We'll hit the Arkansas pretty soon," Charlie Reuschel said. He pulled his hat off, and his bald head shone in the darkness. He was the best shot on the wagon train and had been over the trail, part way at least, once. "When we get there, we'll have to decide what to do."

"What are our choices?" Stuffy asked, chewing vigorously on the tough steak.

"We can either take the Cimarron Cutoff or go straight on across until we hit the Sangre de Cristo Mountains."

"Which way's the easiest?" Stuffy asked. "That's what I want."

"Well, I've never made the whole trip," Jesse said, "but a friend of mine did. He said the Cimarron Cutoff is the quickest, but it's bad desert most of the way and not much water."

"I heard about that cutoff," Herendeen grunted. "It's bad. We'd be fools to take it. I say we go onto the mountains."

"It'll be Rocklin's say," Brodie commented. He looked with some sadness at the steak and threw it out into the darkness. "Antelope's a poor thing for a man to feed himself on."

Rocklin had stopped by before the train started up the next morning. He met Paul Molitor and saw that the man was practically helpless. His hands were trembling, and Rocklin finally said, "I think you'd better ride in the wagon with Kate today, Molitor."

"I — I could use a drink." It had cost Molitor whatever shreds of his pride was left, but he knew before he spoke that it was hopeless.

"That's not what you need. You're going to have to dry out. You drink a lot, don't you?"

"All I can get."

"Poor way to live."

"You don't have to tell me that." Molitor pulled himself up and climbed aboard the wagon. He sat there until Kate got up beside him and picked up the lines. She said nothing until she heard the customary call for starting.

Rocklin yelled, "Stretch out!" and the wagons lurched forward, the wheels making a whining noise on their dry axles as the schooners lurched, moving forward.

Kate said quickly, "If you get to feeling too bad, you can lie down on the bed in the back."

"I'm all right," Molitor said. He tried to smile although his nerves were screaming out for liquor. "I'm sorry to be such a bother."

"Don't be foolish." Kate studied the man. He had shaved early that morning, which made his face look even more cavernous. He had crisp, brown hair that had not been cut, and his eyes were sunk deep into their sockets. He was thin, and there was a twitch at the side of his mouth. Still Kate thought, *He's seen better days than this. I don't know what his story is, but it's probably not a good one.* "We'll be getting to the Arkansas soon.

There should be some wagons on the way back east. You can get on with one of them."

Molitor did not answer. He was holding onto the seat, and his stomach was crying out. He had eaten a little of the mush Kate had fixed for him for breakfast, but all he could think of was getting a drink. He knew that was impossible, and despair settled over him like a heavy, dark mist.

For two days Molitor had endured the ride. The initial craving for drink had gone away although he still had moments when he wanted to scream and at times blow his brains out. On the second day he had joined Mark, who was still condemned to filling the wood boxes. It was late afternoon as he tried to pick up a heavy chunk of wood and felt a weakness. His head seemed to swim, and he slumped to his knees trying not to pass out.

"Here, let me give you a hand with that."

Molitor looked to see a young woman dressed in male attire who had brought her horse close beside him. She stepped out of the saddle and said, "I'm Callie Fortier."

"My name's Paul — Paul Molitor."

The girl reached down, picked up the chunk easily and dumped it in the back of the wagon. "Are you sick?" she asked.

"No, just a drunk," Paul said bitterly. "You don't have any whiskey, do you?"

"No, I don't."

Molitor looked down at his hands, which were trembling. Callie said, "How long has it been since you had a drink?"

"Three days, maybe four. I don't know. I lost track."

"You'll feel better soon. This doesn't last forever."

"It seems like it's going to," he said.

Callie saw that he was still unsteady. "Tell you what. Why don't you ride on my horse awhile. You can ride, can't you?"

"No, I don't think I could even get on."

"Well, you get in the wagon then. I'll pick the wood up."

Molitor stared at her. "Why are you doing this?"

The girl did not answer. She had large eyes, expressive, and there was a firmness about her lips. But at the same time there was a gentleness as she said, "Because I know what it is to be alone and scared."

Her remark went right to Molitor's spirit. He had long ago lost his pride, and now when this girl who came, apparently, from nowhere showed a gentleness, it was almost like getting hit in the face. "Thanks," he said briefly. "Don't waste your sympathy on me. I'm not worth it."

The girl did not answer. She watched him as he went to the wagon and crawled in and fell on his back. He was shocked as tears suddenly rolled down the sides of his face. "I'm no good," he whispered. "Be better off to blow my brains out."

Callie tossed a chunk of wood into the wood box and turned to see Jori, who had ridden up and was watching her.

"Why are you doing that?"

"That man's not able to work. He's in poor shape, him."

"You have your own work to do."

Callie had said very little to Jori Hayden. She was intimidated by her. There was something about her that spoke of pride, and she had been a good, fine lady in Little Rock. This much Callie had found out. Now, however, anger touched Callie's eyes and she said, "You have no gentleness."

Jori's head went up, and an angry reply leaped to her lips. It was the same thing that Rocklin had once said when she had wanted to leave the girl back in Missouri. Without a word she turned her horse and drove her heels into his side. Callie watched her speed away and smiled. "That got to her, it did," she said with a glow of satisfaction.

■ ■ ■ ■

"That fellow Molitor, he ever say where he came from?" Good News was putting an ointment on one of the mules that had rubbed a raw spot in his tough hide.

"No, he doesn't talk about himself much, but he's had a better place at one time," Kate replied.

"So I figured," Good News said. "You know, I like that verse in the Bible. It's the one that says, 'As a bird that wandered from her nest so was a man that wandered from his place.' "

"That's the lonesome verse," Kate said. "You ready for another lesson tonight?"

"If you're ready to waste your time."

"It's not a waste of time," Kate said. The two of them had spent several evenings together by the light of the fire going over letters and words. Good News did have some sense of reading and writing, and he was highly intelligent despite his rough look.

"Where's your place, Good News?"

"Don't guess I have one. I'm like that wandering bird."

"Well," Kate smiled at him, "the Scripture says the steps of a good man are ordered by the Lord. That means you, doesn't it?"

Good News wiped his hands on his handkerchief and smiled at her. "I guess so." He liked the way she was able to quote Scripture, and it humbled him to think that she would take the time to work with him. He had nothing to do with women, at least her kind of woman, and he said, "I'd like to spell a little while tonight."

Jori had gone down to the creek for water. She had been thinking about what the girl Callie had said about her needing to be more gentle. The remark had galled her, but she was honest enough to know that there was truth in it. The creek whispered a sibilant song as she scooped down and got a bucket full of water, and when she straightened up she was startled, for Rocklin had come up behind her so silently she had not heard him.

"I wouldn't go down that way," Rocklin said.

"Why not?" Jori resented his presence, and Callie's reminder that she had no gentleness was fresh on her mind.

"Been some Indian signs the last two days."

His words startled Jori, and she looked quickly down the creek.

"Oh, they're mostly just Cherokee, no

danger, but I wouldn't wander off if I were you. Here, let me take that bucket."

She surrendered the bucket, and asked, "What about Molitor?"

"Seen a lot like him. He's his own worst enemy."

"He needs to change."

"Sometimes a man can't change without help."

Whether it was so or not, she felt that his remark was critical of her. "You think I'm hard, don't you?"

"On the outside. I'd like to see what's on the inside."

Jori could make nothing of his remark for a moment and finally said, "Tell me about the Indians."

"Well, they're like us. A young Indian woman has the same dreams, probably, that you do."

Jori was resentful of the man and knew that it was foolish. "When will we get to the Arkansas?" she asked.

"Probably two days."

"How far have we come?"

"About two hundred and sixty miles," he said. "That's a third of the way." Suddenly he reached out and took her arm. "Quiet," he whispered.

Jori did not know what he meant, but the

remark about Indians frightened her, and she stood absolutely still and was aware of his strong hand on her arm holding her in place. He did not move for what seemed like a long time then he expelled his breath. "Nothing there," he said. He suddenly put the water down and without warning reached out and pulled her into his arms. Before she could react, he kissed her on the lips then released her.

"You — you let me alone!" she said.

"Sure would like to know what's on the inside," Rocklin said. He saw she was struggling with anger and laughed. "The outside looks mighty good. Maybe I'll find out more what the real Jori Hayden's like before we get to Santa Fe."

"Don't you touch me again!"

Rocklin shook his head, as if puzzled by his own behavior. His voice was summer-soft as he said, "Beauty is a funny thing, Jori. Men see it in different things — some in the desert nights, some in the sea. But I think all men look for beauty in a woman. Those fellows who find it in a certain woman and are lucky enough to win her — why, they've got everything."

Jori stood absolutely still, her breast softly rising and falling to her breathing. She had a temper that could charm a man or chill him to the bone. She had listened to the strange falling cadence of Rocklin's voice, and faint color stained her cheeks. His kiss had caught her off guard, but it had stirred her in a way no man's caress ever had — and this shamed her.

"Don't you ever touch me again!" she whispered.

Rocklin picked up the bucket and looked at her as if deliberating some problem. "I probably will," he remarked, dryness rustling in his voice. "Come on, let's get back."

■ ■ ■ ■

PART THREE:
ALONG THE ARKANSAS

■ ■ ■ ■

CHAPTER THIRTEEN

The left front wheel of the wagon dropped into a pothole, and the motion sent an exquisite pain through Jori and almost made her drop the reins. The day had been long, and her father had chosen to ride instead of driving the wagon, so she had accepted the chore — one that she was beginning to hate. Shifting around trying to find a comfortable position, she looked to her right and took in the country which, except for its lack of mountains and sea, actually was quite beautiful. The late spring flowers had sprinkled the prairie profusely with many-hued flowers. The crab apple thickets sometimes carpeted many acres in the pink blossoms as delicate as anything that she had ever seen. She could see a group of wild grapes that she had learned to recognize, for the hands all wanted to stop and pick them. She saw beyond them a specie of mimosa, flowers like purple globes dotting the landscape.

She had grown used to the monotony of the wide prairie that was broken only by deep ravines or at times a very gentle slope. The woods at this point were sometimes thick with tall, stately walnuts and the towering oaks and graceful limbs. Tall cottonwoods sometimes lined the creeks, and at this point there was plenty of cool, sweet water for the stock and for all of them. The sound of a popping whip like a rifle shot drew Jori's eyes toward the wagon over to the far left. They were traveling now five abreast instead of in a single line so that no one actually had to ride in the rear. She watched now without curiosity as Herendeen, walking alongside his team, cracked the whip. It nipped the ear of the leader, and the animal at once quickened the pace. One of the other men called out something to Herendeen, and she heard his husky laughter. She had learned to dislike the man and kept waiting for him to say something that she could use to pull him up short, but he was crafty and sly and kept barely within the boundaries.

"You want me to spell you, Jori?"

Turning to face her father who had ridden up, Jori shook her head. "No, I expect we'll be nooning pretty soon. Maybe then."

"Kind of rough on the body sitting on that hard seat. Why don't you take a quilt or something and make a cushion."

"I'll be all right, Papa."

Leland rode alongside the wagon for a moment, studying his daughter's face. He saw the fatigue etched there and knew that his own face was no different. "Pretty tough going, isn't it?"

"We'll be all right." She found a smile, and he returned it and then turned and rode forward.

It was past noon, and when Jori's stomach growled, she was aware that she was hungry. She reached down into the bag under her feet, mined around inside of it, and fished out a piece of hard rock candy that she popped in her mouth.

The train usually halted at about ten or eleven o'clock, depending on the weather. The routine bored her in all truth, for every day was pretty much the same — they'd pause, the animals would rest, and the men had a light meal. Jori thought it was amusing that they called it breakfast though sometimes it did not come until after twelve o'clock. The men sometimes carried out chores or repaired their gear. The meal was pretty much the same for everyone and included cooked meat and freshly baked skillet bread.

A shout to her right caught Jori's attention. She turned to look and saw something moving into a grove of trees.

"It's a bear — it's a bear!" one of the men called out. Wiley Pratt grabbed a rifle and started after it, but Rocklin's voice brought him up short. "Leave that bear alone, Wiley!"

"Bear meat would go mighty fine."

"I'll take care of the hunting. You take care of your mules."

Wiley Pratt, a tough, short, muscular man with tow hair and hot-tempered hazel eyes, glared at Rocklin, who sat on his horse and met his gaze evenly. Jori drew her breath in, for these were violent men. There was always the chance of something happening. Nothing had so far, but she knew it was the iron control of Rocklin that kept them in line. She expelled her breath as the mule skinner sullenly turned and walked back to the wagon trudging along beside it.

Rocklin turned and found Jori watching him and guided his horse over. "How's it goin', Jori?"

"Why wouldn't you let him go after that bear?"

"Because she had cubs."

Jori stared at Rocklin. "I didn't see

any cubs."

"I did. Two little ones. Not able to take care of themselves yet. You shoot their mother, they'd die."

It was a side of Rocklin that Jori had seen little of. "But that's always the chance when you're hunting, isn't it, that you'll shoot a mother?"

"Yes, it is," Rocklin admitted. "I guess I'm too tenderhearted." He rode easily in the saddle, and his eyes were always moving from point to point. Jori studied him carefully. There wasn't any fat on the man. He had long arms and legs, and the edge of his jaws were sharp against the heavily tanned skin. She noticed something she had missed before, that his nose had a small break at the bridge. He looked solid and tall in the sunlight. He suddenly turned and caught her watching him and smiled at her. She flushed, for since he had kissed her there had been a restraint between the two of them.

"About time for nooning, I reckon."

She arched her back and lifted her head. "Look, there's a river," she said. "Is that the Arkansas?"

"No. That's the Little Arkansas, just a branch. The real river's on a few more miles, but we'll stop before we go to crossing."

He stayed beside her, neither of them saying anything, and finally when they came to the stream Jori caught her breath. "It looks rough."

"All that rain's coming down out of the hills."

"Won't it be dangerous to cross?"

"Won't be easy."

The river, for such it seemed to be, was roiling, and there were small white caps tossed by a breeze. There was a menace in the stream, it seemed to her, and finally she asked, "Can't we wait until it goes down?"

"No tellin' when that will be. It ought to be all right if we keep our heads. I'll drive your wagon across."

"I can do it."

"You probably could, but I'd hate to see you tump over and get all your goods wet." He did not wait for an answer but kicked his horse into a gallop forward and shouted, "Pull up! We'll noon here!"

Paul Molitor stood staring down at the brown waters of the small river. He was so fatigued he could hardly stand there, and every nerve in his body cried out for a drink. He had hoped by this time that some of the desire would have left him, and at times it did. But now it came to him, and he knew he would sell his soul for a bottle of whiskey.

"Looks pretty active."

Molitor turned to see Callie Fortier, who had come up on foot leading her horse. "I don't see how we're going to get across."

"It will not be bad, no. At least nobody should get killed."

Molitor reached down, picked up a stick, and threw it out in the river. It sailed out until it hit the water and instantly was driven downstream by the force of the water. He watched it grimly and shook his head. "We could all drown in this thing."

Callie studied the man. She had wondered about him, for his speech was different from the mule skinners. She knew instinctively that he was educated, and now, as she studied him, she thought, *He would be good-looking if he'd gain weight and shave.* "We'll need help getting the mules across. You want me to pick you out a horse?"

"I'm no rider."

"All you have to do is sit. The horse does all the work."

Molitor suddenly shivered. It was not cold, but the desire for drink did that to him at times. He did not speak but was such a picture of abject misery that Callie felt sorry for him. She did not have a chance to say anything else for a voice cut into her thoughts. "All hands pullin' grass!"

"Pullin' grass? Why for is that?" Callie asked.

"That bank's too steep for a wagon." Rocklin was looking at the slight rise. "We'll pack it down with grass and make sort of a carpet. You OK, Molitor?"

"Yes."

"Well, start pullin' grass then. You, too, Callie."

It took more than grass, and men finally had to fall to with picks and spades and even axes. They leveled out the incline, saw that it was not abrupt, and the dirt was shoveled in. Then the grass, shrubs, and bushes that the crew had gathered were thrown in. In the end it made a carpet strong enough to bear the weight of the wagons, at least Rocklin hoped so. "That ought to do it," he called out. "Let's get across this thing. Herendeen, you take the first wagon."

Herendeen, big and bulky, was staring at the river. "I never like white water," he said. "It ain't nothin' to fool with."

"Like it or not it's there, and we've got to get across. If you can't do it, say so now."

Rocklin's words touched Herendeen's pride, and he straightened up. "I can do anything you can do, Rocklin."

"Well, get across then."

Herendeen's mules balked at the water, but he cursed and slashed at them with his whip until finally, with what seemed almost to be a scream, they plunged in. The force of the current swept them to the left, but Herendeen leaped on the back of the wheeler mule next to the wagon and slashed at them and yelled so that they forged their way across. The water came higher and higher but did not reach above their bellies.

Jesse Burkett took the next wagon across, and Stuffy McGinnis followed him.

Stuffy had trouble getting his mules in, despite his yelling, and finally, when they started across, one of them seemed to tangle in his harness. The current caught the wagon, swinging it around, and Stuffy was unexpectedly jerked by a sudden movement of the mule and went head over heels into the water. He came up hollering, "I can't swim — I can't swim!"

Rocklin at once plunged in and yelled at McGinnis, "You'd better learn to swim quick!" He rode his horse to the lead mule, grabbed the harness, and led them out the other side. McGinnis floundered around and, being a short man, was having little success. Callie drove her horse to him and cried out, "Hold onto his tail, Stuffy!"

Stuffy did as he was directed, and Callie hauled him across. He spat out the river and glared at Rocklin, who was watching this with a mild interest. "I could have drowned out there, Chad."

"You were all right. You just lost your head. Take this wagon on now."

The rest of the crossing was fairly uneventful. Molitor stood watching helplessly, and finally Jori said, "Get in the wagon with me, Molitor."

She watched as he climbed slowly in and settled himself. She saw that he held onto the wagon seat until his knuckles were white. "It's all right. We're making it fine."

"Doesn't matter, I guess. If this river doesn't get us, something else will."

"Why do you want to be so morbid?"

Molitor turned to face her. The ravages of drink had planed him down. She could see that there was a fineness in his face and wondered as others had about the man's background. They could not move, for Pedro and Callie, joined by Addie Joss and Jake Fingers and two other of the mule teams, were getting the stock across. Suddenly Jori asked him, "What are you doing out here in this place, Paul?" It was the first time she had ever called him by his first name. Almost everyone called him Molitor when they called him anything. "You're a city man, used to better things."

"You're asking me, I suppose, how I lost my honor? Why I'm a drunk?"

The bitterness of his tone caught at Jori. "I didn't mean it like that."

"I think you did." He hunched over and gripped his hands together. Staring down at them he said, "Men don't lose their honor all at once. Small rodents come in the night, and they carry it away on their little, tiny feet. A man never notices it's gone — it goes in such small chunks. That's what I'm doing here. I lost my honor in small chunks carried off by rats."

Jori stared at the man. His words were almost poetic despite the bitterness of his tone, and she knew there was not another man in the train, even including her own father, who could speak like this. "You're a young man. You can change. Don't you have a family, someone who cares for you?"

"No."

"Surely there's someone."

"You still believe in love, I see."

Jori was struck by his words. "Why, of course I do. Don't you?"

"No, I don't." He turned to face her, and there was a blank emptiness in his words.

"Love's too short. It doesn't cover every-thing. It's like a short blanket. There's always a head or a leg sticking out in the wind when the cold comes, and it always comes."

Jori was silent. She knew that something had destroyed a man who had great potential, and she was a woman who liked to see on the inside of things. Right now she knew that he was in the depths of some sort of hell that she could not even imagine. "Things will be better, Paul."

"No — they won't."

The clear, flat finality in his tone shut Jori out, but she resolved to find out more about this man who was so different from everyone else.

Jake Fingers was the oldest man on the train. He never spoke his own age, but he had to be in his midfifties. He was short, skinny, and homely with buck teeth and a lined face. He was also scared to death of Indians — so much so that more than one person had asked him why he was headed into Indian territory.

"I don't know. It just happened that way," Jake would admit. "But the Indians won't get me."

Fingers had been assigned the job of finding more firewood. Herendeen had spoken to him roughly, and now Fingers had ranged about a hundred yards from the camp. He had seen a tree stretched out there, and when he got there he was glad to see that it was dead. The tree had been dead for some time and was settled into the earth. Some of the limbs had fallen off, and Jake reached over the main body and started gathering a pile. He leaned over to pick up a chunk at least three inches thick, and as he did, his blood chilled as he heard a deadly buzzing sound. He had only time to turn his head when he saw something white — a huge rattler almost as thick around as his arm. It struck even as Fingers turned his head. He felt the fangs penetrate his neck and stumbled backward yelling and pulling at the snake. He turned and started for the wagon, calling out, but even as he did, he saw Rocklin lift his head and come forward. "What's the matter, Jake?"

"A rattler. It got me . . . in the neck." He saw Rocklin's eyes open wide and said, "The Indians ain't gonna get me. That snake will though."

"You can make it, Jake."

"No, I'm a dead man. . . ."

Jake Fingers died quickly but horribly.

Spasms had shaken his body, and he had formed an arch as the poison coursed through his veins. It had not lasted more than twenty minutes from the time Rocklin came bearing him into the camp. Everyone watched in horror, and it was Jesse Burkett who said, "I guess we could try to suck that poison out, Chad."

"Too late. It got him right in the big vein." Rocklin's voice was cold as he knelt beside the dying man.

"I heard that tobacco juice will help," Eddie Plank suggested.

"It's not going to help him," Charlie Reuschel spoke up. "If it got him in the arm or leg maybe, but in the neck in the big vein, he's a goner."

Five minutes later Jake Fingers had ceased to move. His body had stiffened and then relaxed as if he were going to sleep.

Rocklin rose up and said bleakly to Good News, "Let's go dig him a grave." He looked down at the still form and said, "Well, the Indians didn't get you."

There was something in his tone, a grim finality, that chilled Jori. Her eyes went around the circle, and she saw that most of the men were calloused, not seemingly horrified by the scene. She knew they had seen more of this side of life than she had, but still a pity came into her. Carleen came and pressed close beside her. "I wish he hadn't died. He was nice."

"Yes, he was."

"He liked oranges better than anything else."

"How do you know that?"

"He told me. He said his idea of heaven was to have all the oranges that he could eat."

"Well, he's having his oranges now, I guess," Jori said slowly. "Come along. Let's go back to the wagon."

Jori had been troubled by the death of Jake Fingers. She had stood with the others beside the grave that the men had dug. There had been no rocks to pile over it so they had buried him deep. Good News Brown had quoted a great deal of Scripture and said a few words about the man, but there was still something raw and angular and terrible about a death.

Later on in the afternoon she wandered away from camp and saw Rocklin standing over the grave. Curious, she made her way to join him. He turned to see her and gave a nod, and there was a bleakness in his countenance.

"It's too bad," Jori said.

251

"It always is."

Jori stared down at the raw earth and was restless. "You think it was worth it, Chad?"

"You mean coming on this trip?"

"Yes. Wouldn't it have been better if he had stayed back in Franklin?"

"I'm not the man to ask."

"You've seen men killed before, haven't you?"

"Yes. I've seen men killed over a two-dollar bet at blackjack. Does that mean anything?"

His voice was almost harsh, and Jori was surprised to see that the little man's death troubled him. She waited, not knowing what to say, and finally he said, "I had a good friend once that ran in a burning building to try to rescue a woman who was trapped. He didn't make it. He got burnt up himself, and so did the woman. Was it worth it?"

"I don't know about things like that, but it was a noble way to die." She suddenly felt a touch of fear along her nerves. "This trip frightens me, Chad. We never should have come."

He turned at once to face her. "You want to go back?"

"No, I won't go back."

Chad Rocklin stared at her and said, "I've been meaning to apologize for that kiss."

Jori was taken aback. They had been talking about death, yet the kiss was in his mind. "I've been kissed before."

"I'm sure you have. If you want to go back," he said, "I'll see to it. You're a proud woman."

"You make pride sound like it's a disease."

Rocklin seemed to have pulled a curtain around himself and shut out everything. He was cold and aloof, and Jori knew at that moment that he of all the skinners had felt grief for Jake Fingers. He looked at her and shook his head. "You're a proud woman," he repeated. "And pride kills more people than bullets or knives or sickness."

"I'll be all right, Chad."

He stared at her a minute, and she could tell that something was on his mind. He could not find the words to say it, and she wondered at his silence. Finally he turned and said, "Better get some sleep. We'll leave early in the morning."

CHAPTER FOURTEEN

Mark Hayden stood beside the small stream no more than ten feet across. He stared moodily down at the water, noting a group of minnows that seemed directed by the same brain. Briefly he wondered how they all knew when to turn together all in the same direction at the same instant. Even as he watched they suddenly exploded, making a silvery flash underneath the water, and then were gone.

Overhead the sky was blue and dotted with fleecy clouds that moved majestically across toward the horizon. The sun was hot, and Mark took off his hat and let the breeze ruffle his hair. In his free hand he held a pint bottle of whiskey. He lifted it, measured the contents no more than a half inch, and then quickly swallowed it. As the fiery liquid burned at his throat and hit his stomach, he coughed, and then with a sudden angry gesture he threw the bottle out. It sailed over the stream, landed on the far side and broke against a rock that thrust itself upward from the loam of the prairie.

From far off came the sound of laughter. The train had stopped for nooning, but Mark had no desire for company. He was sick to death of the trip, worn in body, and knew that a hard time was coming, for he had drunk the last of the whiskey that he had brought with him from Franklin. It had been in his mind that they would pass a train headed eastward or catch up with a slower moving train than their own, but they had seen no one for days now, and the monotony was a burden on him.

"Hello, Mark."

Mark turned and saw that Callie had approached on foot. She had a bundle of clothes in her arms, and he assumed she had come down to wash them. His own clothes were filthy, but he had not enough energy or desire, for that matter, to wash them. "Hello, Callie."

"Beautiful day, isn't it?"

"It's all right."

"I thought I'd come down and wash a few clothes out." With these words Callie knelt, dumped the clothes on the ground, and grabbing a shirt, plunged it into the water. She made a lather out of a bar of gritty, yellow soap and was humming under her breath as she performed the task.

Mark squatted down and watched her. The liquor was going to his head, and he felt a slight dizziness. He did not drink well, he knew that, but he had fallen into the habit and now was ill-tempered because he knew he would be cut off from liquor at least for a time.

"I'm tired of gathering wood," Mark said abruptly.

"Well, why don't you get Rocklin to let you help Pedro and me herd the animals."

"I'm not asking him for anything."

Callie looked up. The sun caught the brightness of her hair, and her gray eyes were inquisitive. She had a smooth, ivory complexion, and her teeth were white as she smiled. "Why don't you want to ask him?"

"I don't like to ask favors."

"That's foolish. We all have to ask favors."

Mark wanted to argue. He was ill-tempered, and something about the girl's cheerful disposition irritated him. "You don't have to be so happy about everything."

"Why not? What's to be unhappy about?"

"For you maybe nothing, but I've had better things in life."

"You're spoiled. You're a big baby, you."

256

The truth of Callie's words struck Mark with force. He suddenly straightened up and reached over and pulled her up. The flesh of her arm was warm and firm in his grip, and he could see tiny flecks of gold and blue in her gray eyes. "You can't talk to me like that."

"Let go of me, Mark."

"I'll let go of you when I want to." Mark suddenly reached out, grabbed her other arm and pulled her toward him. She struggled and jerked one arm free, striking him lightly in the chest.

"Let go of me, I said!"

Mark just merely laughed. "I don't have to." He was determined now to kiss her just to show her that she was nothing but a servant. He made a wild grab for her, but suddenly Callie pulled away, and with one swift motion of her free hand struck him with the flat of it against his chest. The force of it knocked Mark off balance, and he took a step backward. His foot hit nothing, however, except the crumbling bank, and with a yell he fell over backward full length into the stream. His head was plunged beneath the surface, and he swallowed some of the muddy water. Rolling to his feet, he came up as angry as he had ever been in his life. He staggered getting up, but the whiskey had made him less than certain. He waded out and started for Callie, grimly intent on having his own way when suddenly a voice caught him.

"Hey, Mark, did you fall into the river?"

Mark wheeled to see Carleen who had come trotting up. She had her pants rolled up, and her eyes were dancing. He knew instantly that she had seen what had happened, and that infuriated him. "Get away from here, Carleen!" he said gruffly.

"I don't have to, Mark," Carleen said. He made a lunge toward her, but she easily evaded him. "You been drinking whiskey again, haven't you?"

"It's none of your business!" Mark shouted. He whirled angrily and stalked away, staggering slightly.

Carleen watched him go and then turned to say, "I know he didn't fall in. You did the right thing to push him into the river."

Callie turned to the young girl and saw that there was a sadness in her. Callie, a discerning young woman, said, "You love your brother, don't you, Carleen?"

"Sure I do." Carleen moved over to the river, slipped her shoes off, and began wading in it. Callie watched her, saying nothing until finally the girl looked up and said with sadness in her tone, "When I was little he played with me all the time, and then when I got older he took me places no one else would." She looked down at the water and then suddenly kicked at it. The drops caught the sun sparkling like diamonds and fell back. "I wish he wouldn't drink, Callie."

Callie studied the young girl, and then an impulse took her. "I like him, too. He'll stop drinking some day, him."

"Do you really think so?"

"Yes. Come, I saw some berries downstream. Let's go pick some."

Carleen brightened up at once. "All right. We'll make us a pie."

"I'm a good pie maker."

"Can we give Mark some?"

Callie laughed. "Yes, if he's good and doesn't fall in the river."

Carleen laughed at this. She was a creature of moods at times, and she found that the young woman was good company. The two made their way downstream to where they found the berries that were plump and delicious. They had nothing to put them in so they simply ate them.

"Let's go back and get a bucket and we'll fill it up," Carleen said. "Then we can —" She stopped suddenly and Callie saw her eyes widen. She was looking at something behind Callie. Turning, Callie froze for there stood two Indians not ten feet away, staring at them. They had come so silently making no noise at all, and now fear rushed through Callie.

Carleen said, "Indians! Run, Callie!" She whirled and began running. Callie fully expected the two Indians to pursue her, but one of them, the tallest of the two, smiled and studied her.

"Why don't you run?" he said in a high tenor voice. Callie had had little dealing with Indians. They each carried a rifle. One was very tall and young and lean, the one who had spoken. The other man was older, in his middle age, short and muscular.

"What — what do you want?"

"Something to eat," the younger man said. "I am Kicking Bird. This is my friend Four Bears."

Callie felt a slight touch of relief. "If you'll come into the camp, I'll cook you something."

"We come," Four Bears said. There was something deadly about the man, or seemed to be, but Kicking Bird was pleasant enough. "You have any whiskey?" he asked.

"I don't think so, but I'll feed you if you'll come with me." She turned, half expecting the two to grab her, but they simply followed along beside her.

I've got to get back to the train and then I'll be all right, Callie thought.

Paul Molitor was watching Good News and Addie Joss work on a wheel. Something was always going wrong with the wagon wheels. As they got into the drier country, the wood would shrink and cause the iron tires to fall off. There was no blacksmith shop along the way to Santa Fe, but Addie Joss had a portable forge and usually he and Good News Brown could devise some sort of a repair.

The two men now were busy driving wedges in between the tire and the wheel until they could do better. Paul Molitor had watched them enough to know that later on, when there was time, they would wrap the rim with some sort of canvas or green hide.

Addie was irritated about the delay, but Good News merely grinned. "All things work together for good for those that love the Lord," he said cheerfully. Paul sometimes grew irritated at the infallible good humor of Good News Brown. "So you're saying it's a good thing that wheel has gone bad?"

"That's what the Book says," Good News said. "Who knows, if it hadn't broke down, we might have made better time and there might have been a bunch of Indians up there waiting to scalp us all. But now we've slowed down, and the Indians are gone."

Suddenly Paul Molitor laughed. It was one of the first times that either of the men had ever heard him. "That's the craziest theology I ever heard, Good News, and it's foolish to think that everything happens for good."

"It don't say that," Good News explained carefully. "It says everything happens for good to those that love the Lord. Those that don't know the Lord, they are on their own, don't you see."

Molitor was about to reply. He liked Good News Brown but felt that he was completely out of line with his religion. The man could quote Scripture by the hour, and nothing ever seemed to trouble him. Perhaps it was this that caused Molitor to be slightly envious. He started to answer, but then suddenly Addie Joss got up and reached for his rifle. "Look, Indians."

Molitor whirled quickly and saw first Carleen Hayden running full tilt toward the train. Behind her fifty yards was Callie Fortier, and accompanying her were two Indians.

"Hold off on that shootin', Addie. Don't

look like they mean trouble."

The rest of the drivers had not seen the Indians, but suddenly Wiley Pratt let out a yelp. "Injuns!" he cried.

Almost at the same time Rocklin walked around from behind one of the wagons where he had been inspecting the running gear. He moved quickly then and stood in front of Pratt. "Keep that gun out of sight, Wiley."

"But them's Indians!"

"I know they are, but they don't mean any harm."

"How do you know that?" Grat Herendeen demanded.

"Those are Comanches. If they had meant harm, most of us would have been dead. You keep a lid on it, you hear me?" He stared the men down and then turned and walked toward the strangers.

"Chad, there's Indians!" Carleen cried out.

"I see them, honey, but it's all right. They're friends of mine."

Callie was close enough to hear Rocklin's words. Her eyes opened, and she watched as Rocklin held his hand up. She turned to see the two Indians making the same sign.

"I see you again," Rocklin said.

"Yes, it is good to see you," the youngest

Indian said. He was grinning now and said, "You keep no guard. We could have taken all your scalps."

"I'm glad you didn't. How are you, Four Bears?"

Four Bears nodded. "Good," he said gutturally.

"You got the word that I sent by White Deer?"

"Yes. He said you're not able to take care of yourself so you need two good men." Kicking Bird spoke good English. He had spent two years in a mission school and had learned English well.

A crowd had gathered now, and Leland Hayden was eyeing the Indians cautiously. "It seems like you found some old friends, Rocklin."

"Yes, we are brothers. I spent four years growing up with these fellows. This is Kicking Bird, and this is Four Bears."

"Do you have anything to eat?" Four Bears demanded.

"We'll find something."

"I've got some meat on the fire," Kate said. She was curious about the Indians as were they all. They were not exactly what she was expecting. "Come and get it."

The Indians appeared to be curious about the train and everything else. They held closely to their rifles and Rocklin asked, "Where are your horses?"

"We hide them. We think maybe you have horse thieves here."

"Nobody could steal a horse from a Comanche," Rocklin grinned. "Not from Four Bears anyway. You remember the raid we went on against the Pawnees when they stole your horse?"

Kicking Bird laughed with delight. His eyes lit up. "The great horse stealer Four Bears had his horse stolen by a miserable Pawnee."

Four Bears gave Kicking Bird a murderous look and then grunted. "I got him back later, and I've got the scalp of the Pawnee that took him."

All of the Haydens were watching carefully, and finally Chad said, "Leland, we're going to need help hunting later on. Game gets scarce from here on, so Kicking Bird and Four Bears will come in handy."

Leland said quickly, "Whatever you say, Chad."

Over to one side Herendeen and the rest of the skinners were talking about the Indians. Herendeen and Wiley Pratt were the two who had the most to say. Pratt hated all Indians and said, "You can't trust none of them. They're all liars and thieves."

"I agree with that," Grat nodded, "but they're good friends with Rocklin. That don't mean nothin'. He always was an Indian lover."

"They don't look too dangerous," Brodie Donahue said, eyeing the two Indians.

"You don't know Indians, Brodie," Grat said shortly.

Jesse Burkett was leaning against the wagon, tall and lanky and a quiet sad man. He shook his head and said, "Rocklin wouldn't let them in here if he didn't know 'em. Maybe they can help us get through the Indian country."

"You can't trust 'em, Jesse," Grat said, his eyes burning. "We got to stick together, but we can't have those Indians trailing along with us."

Brodie grinned. "Why don't you go tell Rocklin that, Grat."

"I will," Grat said. "You think I'm afraid of him?"

"No, I don't think you got sense enough to be afraid of him," Brodie said.

Grat stared at Brodie, who was somewhat smaller than he but still a fighting man. "You just watch this if you think that, Donahue."

Grat Herendeen was a man who could not

bear to think another man better. He had been planning for some time to assert himself against Rocklin. He had no doubt about his ability to crush the smaller man, for he was a notorious brawler. Now he welcomed the idea of making a call that he thought was a good one. He walked right up to the fire where the Hayden family were sitting and glared at the two Indians and then turned to face Rocklin. "You don't intend to let them Indians stay, do you, Rocklin?"

Rocklin got to his feet at once. His eyes narrowed, and he recognized that Grat Herendeen had been waiting for something to create trouble over, and now it had come. "It's none of your business, Grat."

"It's my business if I get my scalp took." He nodded his head toward the two Indians who were watching him closely. "We all agree we ain't goin' no farther until you get rid of them savages."

"It's a long walk back to Franklin, but it's that way. You don't get a horse though."

Grat Herendeen was a man of fiery mood. He took a step closer now, and his eyes were filled with fury. "You think you're the proud coon, don't you? Well —"

Herendeen interrupted his own word by throwing a roundhouse right at Rocklin.

Rocklin had known that trouble was coming, but it caught him off balance. The blow caught him in the chest and drove him backward. Rocklin sprawled, and he heard Herendeen shout a hoarse cry, "I'll kill you!" and saw the big mule skinner launch a kick. Rocklin managed to roll over and take it on his hip then came to his feet.

"I guess I'll have to leave my mark on you, Grat," he said.

The words infuriated Herendeen. He had won most of his fights by his toughness. He had a thick skull and was well padded with muscle. He knew only one style of fighting; that was, do anything you can to destroy your enemy.

Rocklin had known that Herendeen would come roaring in. Chad Rocklin was a faster man, and he planted himself, dodged the assault that came at him, and threw every bit of his strength into a blow that caught Herendeen in the mouth. It stopped Herendeen, but Rocklin knew it would take more than one blow to put him down. Quickly he stepped forward, and when Grat raised his hands to protect his face, he drove a powerful punch into the pit of the stomach exactly where the ribs part.

Herendeen doubled over, expelling his breath. When he dropped his hands, Rocklin's fist came down, cracking the bridge of his nose.

Herendeen stepped back then. Blood was running from his mouth, and his nose was broken, but he was tough as a grizzly. "I'm gonna kill you, Rocklin. I'm gonna break every rib you got." He came in more cautiously, aware of the speed of Rocklin and the power of his blows. He held his hands up so that Rocklin had no chance at a quick punch. The two men circled each other, waiting for a chance.

Jori was horrified by the violence that had seemed to explode in the middle of a beautiful day. The two men circled each other like animals, powerful, strong, both of them trying for a kill. She had expected it of Grat Herendeen, but she had not seen this kind of violence flare out of Chad Rocklin. She knew his record, and she whispered, "Papa, stop it."

"Out of my hands," Leland said in a matter-of-fact tone.

All of the skinners had gathered now so that the two men were in the middle of a circle. The two Indians' eyes were glittering. Though they said nothing, you could tell they were enjoying the fight.

Rocklin stepped forward and aimed a blow at Herendeen's face. Herendeen caught it on his forearm and threw his own jab. He was quicker than Rocklin had thought, and Grat's fist caught him high on the temple. The power of it was chilling, and for a moment the world whirled, shedding brilliant stars. He heard Herendeen grunt with pleasure and backed up, avoiding the rush from Grat. As Herendeen missed, Rocklin stuck his foot out, and Grat sprawled in the dust. He came quickly to his hands, but as he was rising, Rocklin brought his forearm down on the back of the neck with all the force he could muster. It would have broken the neck of a man of less flesh and bone and gristle, but all it did was drive Herendeen back to the ground. He came up and as he did, Rocklin, taking deliberate aim, kicked him full in the face. The sound of the boot striking Herendeen's face made an ugly sound, and Jori closed her eyes. A cry went up from the two Indians, and as for Herendeen, he was unconscious.

Breathing heavily, Rocklin stood staring down at the man and waited, saying nothing. Finally Herendeen's eyes opened, and he got to his feet painfully. His face was bloody, but the fight was knocked out of him at least for a time.

"Make your choice, Grat. Start walkin' or

take orders."

Herendeen stared at Rocklin, hatred visible in his battered face. "There'll be other times, Rocklin," he muttered, then turned and walked away unsteadily.

Four Bears had not stopped eating. He was chewing on a bone, and now he studied it and threw it away. "You should kill him," he remarked.

"No, I need him, Four Bears, to drive a wagon. When you two get filled up, go find us somethin' better to eat. Some bear steaks would go pretty well."

Carleen crept closer to where Grat Herendeen was washing his face in the stream. She had followed him out of camp keeping hidden, but now she came closer.

Herendeen suddenly turned and glared at her. "What do you want, girl?"

"Are you all right?"

Herendeen was still caught in the fury of the fight. "Get out of here!" he said gruffly, but the girl did not move. "What do you want?" he repeated.

"You're hurt pretty bad."

"I've been hurt worse."

Carleen Hayden was incurably inquisitive. She had been afraid of the big man during the fight, but now he seemed harmless

271

enough. "Your face is all cut up."

Herendeen was feeling the aftereffects of the fight. He had been whipped for the first time in his life, and something had gone out of him. He knew that somewhere down the line he would have it out with Rocklin again. He could not believe that the smaller man had beaten him so quickly.

"Carleen, you'd better get back to the wagon."

Paul Molitor had been watching the girl and followed her to the stream. Now he came and looked at the face of the battered Herendeen. "That cut's got to be sewn up, Herendeen."

"It'll be all right."

Paul Molitor shrugged. "It's up to you. I'll fix it if you want."

"You sewed up fellows before?"

"Once or twice."

Herendeen dropped his head for a moment. He hated to take favors, but he knew that his face did need attention. "All right," he said.

"I'll get something to fix it with."

Twenty minutes later Molitor stepped back and looked critically at the job he had done. "That's about the best I can do. Leave those stitches in for a few days. It's going to be painful."

"I can take that."

Carleen had watched Molitor with fascination as he had sewn up the gaping wound. "Golly," she said, "you sew as good as a woman."

Molitor grinned briefly. "Thank you." He turned to leave.

"Much obliged, Molitor," Herendeen said.

"You're welcome."

Carleen came over to stare into Herendeen's battered face. "You look funny," she said, "with those stitches hanging out, but you'll feel better soon."

Grat Herendeen could not understand the girl. He had had nothing to do with children and rather disliked them. This one, however, was different. "Ain't you afraid of me?" he asked.

"No, not really. I'll see you later, Mr. Herendeen."

Herendeen watched as the girl skipped off after Molitor. Finally, despite the pain, he muttered, "That kid has got spunk. Too bad that brother of hers ain't got some of it. . . ."

CHAPTER FIFTEEN

The brilliant light of the noonday sun touched the red hair of Carleen Hayden, and the tint made a colorful dot as the train rumbled along. Of all the members of the train, Carleen was by far the most inquisitive. She rose from her blankets each morning ready to ask questions, and they did not stop until she closed her eyes in sleep at night. She moved back and forth between the wagons, knew all of the skinners better than anyone else, and now, as the Conestogas rumbled over a small stream, she had stopped to dabble in it. For a time she looked for crawdads, and finding none she at last spotted a small snake. With a cry of excitement she ran after it and picked it up. It was a beautiful shade of green, no more than eight inches long and no thicker than her thumb. As the reptile curled itself around her forefinger, she studied it and considered keeping it as a pet.

"I reckon not," she said. "You need the water." She put the snake down, watched as it made its graceful way into the water, and then hurried over to where she saw Paul Molitor, who had become one of the herders for the animals. He was riding a small dark brown horse but had dismounted now and was looking off into the distance.

"Paul — Paul!" Carleen cried and ran over to him. She pulled up in front of him and looked up into his face. "What are you doing?" she asked.

"Don't you ever get tired of asking questions?"

"I caught a snake. It was green and about that long."

"You'd better leave those things alone."

"I'll leave the bad ones alone, but this one wouldn't hurt anybody."

He looked off and saw several of the mules wandering away from the main herd. "I've got to stop those mules," he said.

"I'll go with you."

Molitor looked down at the girl but made no answer. He was not as pale as he had been when he had first joined the train and had gained a few pounds. The good food and the forced abstinence of liquor had brightened his eyes, but there was a sadness about him that was almost physical.

The two walked along and started for the mules, but Carleen said, "Let me get them. I can ride your horse."

"No, you might fall off."

"I don't fall off of things. Please, Paul."

Molitor shook his head. "No. I'm afraid something would happen. I don't need a hurt child on my conscience."

Carleen hurried to get on the right side of Molitor as he walked leading the horse. When they were close enough, she shouted, "Get back there, you ugly mules!" She called one of them a name that she had heard the mule skinners use. She wasn't sure what it meant, but she liked it.

Molitor stared at her. "Don't ever use that word, Carleen."

"Why not?"

"Because it's not a good word — especially for children."

"Oh, it's a cuss word. I know most of the cuss words. You want me to say them for you?"

Molitor suddenly laughed. "No, I think not."

Out of the blue Carleen had the habit of firing questions rapidly of the most intimate nature. "You have a wife, Paul?"

"No."

"Why not?"

"I don't know why not. It just never came my way."

"Most men as old as you have wives. How old are you?"

"I'm thirty-three."

"That's pretty old. I expect you'd better get married pretty soon."

"I'd better not. I might have children, and one of them might ask as many questions as you do."

Carleen seemed not to hear. "Were you ever almost married?"

There was a moment's silence, and then Molitor shrugged, "I guess I was what you call almost married once."

"What was her name?"

"Her name was William."

Carleen looked up at him, her green eyes bright. "William! That's a boy's name."

"William Smith. That was her name all right. You see, before she was born her parents wanted a boy, and when they got a girl they decided if they couldn't have a boy they'd give her a boy's name anyway. Yep, I think about William a lot."

Carleen reached over and struck Molitor with her fist on the arm. "You're funning me, Paul."

Molitor smiled. "Why don't you go pester somebody else with your questions?"

"No, I don't want to." She glanced over and saw Mark trudging along on the other side two hundred yards away, picking up firewood and throwing it in the box. "Mark drinks whiskey too much just like you."

A flush washed across Molitor's face. "You're not supposed to tell people their faults, and you're not supposed to talk about your family to strangers."

"What difference does it make? Everybody knows you and Mark drink too much whiskey."

Molitor did not answer, and a few minutes later Carleen said, "Look, there's Grat Herendeen's wagon. Nobody likes him, but he's not all bad."

"How do you know?"

Astonishment touched Carleen. "Why, I just know! You can just look at someone and know what they're like."

"No, you can't. That doesn't always work."

"It does with me. I can just look at someone, and I know about them."

"You can be wrong." Molitor did not speak for awhile, then finally he lifted his eyes to the horizon. He seemed to see something far away, but actually his eyes were blank. "I thought I knew someone once, but I was wrong."

"Was that William?"

"She let me down."

"Well, maybe you just need to find a good woman, Paul." Then she made an abrupt change. "When I get old enough, I'm going to marry Chad."

Molitor laughed. "He'll be too old for you. He's too old now."

"Sometimes older men marry younger women. There was a man that lived down the road from us. He was sixty-two years old, and he married a woman who was only eighteen."

"Doesn't seem suitable."

"Well, maybe I'll marry you. I'm ten now. Some girls get married when they're fifteen, and you're thirty-three. That means you'll be only thirty-eight by the time I'm old enough to marry."

Molitor suddenly laughed, and his mood lightened. "I will wait with breathless anticipation, Carleen. We'll be the handsomest couple in town."

Pedro eased his horse and looked out at the animals that were plodding along in a docile manner. It was high noon, and he watched as the animals stopped beside the small creek. He turned to Callie, who had joined him while the animals were drinking. "This is Walnut Creek," he said. He pointed and said, "We'll be taking the Cimarron Cutoff pretty soon."

"What happens then?"

"We cross the Arkansas and head south."

"How long will it take?"

"Maybe another month." He pulled a small cigar out of his pocket, lit it with a match, and blew the smoke into the air. "You never been in Santa Fe?"

"No, I never have."

"When we get there, you can buy a dress and be a woman."

"I don't need any dresses, Pedro."

Pedro Marichal eased his tall form backward, his eyes constantly on the move. "You need to get you a man. Every woman needs a man. Someone to take care of her."

"I can take care of myself."

"God made men and women to be together. Don't you ever read the Bible?" Pedro grinned, his teeth white against his olive skin. "He made Adam and then He saw that Adam was lonesome, so He made Eve. That's the way it is."

"I don't need no man. I can take care of myself, me."

"That boy Mark, maybe he likes you."

"No. He may want me, but that's not enough."

"It's enough to start with," Pedro

shrugged. "We need somebody to want. Listen to me, Callie, I've worn out three wives, so I know what I'm talking about."

Callie suddenly laughed. "Well, I'm not going to be number four." She rose and suddenly kicked her horse into action. The mare lifted up into a gallop, and she circled the herd. Far off she saw Carleen talking to Paul Molitor and wondered about the man. He was a different kind of man from anyone else, but he was sad about something.

"Callie, wait a minute."

Callie turned to see Mark Hayden riding toward her. "I need to talk to you."

"What do you want?"

Mark pulled his horse up so that he was alongside of Callie. He seemed awkward and ill at ease, and Callie was cautious.

"I don't have a creek to push you into, but I can shoot you."

Mark Hayden suddenly laughed. He was a clean-cut young man just under six feet and was trimly built. It was the first time she had ever seen him laugh, and the thought crossed her mind, *Too bad he doesn't laugh more. He's better looking.*

"I came to apologize for what happened at the creek. It's taken me this long to work my courage up. I'm not known for my skill in making apologies."

Callie laughed and suddenly felt better about the young man. "Why then I suppose I should apologize for pushing you into the creek."

"No. I'm just glad you didn't shoot me." He glanced at the gun that she always carried. "Do you know how to shoot that thing?"

"Well enough."

"Not many young women carry guns."

"I suppose not."

The two pulled their horses to a stop, and both animals lowered their heads and began grazing. "It's rather strange to find a woman as young as you all alone. Don't you have any family?"

"I had only my papa, and he died not long ago."

"I'm sorry. What did he do?"

"He was a mule skinner, and he taught me how to drive a mule train. I could drive one of those wagons as well as most of the men, but Rocklin won't let me."

"That's a pretty rough life."

"There are things worse than driving mules."

The remark startled Mark. He considered the young woman for a moment and then shook his head. "I guess I've had it so easy. I've never done anything on my own." He looked ahead of the train and saw Rocklin coming back from his daily scout. "I envy men like Rocklin."

"You could be like him."

"I don't know why you should think that. All I've done," he shrugged his shoulders, "is to make a nuisance of myself. Oh, I've managed to get drunk, and I got pushed in the creek. That's about the scope of my accomplishments."

Callie smiled. "Well at least you haven't been hung for stealing, and I don't suppose you ever shot anybody."

"My negative qualities are numerous." Mark suddenly grew serious. "I don't know if I could ever do anything, Callie. I feel like an infant out here. If I got lost and out of sight of this wagon train, I'd die. I can't even take care of myself."

"You're doing better, Mark."

"You think so?"

"Yes, I do."

"Well, that's progress."

The two continued to talk, Mark trying to draw Callie out. He was somewhat shocked at the stark quality of the life she had led. He had moved in a realm of society that was as different from hers as the surface of the moon was to the earth. He had paid her little attention before, but now, as he studied her, he was aware that the girl was a real beauty. Beneath the dusty men's clothing she wore, her body was trim and had all the promise of young womanhood. He guessed her age at somewhere around seventeen or eighteen and tried to picture her dressed in a fine gown at a ball.

As for Callie, she was cautious around men. She found young Mark Hayden interesting. Actually, she had not been displeased when he had tried to take advantage of her; all men did that, and she knew how to handle it. It had amused her that she had pushed him into the creek. Most men would have been humiliated and furious and searching for ways to get even, but there was a good-natured air about this young man.

Callie grew relaxed, and as he began to talk, she was fascinated about the life of someone who was of his station. She was so intent on listening that she did not hear the buzzing sound of a rattlesnake. Her horse suddenly went up in the air in a wild effort to escape the snake, and Callie found herself thrown free, then she hit the ground. Before she could move, the hind foot of the horse caught her in the shoulder, and a pain such as she had never felt went through her.

Mark's horse had also reared up, but he

had managed to stop it. He awkwardly came off his horse, then saw the snake. Running forward he pulled Callie's revolver and fired it. He missed the snake, but the reptile crawled away. He turned then to Callie and saw that her face was pale. "Callie," he said, "are you all right?"

Her right hand went up to her shoulder, and her lips were white. "My shoulder. I think it's broken."

The sound of thundering hoofbeats came, and Mark turned as Pedro came up quickly. "Is she all right?" he said, coming out of his saddle. He held onto the lines of his horse and knelt down. "Are you all right, Callie?"

"My shoulder. It hurts so bad!"

"Can you get up?"

"I — I don't know."

The two men helped her, and she cried out as Mark touched her left arm. "Don't touch me," she said. "It's —"

"We'd better get her to camp, Mark," Pedro said. "A broken shoulder is a bad thing."

"It's going to be all right, Leland," Kate said. She was sitting on the wagon seat driving beside her brother-in-law. She had seen he was discouraged and was trying her best to cheer him up. "It's kind of hard right now, but think how wonderful it will be to get to Santa Fe. We'll have a whole new life there."

Leland turned to face Kate. He shook his head with admiration. "I wish I had your faith, Kate. This has been the toughest thing I have ever known."

"It could actually turn out to be good. You know the Scripture. All things work together for good to those that love God."

"I'm worried about Mark."

"He's had a hard time, but you know, Leland, hard times make good men, not easy times."

The two suddenly straightened for the sound of a gunshot had come to them. "I don't think that was a hunter," Leland said. He pulled the wagon up and saw that the rest of the wagons had totally stopped too.

They came off the wagon and Leland said, "There comes Pedro and Mark. Something's wrong with Callie."

The two moved forward, and at once Mark said, "Callie's had a fall and got kicked by a horse."

Kate saw that the girl's face was pale, and she pulled a box out from the back of the wagon and set it on the ground. "Here, sit down, Callie. Which shoulder is it?"

"Left one," Callie said through clenched teeth.

A crowd began to gather, and several of the teamsters had come to find out what the trouble was. Rocklin, who never seemed to be far away, came at once. He stood before Callie and listened as Mark explained what had happened. "We'll have to fix you a bed in one of the wagons."

"What if it's broken?" Callie whispered.

Rocklin had no answer for that. "We'll just hope it's not. Lots of times you just put a stress on something. You'll probably be all right in a few days."

Carleen pushed her way through those who were watching, and Molitor was beside her. "What happened to Callie? She get shot?"

"No, a horse kicked her. Don't pester her now, Carleen."

"Did it hurt bad, Callie?"

"Of course it hurts bad!" Callie snapped. "A broken bone always hurts."

"I'll go fix a bed for you, Callie."

"I can sit up."

Suddenly Molitor moved to stand beside Callie. "Can you lift your arm at all?"

Callie looked up with surprise. Molitor was watching her carefully. "A little bit," she said.

Paul Molitor reached out and began to run his hands over Callie's shoulder. Callie stared at him, and he said, "Does this hurt?"

"No."

"How about this?"

"Yes! Oh, that hurts ver' bad!"

Everyone was watching Molitor. He seemed like a different man. There was an assurance about him that they had not seen. Everyone's eyes were on him as he ran his hand over the girl's shoulder. He looked up to Rocklin. "It's not broken, just dislocated." He looked back to the girl. "I know that hurts bad enough."

"Dislocated?" Callie asked between tight lips. "What does that mean?"

"It just means that the bones have kind of popped out of place." He hesitated for a moment then said, "I think I can help you, but it might hurt a little at first."

"Anything to stop the hurtin'."

"All right." He came to stand in front of her and said, "Put your left hand on your other shoulder."

"It hurts."

"I know it does, Callie, but you'll feel better in a minute. Just hold it right here." He guided her hand to her shoulder and held it and said, "Now listen, Callie, I'm going to pull your shoulder back into place. It'll hurt. I know it's hard to relax when you know you're going to be hurt. The natural thing is to tense up. You're a strong, young woman, and I'm not all that strong myself, so if you tense up, I'll be pulling against your muscles. And if you resist, I just can't do it."

"What do you want me to do?"

"I want you to be absolutely relaxed for just a moment." He shifted his hands on her, and there was absolute silence in the circle. "I want you to think about yourself as . . . as a big piece of liver — like you didn't have any bones. Can you do that for me?"

"I . . . I can try."

"All right. That's fine. I can tell you're relaxed. I'm going to count to three, and while I'm counting, you try to relax even more so that by the time I get to three you'll be perfectly relaxed. All right?"

"All right."

"Here we go then. One — two —"

And then suddenly Molitor made a move that was so unexpected that no one caught it. Callie was waiting for the three, and she grunted with pain and cried out, but then her eyes flew open with astonishment. "How does it feel now, Callie? Can you lift your arm?"

Callie's arm was at her side, but she began to lift it. "Why — it doesn't hurt hardly at all. It's fixed!" She stared at Molitor. "How did you do that?"

"I'd like to know that myself," Rocklin said.

"Well, I had a friend who was a pretty good man with bones. I saw him do that a few times."

"Is it really all right, Callie?" Carleen demanded. "It doesn't hurt?"

Callie experimented with her arm. "Why, it's a little sore. I've probably got a bruise, but the bone seems all right." She turned to Paul and said, "Are you a doctor?"

Molitor shook his head. "Just a trick, Callie. I'm glad it wasn't worse."

"He looks like a doctor to me. You act like a doctor to me," Kate said abruptly.

Molitor was aware that every eye was fixed on him. "My father was a doctor. I learned a few things from him. I'm glad you're all right, Callie."

Jori followed Rocklin as he moved away. "What did you think of that, Chad?"

"I think it's a good thing we got Paul Molitor here with us."

"You know, I was wrong about Callie."

Rocklin turned and looked at her. "What do you mean?"

"You were right to bring her on the train.

It was cruel of me to even suggest leaving her there with those men."

"I'm glad to hear you say that."

"I know you think I'm hard and I'm spoiled. You must think I'm unbearable."

Rocklin grinned at her. "No, I can bear you well enough, Jori. Besides, if you don't behave, I'm the wagon master and I can always chastise you."

"Why, you wouldn't!"

She saw he was laughing at her and then shook her head. "I need it, I know, at times."

She turned and walked away, and Rocklin looked after her. He was remembering the kiss, and the memory stayed with him like a rich fragrance. He turned abruptly and walked back toward his horse.

CHAPTER SIXTEEN

Slipping a broad knife underneath the pancake in the skillet, Kate flipped it over and looked up at Carleen who was watching every move. "You see how easy it is?"

"Let me do the next one, Aunt Kate."

"Of course you can. You've got to learn how to cook sometime."

"Did you learn how to cook when you were as young as me?"

"Younger than you, sweetheart." Kate's eyes were fixed on the young girl, and she smiled suddenly. "I must not have been more than six when I started learning how to cook."

"You learned very well," Leland said. He had come to sit on a box and was eating one of the pancakes. "You make the best pancakes on earth — or anywhere else for that matter."

"You're just being sweet, so I'll give you another pancake," Kate smiled.

"You know what I want to be when I grow up, Papa?"

"I guess you would like to run away with a circus and do flips off the backs of horses."

"That's silly," Carleen said. "Who'd wanna do a thing like that? No, I want to be a doctor."

"Well, I'm sorry to disappoint you, honey, but you can't be."

"Why not?"

"Because there aren't any woman doctors. All doctors are men."

Carleen stuck her lower lip out in a habitual gesture when she was challenged. "Then I'll be the first," she said.

Kate laughed. "You're stubborn enough. If you make up your mind to it, you might just do it. Here, take this pancake."

Carleen took the pancake on the tin plate, poured molasses over the top, and cut it up into pieces. She got up and started off. "Where are you going, honey?" Leland called after her.

"I'm going to give Herendeen this pancake."

"He won't thank you for it."

"Yes, he will," Carleen said defiantly and continued striding along the line of wagons. She got to the wagon that Herendeen drove and saw him sitting with his back against the wheel. The other drivers had made a fire and were sitting around eating. Herendeen looked up. She came to stand before him and said, "Here, I brought you a pancake for breakfast."

Herendeen's face was still battered from the beating he had taken. His left eye was barely open, and he peered at the girl. "Why you givin' that to me?"

"Because it's hard for you to chew with your mouth all beat up. This pancake will be easy. Here, I've already cut it up and poured molasses all over it."

Grat Herendeen could not answer. He was studying Carleen almost with disbelief. "Why you givin' it to me? I ain't never done nothin' for you."

"I told you. Your mouth is sore, and this is easy to eat. You want me to feed it to you a bite at a time?"

"I don't reckon." Herendeen took the plate, took his knife out, and speared one of the pieces. In truth his mouth was sore, for the inside of his lips had been cut by Rocklin's smashing blows. He chewed carefully, swallowed it, and nodded. "That's good, missy. Did you make it?"

"No, but my Aunt Kate, she's going to teach me how." Carleen sat down directly in front of Herendeen, crossing her legs Indian fashion and watching him as he ate. "Are you married, Herendeen?"

"No, not now."

"You mean you were once?"

"Yes, I had me a wife once."

"Did she die?"

"No, she didn't die. She took up with a gambler in a saloon. The two of 'em ran off and left me. Good thing they did, too."

"Were you real sad when she left?"

Herendeen shook his head. "You ask a lot of questions. I was mostly mad, I guess, to think a woman would take a gambler over me."

"Did you have any children?"

"No. That's a good thing."

"You don't like children?"

"A man can't be a mule skinner and have kids. He'd have to leave 'em behind all the time."

Carleen sat there watching and popping questions faster than Herendeen could answer them. He had been sullen and withdrawn ever since he had taken his beating, and he knew nothing about children. It somehow amused him that she would ask the most intimate questions with total innocence. Finally he asked, "Don't you ever get tired of asking questions?"

"No. That's the way I learn things, Herendeen." She got to her feet and reached out for the tin plate. "Do you want another one? I'll cook it myself."

Herendeen hesitated. "That would be mighty good."

He watched as the girl skipped off, as innocent as if she were one of the flowers that bloomed on the prairie. The thought came to him that one day she would lose that innocence and somehow this saddened him. He was a rough man in all his ways and had little respect for anything in this world, but something in the girl had touched him, and as he sat there waiting, he thought, *She'll probably have a lot more questions. I never saw a young 'un like her before.*

"Good News, I want us to have a service this morning."

Good News was eating the pancakes that Kate had fixed for him. He looked up, his eyes widening. "A service? What kind of a service?"

"We've been on the trail now for weeks, and we haven't had a single service."

"Well, we don't have a preacher."

"That doesn't matter. You know enough Scripture, and you've learned how to read some."

"Well, I'm no preacher. No one would

listen to me."

Kate had risen and looked down on him. When he glanced up at her, he saw an odd expression on her face. "I'd listen to you," she said quietly. "Will you do it?"

Good News laughed. "Well, sister, it'll probably be just you and me, but I'll do the best I can."

"Good. Carleen, you go pass the word around that we're going to have a service. Tell everybody to come."

"Good, Aunt Kate. I'll tell 'em all."

Carleen began her mission with her usual enthusiasm. She went first to the drovers and told Pedro and Callie, and Pedro shook his head. "Somebody's got to watch these critters."

"Will you come, Callie?"

"I guess so. I don't know much about church, though."

"I'll explain it to you," Carleen said. "Hurry up. We're going to start pretty soon."

She ran quickly, up and down the wagons, and finally got to where the mule skinners were sitting around, some of them still eating. She said loudly, "We're gonna have church. All of you need to come."

Jesse Burkett stood while taking a sip of coffee. The tall, lanky man nodded and grinned broadly. "Are you gonna do the preaching, Carleen?"

"No. Good News is gonna do the preaching."

Wiley Pratt shook his head and grunted. "I ain't needin' to hear no preachin' from no mule skinner."

"Why, it'd do you good, Wiley," Stuffy McGinnis said. "Maybe even get you a pass to the pearly gates."

Brodie Donahue and Eddie Plank, both big men, were seated across the fire from each other. Brodie winked and said, "Eddie, there's your chance. I reckon you could use a little religion."

Eddie Plank glared at Brodie. "I've got as much religion as you have, I reckon."

"All of you need to come," Carleen said and stood waiting.

Wiley Pratt said with a curse, "Get out of here, girl, we don't need you or no preachin'!"

"Let the girl alone, Wiley. If you don't want to go, that's fine, but otherwise keep your mouth shut."

Herendeen had suddenly appeared and loomed over the group. His eyes locked with Wiley Pratt, a hot-tempered man himself. Wiley started to answer, but something in Herendeen's attitude caused him to be silent. Finally he grunted, "None of my business. Go on if you want to."

Brodie Donahue was examining Herendeen carefully. All of them had been shocked when Rocklin had beaten Herendeen. None of them had thought it was possible. Donahue asked cautiously, "You reckon you'll be goin' to the preachin', Grat?"

"Yeah, I'm goin'."

Grat Herendeen stared at Brodie, who shrugged and said, "Well, if it's good enough for you, I reckon it's good enough for me. Come on, let's go hear what Good News has got to say."

Good News stood rather awkwardly in front of the group that had gathered. They were all standing and waiting for him, and, though he was a man of firm convictions and never shirked from declaring his faith, something in the eyes of his fellow mule skinners intimidated him.

Kate saw this at once and said, "Leland, I think you ought to say something to get the meeting started."

"Me?" Leland was startled. He started to speak and deny the honor, but he saw Kate watching him. "Why, I'm no preacher, and I guess I'll have to admit that I haven't served God the way I should have. But I know He's real, and I'm trusting in Jesus Christ for my salvation."

Jori listened with surprise as her father spoke. Religion with him had been a private thing, but she was impressed at how sincere he was. She knew him well enough to understand that he was not just mouthing words. *Something in Papa has changed. I think the loss of everything and having to start over again has broken him, but he means what he's saying.*

Finally Leland shuffled his feet and said, "God's never failed me yet, and I don't think He ever will."

When Leland fell silent, Kate spoke up and said, "Well, that's a fine testimony, Leland. I think before Good News gives us something from the Word of God we ought to sing a hymn." Without hesitation she raised her voice and began to sing:

When I survey the wondrous cross,
On which the Prince of glory died,
My richest gain I count but loss,
And pour content on all my pride.

Jori knew the song and joined in. She had a strong alto voice and had learned to sing parts with her aunt when she was but a girl. Now she glanced around and saw to her surprise that Chad Rocklin's lips were moving. *He knows the song,* she thought with surprise and saw that there was a strange expression on his face. She could not know what he was thinking, but he joined in with the rest of the verses ending with the final one:

Were the whole realm of nature mine,
That were a present far too small;
Love so amazing, so divine,
Demands my soul, my life, my all.

Kate sang three more hymns, and, although the Haydens were familiar with them all, most of the mule skinners did not know any of them. Jori saw that Callie was totally silent, making no attempt to join in, and the thought came to her, *She doesn't know anything about all this.*

Finally Kate turned and nodded at Good News who at once stepped forward. He had a Bible in his hands, and there was a light of gladness in his eyes and a sound of joy in his voice. "I don't have to tell any of you fellows here that I'm no preacher, but I am a believer in the Lord Jesus. Miss Kate's been teaching me how to read, and it's been the finest thing in my life to be able to read the Word of God. I've learned to read enough to give you a few verses right out of the Book. The first one is found in the Gospel of John, the third chapter. Most of you probably heard the sixteenth verse. It goes, 'For God so loved the world, that he gave his only begotten Son, that whosoever believeth in him should not perish, but have everlasting life.' I reckon that's everybody's favorite verse, but for a long time I've been thinkin' on verses fourteen and fifteen, which come just before this one, of course." He opened his Bible and ran his finger along the words. His voice was halted but clear, " 'And as Moses . . . lifted up the serpent in the wilderness, . . . even so must the Son of man be lifted up: . . . That whosoever believeth in him . . . should not perish, but have eternal life.' "

Good News obviously was proud of being able to read the words, as faltering as it might have been. "I didn't understand that verse for a long time, folks. I couldn't read the Bible, and I didn't know what it meant when it talked about a serpent. But since Miss Kate has been teaching me, I found in the old Book, the Old Testament, that is, what it's all about. Maybe you heard how that God delivered the children of Israel out of bondage, out of the land of Egypt across the Red Sea to dry land. Well, they was on their way to the Promised Land, and the Bible says in the book of Numbers, the twenty-first Chapter and starting with verse four, a little story there that makes the words of Jesus be a help to us." He stumbled through the verse and began to read again in the same faltering fashion. " 'And they journeyed from mount Hor by the way of the Red Sea, to compass the land of Edom: and the soul of the people was much discouraged because of the way. And the people spake against God, and against Moses. Wherefore have ye brought us up out of Egypt to die in the wilderness? For there is no bread, neither is there any water; and our soul loatheth this light bread. And the Lord sent fiery serpents among the people, and they bit the people; and much people of Israel died.' "

Good News looked up and shook his head. "I guess people aren't a lot different today. I don't think we had gotten out of Franklin before some of us started gripin' and bellyachin' about the hardships. We didn't have anything like the children of Israel. They didn't have any food or any water. They didn't know where they were goin', and they were mighty scared, so they began to complain. And as I just read to you out of the Book, God sent fiery serpents to bite 'em. I guess the preachers would all tell us that we don't need to complain about anything that happens to us. God was gonna take care of the Israelites, and I'm believin' that God's gonna take care of me — and of you, too. Anyway, them fiery snakes, they began to bite people. We've seen that when poor old Jake Fingers got snakebit. I reckon all of us saw him die — a hard death it was, too. I think we'd have given anything if we could have saved old Jake, but there wasn't anything we could do. We just had to stand there and watch him die. But look at what verse seven says." He began to read again, and it was obvious that he had read it many times.

" 'Therefore the people came to Moses, and said, We have sinned, for we have spoken against the Lord, and against thee; pray unto the Lord, that he take away the serpents from us. And Moses prayed for the people. And the Lord said unto Moses, Make thee a fiery serpent, and set it upon a pole: and it shall come to pass, that every one that is bitten, when he looketh upon it, shall live. And Moses made a serpent of brass, and put it upon a pole, and it came to pass, that if a serpent had bitten any man, when he beheld the serpent of brass, he lived.'

"Well, glory, ain't that a fine, fine thing that God done for the people?" Good News lifted his voice and his eyes flashed. "Just imagine if there'd been something like that for old Jake. When he was a dyin', if he had just had somethin' to look at like that brass serpent. And the Book says it, so it's true. And that's what Jesus meant when He said if anybody wants God, all he has to do is look to Me. Just like Moses lifted up that serpent, I'm gonna be lifted up, and I'm the way that will save everybody that will just look."

Good News got carried away and spoke vehemently and with great excitement. He ended by saying, "Well, I'm talkin' too much maybe, but I remember the day I looked to Jesus. I was worse off than anybody with a snakebite. My soul was dyin'. I was headed straight for hell, but I remember that day as if it was yesterday. I called out to Jesus, and I looked to Him and right at that moment, folks, God came into my heart. The Lord Jesus took up residence, and He ain't never left and He never will." Tears suddenly came into Good News' eyes, and he said, "I know there are men that could have said this better, but all I know is that Jesus saves sinners because He saved me."

Callie had listened with some astonishment to the sermon. She had never been to church in her life and knew absolutely nothing. The name of God she had heard blasphemously from the rough men she had grown up around, but something about the words that Good News said had touched her. Her eyes had gone around the crowd, and she was shocked to see that Molitor had tears in his eyes. When the crowd broke up, she went over to him and said, "Paul, what is it? Why are you crying?"

Molitor pulled his handkerchief out and wiped his eyes and said, "I envy Good News, at least his faith." A sadness came over him that was obvious from the expression of his eyes and the way his face was drawn. "I had faith once, but I ruined it."

Callie did not understand what he meant, but her heart suddenly grew warm. "You're a good man, Paul. It's never too late for a man to change."

"That's a kind heart speaking, Callie," Paul Molitor said. He cleared his throat but then murmured, "For me it's too late."

Callie watched him go, and Kate, who had been standing close enough to hear the conversation, came over. "Paul's a very sad man, isn't he, Callie?"

"I don't understand him. He's educated. He could do anything."

"His heart's empty. When a man's heart is empty, Callie, it doesn't matter what he does." She suddenly said, "What about you? Do you know Jesus?"

Callie shook her head. "No. I don't know anything about religion."

Kate put her arm around the girl. "Well, we'll have to talk about that if it's all right with you."

Callie had known little of the love of women. She had lost her mother early, and that mother, indeed, had never been demonstrative. "All right," she said, "I'll listen to you."

Herendeen had not spoken to Rocklin directly since the fight, but he came upon him abruptly early one morning and said, "Rocklin, my mules ain't gonna make it. They're played out."

"I reckon you're right, Grat, but we've got to keep goin'."

Herendeen shook his head. "They'll never make it to Santa Fe."

"I know it, but I got good news. Four Bears and Kicking Bird came in last night.

There's a bunch of Pawnees right up ahead. We'll have a meeting with them."

"A meeting with Injuns? What for?"

"They got mules, Grat. Probably in good shape, too."

"You can't trust Injuns."

"You don't trust anybody, do you, Grat? We'll keep our eyes open, but we'll be all right."

Rocklin was aware that Herendeen would spread the word, and he knew that most of the mule skinners hated Indians and feared them. But he himself was glad.

Jori saw him and said, "What's going on, Chad?"

"We're about to get some new stock, Jori." He nodded toward the long low ridge that lay ahead of them. "Right over that ridge there's plenty of mules, all we need."

"Mules?" Jori asked with surprise, "What are mules doing out here?"

"The Pawnees raid the Spanish villages. They go to the south and steal the mules. Now we're going to trade 'em out of some of 'em."

"Indians? But won't they attack us?"

"Not these. Four Bears said it's not a war party. Just a few of the older men and some of the young boys and their squaws, of course."

He saw that she was troubled and said, "Don't worry. There'll be no trouble with these Indians. Maybe later on we'll run into some tougher ones, but this will be all right."

The trade for the mules went very smoothly. Jori was shocked when she saw the Indians. She had been brought up on the stories of the Wild West and the noble redskin with strong, fiery warriors, but there was nothing like this in the group that she saw. It was mostly squaws and children, and they were led by a very skinny man who seemed age-less. The lines in his face were scored deep. It was with him that Chad did most of the trading.

Jori watched as the group came on, and she asked Chad, "Where are the mules?"

"They've got 'em staked out somewhere. They wouldn't show them to us until we show 'em what we have to trade. Come along," he grinned. "You can brag to your grandchildren how you met wild Indians on your way to Santa Fe."

Jori was indeed eager and accompanied Rocklin. The skinny man, whose unpro-nounceable name meant *flying arrow* in English, was old but not feeble. His eyes were the liveliest thing about him, and he obviously expected a great ceremony and

Rocklin obliged him. The Indians came closer, and Rocklin had left strict orders that there would be no show of guns. This went against the grain for those like Wiley Pratt who hated Indians, but they knew better than to disobey Rocklin's orders.

The swap took place over a long period of time. Kate had fixed food that was snatched and gobbled down by the Indians. Jori, of course, could not understand a word, but Chad did. He interpreted for her, and once he smiled. "What did he say, Chad?"

"He wanted to know if you were my woman. He said that you weren't strong enough. I needed to get two or three more just like you. A man needs more than one wife, he says."

Jori felt her face glow and saw that Chad was laughing at her. She made herself smile. "You give him the truth of that because I'm not anyone's squaw."

"He won't understand that. They hate to see a good woman wasted."

Finally the trade goods were set out: blankets, cloth, beads, mirrors, needles, crockery, kettles. It took a great deal of time for the Indians to settle, and Jori was shocked at how happy they were over pieces that she would have considered worthless.

Finally the mules were brought in, and

Jori was shocked. "I've never seen so many mules! There must be a hundred."

"More like two hundred," Rocklin said. "Their men have been raiding for awhile. We'll be well-fixed for animals for the rest of the trip."

The trading lasted all day. After night came, Jori went to Chad who had moved to the outer fringe of the camp, standing in the shelter of a clump of stunted trees.

"I found out something from the old chief," Chad said. "He says that Santana has been in this part of the country."

"Santana? Who's he?"

"A great war chief of the Kiowas. He's a mean one."

"You know him?"

"Yes. We're enemies."

"Did something happen when you were with the Comanches?"

"Yes. That's the way it was."

The stars glittered overhead as he spoke, and he said no more. Finally he turned and said, "Are you afraid, Jori?"

"Yes, I am."

"Nothing wrong with that," Chad said.

"It's not just of Indians, Chad. It's — I'm afraid of something else."

"Of what?"

"You're not afraid, are you, Chad? You wouldn't understand."

Rocklin shifted his weight, glanced up at the stars, then murmured, "I'm not so much afraid of death. I've seen too much of it, I guess. I'm afraid of some things though."

"I'd like to know what they are."

"I guess I'm afraid of missing something. Don't know how to explain it, Jori." He lifted his head, for a coyote had lifted its plaintive howl. He waited until the sound died away, then said, "I was a partner once with a young fellow named Clyde. We had brushed up against a war party of Crows, and he had taken an arrow in his liver. I knew he was dying. There wasn't anything I could do for him. He wasn't hurtin' a great deal, but he was fading out. I'll never forget what he said. 'I'm not so much afraid of what comes after I die, but I never got done what I was put here to do.' "

"What a strange thing! What was he put here to do?"

"He didn't know — just like I don't know."

"I've never thought about things like dying or finding out what we're here for. My life's been filled up with dresses and balls, and now that I think of it, I'm afraid of that too."

"That may not be a bad thing, Jori. The people I've admired the most are those who knew what they were here for."

The moon was bright overhead, and Rocklin looked up and said, "That's a Comanche moon."

"What does that mean?"

"The Comanches wait until the moon looks like that before they go on raids." He started to speak and suddenly he broke off. With one swift motion he pulled his revolver and with his other arm grabbed Jori and pulled her down to the ground. She knelt helpless in the paralyzing grip of his arms. She silently stared out over the moonlit prairie.

Finally he put his gun back but kept his arm around her. "I reckon it was nothing," he said. "I'm just sort of jumpy." Instead of releasing her, however, he pulled her around and held her tight in his embrace. "I kissed you once, Jori, and I could never forget it." He pulled her against his chest and kissed her, and Jori surrendered to him in a way that shocked her. She did not know what it was, but somehow she felt safe, which was strange considering that they were alone in the night and he was a strong man. She had always had control over men, but now she discovered she could not even control herself. She felt a weakness, and for some perverse reason that pleased her. She could not understand it. Always she had valued her strength, but now it was Rocklin's strength she found exhilarating. Finally she pulled back and said, "Have you ever loved a woman?"

"I've known women."

"That's not what I mean."

"I know what you mean. I've seen it a few times. A man and a woman lived in each other and for each other. Those people have the real thing. I've always thought they had everything."

Jori got to her feet, and he rose with her. She studied his face in the moonlight and said, "How were they different, those people?"

"I don't know. Most people are selfish, I think. Most men want what they can get from a woman — and maybe women are the same. But I knew a man and his wife, Ed and Della Singleton. They had a little farm close to us. They were nothing special for looks or anything else, but Ed always thought of Della, what would be best for her, and she was the same. I asked him one time how he and Della had come to love each other so much, and he grinned and said, 'I always wanted to be a king, Chad, so when I got Della, I made her a queen. Every fella married to a queen,' he said, 'must be a king. Ain't that right?' "

A warm breeze stirred Rocklin's hair. He had taken off his hat and put it down. He was staring off into the darkness, but now he turned to her and put his hands on her shoulders. "So that's what I'll do, Jori. I'll find me a woman, and make her a queen."

Jori was acutely aware of his hands on her shoulders. "And what if she's not all that Della was?"

Rocklin suddenly laughed softly. "Haven't got that all figured out yet."

Jori stood there for a moment then said, "I've got to go. Good night." She made her way back to the tent and went to bed at once. She lay there for a long time thinking of what Rocklin had said and wondered if the man she got would make her a queen.

CHAPTER SEVENTEEN

A rolling front of snow-white clouds pushed its way across the blueness of the sky as Kate and Good News walked through the ankle-high prairie grass. It was the midpoint in June now, and the hot breath of the desert from the southwest could be felt on their faces. Kate stooped down and began to pluck some long, green-looking weeds — or at least so it seemed to Good News. "What are those, Kate?"

"This is lamb's quarter." She held them up, saying, "We can make greens out of it."

"I can remember poke salad and crest and even dandelions, but I don't know that one."

"When I was a girl it was my job to go pick the wild greens. I always liked to pick the spring flowers, and sometimes I would come home with a basketful of new, ripe, wild strawberries."

"We had a herb woman back when I was a boy. She said there was some kind of herb that could heal anything. Her name was Keziah. It came out of the Bible, I think." He stooped down beside her and began to help her pick the stems. "She had a white line around the end of her finger, I remember, like someone had drawn it with white ink. I asked her what it was one time, and she told me her brother had cut it off with an ax. I asked her what for. I remember she was a little bit batty. She said she didn't know. She just put it on the block and said, 'Chop her off!' and he chopped her off."

Kate laughed. "You're making that up."

"No, I'm not. It really happened. She had this little white line. I asked her if it hurt, and she said of course it did."

The sound of the wagons creaking along behind laid on the air. Good News glanced at them, took it all in, and said, "I guess we all have little white lines drawn around us that remind us of somethin' that went on in the past."

"I think so. Even the people that have lots of money have things like that." She straightened up and put a bunch of the greenery in the basket, then hooked it over her arm with the bad hand. Good News thought, *She doesn't think about trying to hide her bad hand from me anymore. I think that's good.*

"I guess life is like a tree," Kate said

quietly. "It gets new branches, and some of the old branches die and have to be broken off. Old things are passed away. That's in the Bible somewhere. I think it's best to try to move on from the bad things and look at the good things."

The two walked on, and her eyes moved constantly, looking for new herbs. Suddenly she said, "How come you never married, Good News?"

"Well, I just never knew how to talk to a woman, I reckon, a good woman that is."

Kate suddenly laughed. "You're talking like a magpie to me. What does that mean?"

"You're an easy woman to talk to."

The compliment pleased her. A summer darkness lay over her skin, and Good News noticed the ivory shading on her neck and the turn of her lips. Her smile was a small whiteness around her mouth, and a dimple appeared at the left of her lips. Now the light danced in her eyes. "I think you're probably funning me. You're probably a devil where women are concerned."

"No, I'm not," Good News protested, then he saw that she was laughing at him. "You're teasing me."

"I guess I am. What are you going to do after we get to Santa Fe?"

"Got no idea."

"Well, you must have some notion. Are you going to turn around and go back to Franklin, or are you going on to California?"

"I just don't have no idea, Kate. I'm just like a ship without a rudder, I guess."

"Didn't you ever have the desire to be anything, a doctor or a lawyer?"

"Neither one of those things. I did want —" He broke off abruptly, and Kate turned to face him quickly.

"You wanted what?"

"Well, I always wanted to be a preacher, but we can't have what we want."

Kate moved closer to him. She reached out and took his arm with her good hand. "I think that's a good idea. You should do it."

"But I've got no education."

"Look, we've been on the trail for just a few weeks, and you've already learned to read. If you put your mind to it, you could do it. It would be a wonderful thing."

"Why — it's just been a dream, Kate," Good News protested.

"Dreams are things that we need to reach out for. God can use you, though you'll never be a smooth, sophisticated man that wears a fancy suit and stands behind a mahogany pulpit. But there are people out in this country that need a preacher. Look at these mule skinners. You've gained their trust. You could start a church."

Good News seemed stunned, and finally Kate glanced at him. She saw that he had gone into some sort of a state and had forgotten that he was walking along the prairie halfway between Franklin and Santa Fe. He turned suddenly and looked at her, and his warm brown eyes took her in. "Something to think about, Kate. It's something to think about. . . ."

Callie had gotten off her horse and was walking along the stream that was no more than two feet across. It would take awhile to water all the animals, but water was scarce, and she knew they wouldn't leave until they had filled up their water barrels and all the stock had drunk their fill. She stooped down and ran her hand through the water, which was warm. The water was clear, and she moved down to where a bend had formed a pool six or seven feet wide. It had dug out the gravel until it looked to be at least two or three feet deep at the deepest part.

"Are you thinkin' about taking a bath?"

Callie whirled and saw that Mark Hayden had come upon her. She was embarrassed at being caught off guard, but she saw the gleam in his eyes and knew that he was pleased at surprising her. "I'm just looking for a place big enough to push you in, Mark."

Mark laughed. "You'll never let me forget that, will you?"

"A girl has to stay on her guard around a ladies' man like you."

"Why, I'm no ladies' man," Mark said.

"Yes, you are." She looked down at the water and, stooping down, ran her hand through it. "I've got dust on me a half-inch thick. It'd be nice to take a bath."

Mark took a step closer, and when she turned to look at him, he was grinning. He winked and said, "Why don't we?"

"You stay away from me, Mark Hayden! I knew you'd have to come out with something like that."

"Why, I was just teasing, Callie," Mark said, surprised by her vehemence. "Nothing wrong with that. It's the way of life for a man to be drawn to a pretty girl."

"I know why you're drawn to me," Callie said.

He saw also the hint of her will and her pride in the corners of her lips and eyes. "You're like a porcupine, all spines and stickers. Why do you have to be that way?"

"You never look at me as a woman you would marry."

Callie's statement stopped Mark cold, for he knew that she had spoken the exact truth. Weakly he said, "I can't afford a wife, Callie. I don't have anything."

"You think marriage is about a house and a fancy carriage and furniture?"

"That's part of it."

"No, that's not part of it. Marriage is something that goes on between a man and a woman. Got nothing to do with those things." Mark stood there speechless for a moment. He realized that there was a depth to this young woman that he lacked, and he said quietly, "I think you're right about that and I'm wrong. But at least, Callie, we could be friends, can't we?"

Callie had expected Mark to become angry, but she saw something different in him now. She was a lonely young woman and had learned to be wary of men. But something about Mark Hayden struck her at the moment, and she knew that it would be good to have him for a friend. "I guess so," she said cautiously. Then she laughed. "From what I hear this may be the last water to push you into for quite a few miles."

"You've always got your pistol," he said.

Callie shook her head. "No, Rocklin needs you, and besides I like your family. They'd all be angry if I shot their baby boy."

Mark suddenly flushed. "I guess that's what I am, the baby of the family. Even Carleen's got more backbone than I have."

The confession surprised Callie. "Well," she said, "maybe you'll grow up on this trip." She turned and said, "Look, there are minnows in there." She watched them, with Mark silent as he stood beside her. The conversation had wounded him somehow. He had come to see himself on this trip for what he was, a helpless weakling, and as he stood there, a resolution came to him that by the time they got to Santa Fe some of that would be changed.

The fire crackled and made a bright yellow dot in the growing darkness. Kate and Jori had fixed the evening meal. Food had become rather scarce, and all of them were hungry.

"Where is this place, Chad?" Leland asked. He was sitting with his back against the wagon wheel, a tin cup filled with coffee in his hand.

"It's called the Upper Springs."

"How far is it from here to Santa Fe?" Jori asked. She was weary and tired of the trip and longed to get some place.

"Maybe two hundred and fifty miles,"

Rocklin said. He was sitting close to the fire, and now he picked up a stick and poked it into the yellow flame. He waited until it caught, held it up, and watched it burn. Finally he blew it out, tossed the stick in, and shrugged. "I guess we're about two-thirds of the way to where we're goin'."

"I wish we were there now," Jori said. She shook her head, and a look of discouragement shaded her features.

Paul Molitor had joined them for supper. He had been quiet during the meal, and now he said, "We've been pretty lucky, Jori."

"You're right about that, Paul," Chad said at once. "All we've had is one death by snakebite. Back five years ago a train went across here with ten wagons and over fifty people. They got jumped by a big Sioux war party. Killed every one of them."

Rocklin's words seemed to cast a pall after that, and Molitor finally said, "My turn to go stand guard." He picked up the rifle and grinned suddenly at Rocklin. "You might as well send Carleen out there."

"Don't you think you could shoot an Indian if he was trying to take your scalp?"

"I doubt if I could hit an elephant from ten yards away."

"Well, if a Comanche came, you'd never see him. He'd have your throat cut before you could look up."

"That's a cheerful thought." Molitor left the campfire and moved outside of the ring of wagons. He had taken instructions from Rocklin on how to keep guard, and the moon was fairly bright. There were practically no trees in this part of the world, so he felt exposed, but he knew he composed one part of a line that circled the camp. Far off to his right he knew Brodie Donahue was on guard. To his left was Stuffy McGinnis, and on the other side Eddie Plank formed the circle. He stood gazing out to the west, but the sun had disappeared completely. He was occupied with his own thoughts when he heard the sound of footsteps coming from his left. His breath quickened and he held his rifle up, but then he saw that it was no Indian. "Hello, Callie," he said.

"Hello, Paul. You on guard here?"

"That's my assignment. I was just telling Chad I don't think I could hit an Indian if I saw one."

Callie came over and sat down. He eased himself down and said, "Is the stock all right tonight?"

"Yes, they're too tired and thirsty to run off."

Callie was intensely curious about Paul Molitor. She had come on purpose to find him. Now she began to ask him questions about himself. She noticed that he revealed as little as possible, and finally she said, "I think Mark Hayden likes me."

"Really? Well, that's not surprising."

"What about you, Paul? Do you like me?"

The straightforward question caught Paul Molitor off guard. He grinned suddenly and said, "I'm old enough to be your father."

"How old are you?"

"I'm thirty-three."

"Well, I'm almost eighteen. You might be my big brother."

"I'd be honored."

"Do you have any sisters?"

"No, nor a brother either. I was an only child." He turned to face her. "Do you like Mark?"

"Oh, well enough, but he would never marry a girl like me."

"Why do you say that?"

"He's a rich man."

"Not anymore if what I hear is true. If this wagon train thing doesn't work, the whole Hayden family will be busted."

"No, he's tried to kiss me, but he'd try that with any girl." She suddenly leaned forward so she could look into his face. "You've never tried to kiss me, Paul."

"No, I haven't."

"Why not?"

"It wouldn't be right."

"Men don't worry about things like that."

"Some of us do."

Callie was intrigued by the man. As far as she could remember, he was the only man that she had been around for any length of time who had not tried her virtue. She suddenly had an idea and said innocently, "My shoulder hurt a little bit today. Do you think it's all right?"

"It hurt? Let's see." Molitor laid the rifle down carefully, then turned. He reached out and put his hand on her shoulder. "Where does it hurt? Here?"

She took his hand and guided it. "No. More like here, I think. Just a twinge."

Molitor said, "Raise your arm — now move it back and forth." He put one hand behind her shoulder and one in front so that he was holding her tightly. He could feel the firmness of the muscle, yet there was the softness of a woman there, too. Suddenly he realized that he had his hands on a young woman and old hungers took him. He knew that Callie was aware of this, and his face grew warm.

"Now," Callie said, tilting her head back, "you'll try to kiss me."

"I'm tempted, Callie, I really am." He

released her and picked up the gun and for a moment was silent. "You don't need a problem like me, Callie."

Somehow Callie's feelings were hurt. She had spent so much time fighting off the attentions of men, and this one who she liked was not interested. "You see. You come from the same world as Mark. I can tell. You had money and nice things. You're educated. You wouldn't think of me as a wife."

"I wouldn't think of anyone for a wife now, Callie, but it's not because you're not a fine woman and pretty, too."

"Why not then, Paul?"

"I've got nothing to bring to you."

Callie could not understand this. She thought for a long moment and then she said, "You have yourself, Paul."

Molitor suddenly stood up. The encounter had troubled him. Callie rose and said nothing. He reached out and touched her cheek. "Be careful, Callie. I'm not a man you should trust. Now you need to leave here."

Callie did not move for a moment, and Molitor saw then that there were tears in her eyes. "I didn't mean to hurt you," he said, but she had already turned and walked away into the darkness.

"Well, there they are, Jori."

Jori was riding alongside of Rocklin. She had tired of the wagon and was tired of walking, and she had joined him without invitation. His horse was moving slowly about a half mile ahead of the wagons. She looked in the direction of his gesture. "There what are?" she asked.

"Don't you see them? It's buffalo."

Jori narrowed her eyes and stared ahead. It suddenly seemed like the ground was moving. "That's buffalo!" she exclaimed.

"Not a very big herd, but we'll have good eats tonight. Come on, I'll let you shoot one."

"No, I don't want to, but I'll watch you."

The two rode on, and Jori was astonished at the size of the herd. As they drew nearer it seemed to stretch out for miles.

"This is a big herd!" she exclaimed.

"Sometimes it takes half a day to get through a herd. It's pretty handy here. I'll drop one and we'll camp. Sometimes you have to drag the things back for miles to get to a camp." He pulled his rifle and the two rode right up, walking their horses at a slow pace.

"Why don't they run away?"

"They haven't been spooked yet. They're just like cattle, but if they do stampede, it's a pretty serious thing." He lifted the rifle, and the explosion shattered the afternoon air.

"You missed."

"No. Watch him now, that big one right over there."

Jori watched as the big, woolly animal walked steadily. Even as she watched, his front legs seemed to collapse, and he rolled over sending a cloud of dust high in the air.

"You have to hit 'em just right. Here, you hold my horse, and I'll get started on the skinning."

"I never knew anything could be so good," Leland Hayden said. They had eaten the tongue and the hump of the buffalo, and Leland said, "I know now what you meant about bein' satisfied with buffalo meat."

"Pretty near all you need," Rocklin nodded. "You never get tired of it either, not like other meats."

It was the second day of the feast on the buffalo. The men had gone off on a hunt and had killed several more. Kate had protested, "Why shoot them?"

"That's the way men are. They love to shoot things," Rocklin said. But Kate knew he didn't like it either.

As for Jori, she had discovered it was the best meat she had ever had. "I don't know why it is, but I can eat all I can hold and three or four hours later I can eat all over again."

Mark was gnawing on a bone, and he grinned suddenly. "Some of the mule skinners ate the livers raw. I don't think I could handle that."

They were interrupted when Rocklin stood up.

"What is it, Chad?" Jori asked quickly.

"Someone coming."

"I didn't hear anything," Mark said.

But no sooner had he spoken than Kicking Bird and Four Bears stepped into the ring made by the wagons.

"How'd you two get past the guards?" Mark asked with astonishment.

"You might as well put puppies out for guards," Kicking Bird grinned.

"Here, plenty of buffalo left. Sit down and eat."

The two Indians sat and ate an astonishing amount of the buffalo meat. They ate with a gusto that amused Jori, but she realized she was no better.

"What did you find, Bird?" Rocklin asked.

Kicking Bird wiped his mouth with his forearm. The grease was running down his chin. "Big war party over there." He motioned toward the north.

"Kiowa?"

"I think yes," Four Bears said. "I think maybe Santana."

Instantly something changed in Rocklin. He grew rigid, and his face grew harsh.

"Did you see him?"

"No, but his band likes this place."

Rocklin said no more, but before he left to go on guard that night he stopped by and said, "Jori, stay close to the wagons. Don't wander off, and watch out for Carleen. Pass the word."

"You think it's bad, don't you?"

"Maybe not."

"I'm afraid, Chad."

"That's a good thing. You hang onto that." He suddenly smiled, reached out and put his hand on her upper arm. "You'll make it fine," he said. "Just be careful."

CHAPTER EIGHTEEN

The threat of hostile Indians changed the nature of the entire train. Rocklin sent riders out, including the Indians, as sentinels. He also sent flankers out on each side, and a close guard was kept in the rear. A stricter guard was kept at night, and everyone's nerves were on edge continually.

The land itself had changed, for the Cimarron Cutoff leading into the south dipped into the Llano Estacado. The land was no longer level but dipped almost violently at times, then rose again in ridges that caused a strain on the animals. The vegetation grew scarce, sometimes vanishing and at other times decorated with skimpy oaks and cottonwoods. The only grass for the animals was clumpy and tough. To Jori the worst thing about it was the vastness. It seemed as empty and alien as the surface of the moon! She wanted to rush ahead to get through it, to arrive at Santa Fe. There seemed to be no end to the travel, and sometimes it was difficult to make out where the line of the sky met the horizon of the earth.

Every day seemed to grow hotter. The sun seemed to burn into her brain and strike her almost with a physical force. The days were miserable, but the nights, for some strange reason, seemed to be better. The sky seemed to be much closer now to earth, and the stars were brighter and glittered like scattered jewels across the sky. All sound seemed to be magnified. The clink of two utensils carried like a gunshot, and the barking and howling of the coyotes seemed so close that many times she would look up expecting to see one. As several days passed, Jori grew weary of the greasewood, the stunted cactus, the patchy grass, and the crumbling earth mixed with sand. Strangely enough she was, at odd times, caught with the unearthly beauty of the land. The sky, especially at night when the sun was low, would turn gold with dark stripes of shadows. It was a terrible, desolate kind of beauty and one that frightened her.

On the twenty-eighth of June, Jori looked up to see Rocklin. He stopped in front of her and studied her face. "You're sunburned," he said. "You need to put some grease on that."

"I don't know if we have any."

"Somebody will have some. Use axle grease if nothing else."

Jori suddenly laughed. "Wouldn't I be a sight then? Kate usually has something for any kind of ailment. Where are we?"

"We'll be at Rabbit Ear Creek by nightfall."

"I hope it's a nice, clean creek."

"Probably be dry this time of year."

"It's a terrible land, Rocklin. Is Santa Fe any better?"

"There's a river there, but it's not like Little Rock."

"I miss the forest and the trees from back home."

"Like I say, this isn't your home." He turned sideways in the saddle and studied her. Her face in its habitual repose had an expression that stirred his curiosity until he found himself trying to find a name for it. It was something like the gravity that comes when someone has seen too much and needs a place of quiet repose. "You're a little bit down today."

"I have been for a long time. The worst thing is I don't even know why I'm unhappy."

"Maybe we'll make it without anything bad happening."

The two rode along silently, and Jori thought it strange how Rocklin's silences were comfortable. He was not a man who had to make talk, and she had picked up some of his habits. "I don't know why I'm unhappy," she said.

"I know that feeling."

"You're not unhappy, are you?"

Rocklin reached down and patted his red horse on the neck. "I've got plenty to eat today, no bones broken. I'm not sick. Not dodging a Kiowa war party."

"And that's happiness for you?"

Her question seemed to trouble Rocklin, and for a time he didn't answer. Finally he shrugged his shoulders, saying, "I don't have any answers for that. A good time and some laughter, the memory of a good friend's greeting, a woman's face half hidden behind a fan — these are a few fading memories. That's about all I have, Jori." Rocklin suddenly laughed. "Don't ask me to be a philosopher. I don't have any of that in me."

"You've had a hard life, haven't you?"

"No worse than some." Something like humor came to him then. "The last time I was in St. Louis there was a man passing out advertisements. He was a thug, beat up people for a living. He had a list of all his services with the prices. At the top of the paper it said 'Rates for Crime' and then it said:

"Number One, both eyes blacked, four dollars.

"Number Two, nose and jaw broke, ten dollars.

"Number Three, ear shot off, fifteen dollars.

"I don't remember the rest. A shot in the leg, I think, was twenty-five. The last one was doing the big job. He had *Big* and *Job* capitalized, one hundred dollars. Now that fellow had a rough life."

She said nothing, and he turned to study her, then asked abruptly, "Do you dream much?"

"Sometimes. I dreamed last night I was chasing a woman down a long canyon about like that one we passed through three days ago. I ran and ran. I somehow knew I just had to catch her, but I didn't know why. And finally I caught her by the shoulders and turned her around — and she had my face."

"I guess that has some meaning, but I don't know what it is."

"All I can think of is, all my life I haven't known who I was. Now, here on this trail, dodging Indians, with my face burned to a crisp, I'm beginning to see who I am."

Rocklin was interested. He turned and studied her carefully. "Most people never figure out, really, who they are. I'll be interested to know what you find out about yourself."

They both fell silent, and a breeze stirred musty and pungent odors as they rode along. Suddenly he said, "I've come to feel something for you, Jori."

Startled, Jori turned and faced him. "What are you talking about?"

Rocklin eased himself up in the stirrups taking time to think. When he turned, the brilliant sunlight caused him to squint his eyes as he studied her. Again she thought he had the bluest eyes of any man she had ever seen. "I think every fellow carries a picture of a woman around in his mind. He sees one woman with beauty, another who has gentleness, another who has inner strength, and he starts looking for that woman with all these qualities."

Jori could not help but smile. "That's not very fair to the woman. No woman could have all of that."

"Maybe not, but when a man finds a woman he wants to live with the rest of his life, he sees the thing in her that he wants to see." Chad saw that the guard was up in her eyes and murmured, "Tough on me, but you've got the kind of beauty I see nowhere else."

"Why, we're nothing alike!"

"I'm not looking for somebody like me. That would be boring, wouldn't it?" Suddenly he reached over and took her hand. He held it for a long time, and she allowed it. His touch seemed to reach farther than her hand in a way that she could not understand.

"I don't know what you mean by all this, Chad."

For one instant Rocklin's urges made a turbulent eddy around them both. She understood it as well as he. She knew that they could never go back to what they were before. Something had changed, and she knew that he recognized it as well as she.

"Funny thing about a man and a woman," Rocklin said. "If I had never met you, I would never have felt like this."

"You would have found another woman."

"I'm trying to tell you it doesn't work like that," Rocklin said.

"Are you telling me, Chad, that you think God makes one man for one woman?"

"I don't know much about things like that, but I know I can't go back to what I was before I met you." He released her hand

and said, "You probably think I'm loco." When she didn't answer, he shook his head. "Maybe I shouldn't have told you all this. I've got to go out and check the scout. Stay close to the wagons and keep an eye on Carleen." Without another word he wheeled his horse around and rode away at a fast gallop. She stood there watching him, not knowing what to think about the strange things that he had said. No man had ever talked to her like this before, and she knew she would not be able to forget it.

All morning Jori tried to put the scene out of her mind, but it kept filtering back. She could remember the exact words that he had said. He puzzled her. She had not liked him in the least when she had first met him, but now she realized that the time together on this trip had done something to her. She had changed, and she did not know exactly why.

During the midday break she was quiet, and finally, when it was time for the train to start up, she heard Kate speak to her. "Have you seen Carleen, Jori?"

"Why, no. She was here to eat, wasn't she?"

"She eats with the mule skinners sometimes." Kate's eyes brightened. "She can get along with anybody."

"Well, she's probably with them. I'll go see."

Jori left and went down the line of wagons looking for Carleen. Finally she got to the last one and saw Grat Herendeen standing beside the mules. His face was still somewhat battered from the beating that he had taken from Rocklin, and he said nothing as she approached. "Have you seen Carleen, Grat?"

"She was here just before we ate. Said she was going over there to that grove of trees." He pointed to a line of cottonwood that traced the bank of the small creek where they had stopped.

"She shouldn't have wandered away," Herendeen said. "I told her not to, but she's a stubborn kid."

"Yes, she is."

Jori had a trace of fear. She walked back, mounted her horse, but she said nothing to Kate or her father. She rode over toward the trees, which seemed to get thicker. They were on the far side of a small canyon, and she had to hang on while her horse went down the steep incline then scrambled up the other side. The creek made a serpentine curve and she called out, "Carleen!" and waited but heard no answer. She rode forward into the grove and called again, and then suddenly a faint sound came to her. She turned and saw an Indian moving toward her at an incredibly fast rate. She kicked the horse, but two more Indians had appeared in front of her. They grabbed the bridle, and the one who had come from behind had pulled her off her horse. She started to scream, but his hand clamped down over her mouth. He smelled rank, and his face was painted in a strange pattern.

Several more Indians came out then, and one of them was pushing Carleen ahead of him. Carleen's hands were tied behind her back, and she was gagged. Her eyes were wide, and she struggled to come forward, but the smallest Indian held her back.

One of the smaller Indians appeared to be the leader. He came over toward her, and all the fears that Jori had nurtured about the savage treatment that Indians dealt out to their prisoners became a stark reality.

The Indian stopped right in front of her. His eyes were so black they seemed to have no pupil. He did not move for a moment, and then he uttered a guttural command. At once two of the Indians forced Jori back into the saddle. One of them tied her feet tightly to the horse's belly with strips of rawhide. Once she started to speak, but the leader shook his head and said something she didn't understand. He took out a knife and held it toward Carleen's throat, and Jori cried out, "Don't hurt her!"

"Be still," the leader said. "I am Santana." She could not help but react and knew that he saw her fear. He uttered a few short words of command, and one of the Indians pulled her horse forward. They moved to where the horses of the war party were held by other braves. There were only nine of them in all. Santana nodded toward one of the larger Indians and gave a command. The larger Indian picked up Carleen, threw her on a horse, and leaped on behind her. All the Indians mounted then, and with one single word Santana sent them out. They headed directly away from the train.

Jori Hayden knew then that she and Carleen were lost. The very worst nightmare had come to pass, and she twisted to look back toward the train, but she could not see it for the line of trees. The Indian riding beside her reached out and struck her a blow. She bowed her head and tried to pray.

■ ■ ■ ■

PART FOUR:
JOURNEY'S END

■ ■ ■ ■

CHAPTER NINETEEN

Letting Red pick his own way, Rocklin sat easily in the saddle. He was relaxed except for his eyes that continually moved over the landscape. The trail was monotonous to be sure, broken only by ranges of hills or low divides, and distances were deceiving. The novice on the trail could fix his eye on an object and after hours of plodding straight toward it, find himself to be no nearer his goal.

Rocklin straightened up and arched his back. He liked the air of the desert. It seemed that every vapor was eliminated from it so that the atmosphere was clearer. He turned toward his right and saw what appeared to be a lake shimmering. This, too, was an illusion. There were no lakes on the Cimarron Cutoff! One was fortunate to find water in the mudholes or at times seeping out in tiny dribbles from the rocks. But the mirages fascinated him. He had seen them make fantastic shapes. A memory came to him from the past, touched his mind and made him smile. He had once seen a herd of buffalo that appeared to be high in the air, not with their feet on the ground. The thought of how shocked he had been to see buffalo a hundred feet in the air amused him.

Pulling his mind back to the present, he began to calculate the myriad of details that were his to look over. He ran over the food supplies that had to do them until they reached Santa Fe. One by one he went over the wagons in his mind, thinking of the spare parts available and hoping he wouldn't have to jettison any of them. Such a thing was not unusual, for he had been on trains where wagons had given out completely. The loads had been redistributed, but that could not happen with this train because the wagons all were loaded with all they could take. He looked back over his shoulder with a sense of satisfaction. He had found water only ten miles ahead, a great deal of it for this part of the world. He gauged the time, and knowing that they could reach there before nightfall brought a sense of satisfaction to him. He was a man who liked to accomplish things, and the challenge of getting the wagons through had consumed him over the past weeks.

Now with two-thirds of the journey behind him, he felt confident, but he had been in the West too long to grow careless. There was always a chance of a storm that could wreck the wagons and even a greater chance of an Indian attack. He had learned to confine his fears into a small part of his mind where he could handle them. It was the only way that a man could exist in a land where danger was as much a part of the landscape as sky or trees or land.

The loneliness of the land found the counterpart in Rocklin as he urged his horse to a faster pace. He had been alone most of his life, and the sense of isolation had become a part of him. Now, however, there was a restlessness that had come to him so gradually he had not recognized it. Now he understood that something had changed in his life. A sudden memory came to him. An ex-school teacher who had given up the classroom to become a mountain man had said something once that had stuck in Rocklin's memory. His name had been Jurgens, and he had been a strange fellow to Rocklin. Jurgens had said, "We're made of memories. They say ninety-five percent of us is water, but they're wrong. Most of us are made up of memories."

As the words came to Rocklin out of the past, he shook his head and a wry smile touched his broad lips. *I guess my memories are all snarled and tangled like a line on a reel that's got to be cut away. I don't reckon anybody could straighten them out.*

Even as this thought came to him, another memory came of a woman's voice. He had been walking down the streets of a small Kansas town and had passed a house. The darkness had swallowed the earth, but that one house was marked by the yellow lamplight that flooded out from inside and threw its beam on the street outside. The woman had been singing a song that Rocklin had never heard. Her voice had been smooth and sweet, and something about it had pulled him to a stop. He remembered standing there outside, looking at the house and wondering who the woman was. Even now he wondered about her. Was she married? Did she have a lover? Was she happy? Did she have children? The memory was as clear to him as the wagons he approached, and he shook his head, then brought Red up to a gallop. There was nothing to be done for a man's loneliness except a woman, and no woman had ever offered herself to fill this vacancy that he now felt.

As he approached the camp, he knew

something was wrong even before he reached the lead wagon. Leland and Kate had seen his approach and were standing there, and something in their attitude, the way they stood, gave Rocklin a warning as clearly as a shout. He came off his horse in one smooth motion and asked, "What's the matter?"

Leland Hayden swallowed hard. His face was pale, and then the words came tumbling out. "It's Jori and Carleen. They're gone. We don't know where they are."

The alarm increased in Rocklin, and his jaw grew tense. "When did you see them last?"

"Sometime around noon," Leland said. "We've got to go back and look for them."

Kate was watching Rocklin's face as if there were an answer to be found there. "I'm afraid for them, Chad," she whispered. "Where could they be?"

"Probably just wandered away and got lost. I'll find them," he said.

Swinging back into the saddle, he rode at once back to where Pedro and Callie were herding the mules. "When was the last time you saw Carleen or Jori?" he asked.

Pedro was startled. "We have not seen them all day, not since this morning."

"What about you, Callie?"

"No, I haven't seen them either," Callie said. Her eyes were wide, and her expression revealed that she knew something was wrong. "How could they get lost out here?"

"Don't know," Rocklin said. He wheeled his horse and rode back toward the train. He stopped at each wagon asking in a hard, spare tone for any information, but not until he reached Herendeen did he find out anything. Herendeen was standing beside the wagon, his eyes fixed on Rocklin.

"Have you seen Miss Jori or Carleen, Grat?"

"Not since noon. I heard they had gotten lost."

"Where'd you see 'em at noon?"

"You remember that old riverbed with the cottonwoods beside it? I think it was all dry. I saw Carleen headed over that way. You know how she is." He shrugged his beefy shoulders. "Always wantin' to see stuff." His brow furrowed, and he said, "You say Miss Jori's gone, too?"

"Yes."

"Let me get on my horse. I'll help you look for 'em."

"You stay here, Grat. Let me do a little looking, then we'll see."

Rocklin wheeled around and galloped back toward where the family was waiting.

Mark had joined them, and his face was pale. "We've already asked everybody," he said before Rocklin could speak. "We've got to find them!"

"Herendeen saw them," Rocklin replied, "way back by the spot where we nooned. I'll ride back and pick up their tracks."

"I'm going with you," Mark said.

"Be better if you stay here."

"No, I'm going."

"All right. Catch up a horse then."

Mark ran to saddle a horse, and Rocklin dismounted and stood, trying to think of some way to put this matter in the best light. He knew the fears that now racked the Hayden family, and he said, "Probably they just wandered off. That happens sometimes."

"I warned Carleen so many times," Leland whispered, and he shook his head. "I can't believe she'd go so far."

"It'd be hard to get lost in this country. It's so level and bare."

"I got lost once in a desert," Rocklin said quickly. "You get turned around and head in the wrong direction, and before long you don't know which way is up. In the country with mountains you can always fix on a peak. I never got lost in the Yellowstone country, but the prairie is different."

Mark was back now, and Rocklin swung into the saddle. "I'll come back as soon as I find out something."

Rocklin kicked the stallion into a dead run and did not even look back. He kept up a torrid pace until they reached the point where the riverbed and the cottonwoods were visible. He kept watch until he found signs of several fires that they had made. "This is where we nooned," Mark said. He looked around and said, "How do you know where to start looking?"

"Herendeen said he saw Carleen headed for those trees over there. You stay behind me. I don't want you to mess up any tracks."

Mark pulled his horse up and watched as Rocklin leaned over. He found, apparently, what he was looking for, but he didn't speak until they were halfway to the old riverbed. "I see Carleen's tracks here and Jori's pony both going in, none coming out."

When they reached the riverbed, Rocklin dismounted and gave the reins to Mark. "Hold my horse," he said. Without another word he moved forward toward the line of trees bent over. *He was like a hound,* Mark thought, *sniffing on a trail.* He knew he would be utterly helpless and useless in such a situation, and as he sat there, the fear that had been birthed in him grew until it made his hands tremble.

Moments went by that seemed longer than they were, and finally Mark saw Rocklin emerging from the trees. He was running, and when he got there his lips were drawn into a tight line. Something in his eyes frightened Mark. "What is it, Chad?"

"Indian war party took 'em."

Mark shot a frightened glance at Rocklin, and quicker breath stirred in him. "Are you sure?"

"Yes. Kiowa, I think." Rocklin's face had a drawn expression. Mark had seen it before. It always came when the big man was facing a disagreeable thing. "What'll we do?"

"Go back to camp."

"But we've got to go after them, Chad."

"We'll have to tell your folks what happened."

There was a dismal ring in Rocklin's voice that tolled like a funeral bell to Mark. He felt a deep emptiness inside, and the world around him seemed to have closed like a curtain of darkness.

"I'm going with you, Chad." Leland Hayden's face was stiff as parchment. He had taken the news that Rocklin and Mark had brought back badly, and his hands were unsteady.

"That won't do, Leland. You stay here and take care of things. I can do this better by myself."

"Is there any hope, Chad?"

Rocklin shifted his gaze to Kate. He saw the fugitive shadows chase themselves in and around the corners of her mouth as she tried to hide the fear. "Always a chance. It was a small party." He didn't mention the fact that a small party could be just as devastating in their cruelty as a large one. There was no way to comfort this family, so he moved quickly, filling his canteen with water and giving instructions. He saw Mark filling his own canteen and shook his head. "You can't go, Mark."

"I'm going." Mark's voice was flat and level, and there was a stubbornness in him that Rocklin had not seen before.

"You wouldn't be any good to me. You can't read a sign. You don't know Indians."

"I'm going after my sisters, Rocklin," Mark said. "If you leave me, I'll follow as best I can, but I'm going."

"I reckon I think better of you for it. All right, Kate, fix us something to eat, some dried meat maybe, and we'll take some extra guns."

The two were quickly prepared for their

mission, and as they were getting ready to ride out, Herendeen and Wiley Pratt came to stand before them. "I'm goin' with you," Pratt said. "I'll help you kill them devils."

"No, you stay here, Wiley."

"I want to go," Herendeen said. His eyes were smoldering. "I'd like to help get those two back."

"Grat, you're in charge of the train while I'm gone. I'm depending on you to keep things going." He saw refusal beginning to form in Herendeen's eyes, and he said, "This is what you do best, Grat. Now, there's water ahead ten miles. I'll draw you a map. Take the train on in there as quick as you can and draw up in a defensive position. Those Indians know how many we are. They may come back."

"I hope they do," Grat's voice grated. "I'd like to kill 'em all. I'd like to go with you though." Something wistful touched the big man's face, an unusual sight to Rocklin. "I like that little girl."

"We all do, but you wouldn't be much use huntin' a Kiowa war party. You are good at your job, so take care of things."

Kicking Bird was staring at Rocklin, his eyes inscrutable. "I think it is Santana," he said, a warning in his obsidian eyes.

"What makes you think that?" Rocklin

demanded.

"His camp, it is over there two or three days' ride. He'll go back there, I think."

"I think so, too," Four Bears spoke up. "It is bad to tackle Santana without a big war party beside us."

"Well, we don't have a big war party, Four Bears." He waited for the Indians to say that they would not go. Indians had no shame about backing off from a fight when they saw they were outnumbered or in a bad situation. Rocklin agreed with them, for the most part. He knew that words would not convince them, and he said finally, "I've got to go after the women. I wish you'd go with me. I'll make it worth your while. Buy you whatever you want."

"Dead men can't use much," Kicking Bird suddenly grinned, "but I will go with you. I never liked Santana."

"But Santana would like to get his hands on you," Four Bears said. "You remember him."

"I remember him. He won't take me alive."

"We need good horses," Kicking Bird said.

"We'll take three horses apiece, the best horses in the herd. Let's go pick 'em out now."

■ ■ ■ ■

Mark was so weary he was about to fall off his horse. His arm ached from holding the lines that held his extra two mounts along beside him. Sometimes they lagged and nearly jerked him out of the saddle.

The sun was going down now, and it was all he could do to keep up. He noticed that nobody had looked to see if he was coming, and he knew that if he fell behind, he would be on his own.

They had been traveling for six hours, and finally Four Bears, who was the best tracker, pulled his mount up and turned. "We camp here. Too dark."

Relief washed through Mark. He sat in the saddle, aching and wondering if he had the strength to stand up. He forced himself out of the saddle, and his legs nearly collapsed. Glancing around quickly, he saw that nobody was paying him any attention. Kicking Bird took his horses. "I'll take care of the horses," he said.

"Mark, catch up some wood if you can find any."

"All right, Chad."

Mark began walking around. Wood was scarce, but he found a small tree that had died, apparently, of the heat. He broke it up, came back, and soon he had a fire going.

"How far ahead do you think they are, Chad?"

"Four Bears thinks maybe twelve hours, a day's ride. It could be more." Rocklin's voice was hard as stone, and he sat before the small fire adding sticks to it.

When the fire was going well, the Indians came in. They sat down cross-legged, and Four Bears stared at Rocklin. "They're headed straight for Santana's camp. Many braves there."

"How many?" Rocklin asked.

"Who knows. Maybe a hundred."

Alarm ran through Mark. "Why, we can't fight a hundred Indians!" They had half a dozen guns between them, but the Indians had guns, too. He waited for Rocklin to speak, to give some sort of indication of how things were going, but he did not. Mark said, "I guess we can eat this food that Kate put up."

He got up, found the meat and the bread, and the four ate silently. There was no water available. It was a dry camp, so they had to drink out of their canteens.

As soon as they had eaten, the two Indians lay down and seemed to go to sleep instantly. Mark had no thought of sleep. He stared into the fire and, from time to time, lifted his eyes toward Rocklin. Finally he said, "I can't help thinking what could be happening to Jori and Carleen. I've heard awful tales about how Indians treat captive women."

Rocklin stared across the fire, the flickering shadows changing his face and obscuring his thoughts. "There's no sense fooling yourself, Mark. They'll be treated rough, but they'll be alive, and that's what counts."

"How can you be sure of that?"

"They capture women for a purpose. They want to make squaws out of them, but they'll be alive."

The crackling of the dry wood made popping sounds and sent sparks flying outward. They looked like miniature stars while overhead the real stars glittered. The two men sat there silently for a long time, and finally Mark said, "I hate to tell you, Chad, but I'm scared stiff."

"Nothing wrong with that."

"I want to pray, but I haven't been a praying man. I've never given God much of a thought. How can I go to Him when I need something and cry like a baby?"

Rocklin picked up a small piece of the wood, laid it on the fire, and then another.

Finally he said softly, "I reckon if we waited until we were good enough to go to God, none of us would ever go. I'm like you though. I wish I were a praying man."

"How in the world are we ever going to deal with a hundred Indians?"

"Best chance is to catch 'em before they get there. I figure there's nine of them. We can handle that many. Come daylight we'll ride as hard as we can. We just have to wait and see how it goes."

"Maybe we can catch 'em by surprise."

Rocklin shook his head. "If it's Santana, we won't catch him by surprise."

"You know about him?"

"He's always been the enemy of the Comanches. When I was growing up, I heard tales about him, not nice ones. Nothing you'd want to hear. He'd like to take me alive though."

"Why you especially?"

"I killed his son on a raid. He's never forgotten it." He suddenly said, "Go to sleep if you can, Mark. It's liable to be a long day tomorrow."

CHAPTER TWENTY

Santana set a hard pace, driving the horse at a dead run at times. After an hour the Indian carrying Carleen, at the command from the leader, removed the gag and untied her hands. Carleen at once began to fight, but the Indian merely doubled his fist up and struck her in the temple. She would have fallen if he had not caught her. He laughed and said something that made the other Indians laugh as well.

Jori was almost numb with fear. She was aware that they were climbing a ridge, and when they were near the top, she looked back but could see nothing but the emptiness of the plain. She was torn apart, could hardly breathe for the tears that she tried to withhold, and there was the knowledge that the future held nothing for her but pain and agony and misery. She had heard stories of how the Indians tortured people. They were noted for their cruelty, but everyone said they were so brave that you could strip the skin off of them and they would never make a sound. She had heard also that they admired anyone who could undergo torture without showing fear.

Finally Santana called a halt. A small water hole fed by a stream apparently filled in a slight indentation, and the Indians all stopped and took turns drinking. When all the Indians were finished, they stood around laughing and talking. Santana motioned to Jori and said, "Drink." One of the Indians cut the rope from under her feet, and she dismounted. She started for Carleen, but one of the Indians, whom she later discovered was named Fox, grabbed her. His eyes were wide, and he grabbed her blouse and ripped it away. His intentions were plain, but Jori determined to fight to the best of her ability. She struck out at Fox and caught him in the throat. He grunted and struck her a blow in the temple. She staggered backward, and he yelled and made for her. At that moment Carleen ran and jumped on his back. It caught him off guard, and her arms came around him and her nails bit into his face as she raked at him. She was yelling, and Jori caught her balance and shook her head from the effects of the blow. She saw Fox reach for his knife and start for the girl, but Santana called out something in their language and he stopped. An argument ensued, and finally Fox snarled and backed off.

Santana advanced. He was not as large as most of the other Indians, looking almost slight, but there was something fierce about him. He came to stand before Carleen, and she glared at him. "I ain't afraid of you!" she yelled.

Santana laughed and looked at Jori. "This one is brave. She will make a good squaw."

"What do you want with us?" Jori asked, hardly able to form the words. "My people will pay you to get us back."

"I am Santana. I will take you to the village and leave you. Then I will bring all my braves, and we will kill everyone at the wagons and we'll take all. We will take everything. Now," he said, "drink and we will go."

At that moment a resolution formed in Jori. It was a simple one. *Stay alive!* She turned and said, "Carleen, drink." She herself stooped down and drank. When they were finished, Santana motioned to the horses, and she went back, mounted up, and Santana said, "You ride with her," speaking to Carleen. Carleen came at once and got on the horse behind Jori. Santana and the

Indians mounted up, and they left the spring at a gallop.

At sunset the party stopped. Several buffalo were grouped together, and the thickset Indian called Fox asked a question. Santana nodded, and all of the Indians whooped and took off after the buffalo.

Carleen slipped off to the ground, and Jori dismounted. They both looked at Santana, who was watching them curiously. "We will eat," he said. "Do not try to run away."

Indeed, there was no place to run. Jori saw that, and she stiffly stood there. She went over and put her arm around Carleen's shoulders. "We'll be all right, honey," she said.

"Are they going to kill us, Jori?"

"No, but they may be mean."

"I ain't afraid of them," Carleen said.

"Try not to make them mad."

Carleen said, "If we could knock that old Santana on the head and the other one watching the horses, we could get away."

"We can't do that."

Santana ignored them. He appeared to be thinking deeply about something. He moved twenty yards away and stood there with his back to them, studying the sunset.

There was nothing to do, and Carleen and

Jori simply waited. It seemed like a long time, and darkness had completely fallen when the party came back. They had evidently killed a buffalo and cut it into chunks, for they quickly made up a fire. Some of them could not wait but began eating the liver and the tongue raw. Santana accepted a chunk of the meat, thrust it onto the point of a stick, and held it over the fire that the young men had made. He said something, and one of the warriors hacked off a chunk of meat and threw it in the general direction of the two captives. It fell in the dirt, and Santana gave another command. The same Indian that had thrown the meat hacked off a sapling, sharpened the point and tossed it to them.

"Eat," Santana said, his face impassive, his eyes fixed on the meat that was sizzling in the fire.

"I don't want their old meat," Carleen said, but Jori shook her head. "We have to be strong," she said and thrust the point of the stick into the meat. She cooked it, at least seared the outside of it, and then ate what she could. Carleen did the same. The Indians ate until they were gorged. Two of them disappeared out into the darkness and the rest simply lay down and went to sleep.

Santana had said nothing during the meal.

Now he looked across the fire where the two sat, Jori with her arm around Carleen.

Carleen said, "When can we go home?"

Santana shook his head. "You never go home. You will be Kiowa woman. I will give you to one of my warriors."

Carleen shook her head violently, her eyes fixed on the savage. "God won't let that happen."

The youngster's words caught the attention of Santana, and he grinned faintly. He was a good-looking Indian with regular features beginning to show a little age now but still strong, and his eyes were alive. "Your God is weak," he remarked.

"No, he's not!" Jori said strongly. "He's a strong God."

Santana turned to face her. "I have heard many who believed in Jesus God. I have seen them die under torture, but Jesus God never came to save them."

"He'll save us," Carleen said stoutly. "He'll send Rocklin to get us."

Santana's eyes glittered. "I saw Rocklin in your camp."

"You know him?" Jori asked.

"Yes. He was a Comanche." He fell silent for a time, and finally he said, "He raided my village with a war party and killed my son. I've always known that I would kill him."

There was utter finality in the Indian's words, and Jori realized that nothing on earth could change the mind of this man. Rocklin had told her how strong family ties were among the Indians, and now she knew even more fear.

"You believe in Jesus God?"

Jori was caught off guard. "Yes, I do."

But even as Jori spoke, there was a knowledge in her that the words did not reflect what she was. She had always attended church, for that was the family tradition. Kate was a devout believer, and her father was at least a nominal Christian. Mark was not, but he went through the motions as did the rest of them. As she sat there in the stillness of the desert air at the complete and total mercy of this savage who would pull her apart, taking one finger after another if he so chose, she suddenly knew that she could not call on God. *I don't really know God,* she thought. *I thought I did, but now I see that I don't know anything about Him.*

Santana seemed to be able to read what was going on inside Jori's mind, and his eyes were fixed on her. "Jesus God will not save you. You will see. No one can save you." He gave a command, and one of the Indians apparently awakened. He listened as Santana spoke. He came and tied the hands of both the captives with rawhide behind their backs.

It was cold in the night air, and the two huddled together the best they could with their hands tied. "It'll be all right. Chad will come for us," Carleen whispered.

The words brought no comfort to Jori. She was struggling with the knowledge that calling on God was impossible for her. She had not known this, and now a greater fear than ever came. She had somehow imagined that she could always call on God and he would answer, but now when she tried to pray she heard nothing but the silence of the desert.

The second day found Jori even more hopeless than she had felt the night before. Santana seemed quick to keep the two of them safe from the attentions of the other Indians, but her heart was sick with the knowledge that all of her life she had, more or less, used God. She decided that religion had been a convenience for her. Now as she rode with the band headed for Santana's home village, the future was dark, not only because of the atrocities that she might encounter at the hands of the Kiowa but the knowledge that her whole life had been a lie as far as religion was concerned.

They stopped at noon, and two scouts went out while the rest were content to eat what was left of the meat of the buffalo. Santana had kept two men to watch the spare horses, and late that afternoon as the sun began dropping in the sky, he came to stand before the two of them. His eyes were fixed on Carleen. He seemed to find her fascinating. "You have courage," he said. "You will make a fine Kiowa."

"No, I won't ever be an Indian," Carleen said. She stood straight and faced him fearlessly, so much so that Jori wondered how one small child had such lack of fear.

"You must learn our ways," Santana said, "or you will die." He turned to Jori and said, "You will be the squaw of one of my band."

"I can't do that."

"You have little choice, but it will be harder for you than for the child." He thought for a moment and then added, "We captured a woman once when I was a young man. She felt as you felt, that she could never be Kiowa, but she was given to my uncle as his squaw. We kept her for years, but many years later we were trapped by soldiers. They recaptured the woman. We heard what happened to her later."

"What happened?"

"She had forgotten how to speak her tongue almost. She cried to be allowed to come back to her Kiowa husband and to her children. She had stopped being a white eyes and had become a Kiowa. She did not know any of the life. The girl will be like that. It will be harder for you." He shook his head and said, "Do not hope. It's useless. One day I will die. It will be as the gods ordain. Now, the gods have given you into the hands of the Kiowa. You will be a Kiowa woman. It would be happier if you'd accept this. It is not a bad life. It is different from anything you have known. You will find a way and a place."

"I won't ever be a Kiowa!" Carleen said, glaring at Santana. He merely laughed at her and turned away. Carleen went over and put her arm around Jori's waist. "Don't listen to him, Jori. We'll get away. Chad will come for us. You'll see he will."

But Jori had lost hope. She did not respond but simply held onto the young girl and tried to keep the tears from falling.

"It'll be up to you, Mr. Hayden." Grat Herendeen was facing Leland, and the sunrise was throwing its bright light over the landscape. The two were looking back over the track that they had followed, and both were thinking of the two captives. The wagons were drawn up in a defensive position, and scouts had been out all night. The water was good, and there was enough graze for all of the animals. But Herendeen was worried. "We can stay here for awhile, but I'm worried about those Indians comin' back. They saw how few of us there are, and if they find some more of their kind, they might attack."

"I can't just go off and leave my girls." Leland Hayden seemed to have shrunk with the crisis. His shoulders were slumped, and dark circles were under his eyes.

"I'm right sorry about your girls, but Rocklin's a good man. Him and them Indians, they got a chance of gettin' 'em back. You want to stay here again today and see what happens?"

"Yes. I want to do that."

"All right, Mr. Hayden. We'll keep good watch tonight. I hope we find them."

Leland walked slowly back to his own wagon and joined Kate. The two of them had spoken little, and now he said briefly, "I want us to stay here at least for awhile and wait and see if Rocklin comes back with them."

"I'm glad we're going to do that," Kate said. "Leland, God's going to help us in this. I know He is. Jesus said if we had as much faith as a grain of mustard seed, we could be heard. So let's pray."

"All right," Leland said heavily, and the two of them fell upon their knees and began to call upon God.

"I'm right scared about what's happened to those girls, Paul."

Paul Molitor had come to help stand guard over the extra mounts. Callie had joined him, and both of them were thinking of the captives. It was impossible to get such things out of your mind, they had both discovered.

"I've heard awful things about what Indians do to white women. I'd kill myself before I'd let the Indians have me."

Molitor turned to face the young woman. A strange feeling sliced through him as he saw how young and vulnerable she was. He saw the desire in her for the two captured women to be all right, and behind the worried expression a little girl's eagerness vaguely stirred and displayed itself. There was a sweetness in this girl that somehow she had managed to keep despite her hard life. He suddenly wanted to comfort her and spoke softly, "Did you ever think, Callie, how close heaven is to us and yet how far off it is when we lift our hands to touch it?"

"Do you really think so, Paul?" She turned to him then and for that instant something warm lay between them, strong and unsettling. Both of them were still. A thin moon lay askew in the low south, and the small creek was a dull silver ribbon freckled with the shadows of the woods. Suddenly long, undulant waves, the sound of a breeze, washed across the land, and the sad wild cry of a coyote added a note of sadness to the night. As they watched a star fell and made a brilliant scratch on the heavens and then died.

"A falling star," she whispered. "I always make a wish."

"I guess I know what it is this time."

"That Jori and Carleen will be all right."

"That's a good wish."

"What will happen, Paul, if Rocklin and the Indians can't catch up to them?"

"I don't know. I don't like to think about it."

"Do you believe in prayer, Paul — that God hears us?"

"Yes, I do. Sometimes it doesn't seem like it, but I believe it."

"I'm glad you do. I want to believe it, too."

"Well, we'll believe together. God answers the prayers of bad people sometimes, I think. I haven't been a good man, but this is a good thing to pray for."

"Don't say that!" She suddenly reached out and put her hand on his chest. "You're not a bad man. You're a good man."

At that moment Paul Molitor felt something that had not touched him for years. He had known women long ago, and the sadness and the disaster of his own life had removed them from his thoughts. Now as Callie stood there, the tone of her presence was an urgency, straining against his sense of propriety.

"We'll pray together about it. It's a good thing to pray about." He saw the glow come into her eyes, and a slight happiness shaped her lips. The moonlight lay against her, brightening her eyes, and the two sat there for a long time without speaking — but each knew that something deep within had touched them both.

Jori woke up abruptly, not in stages as she had the previous morning. She lifted her head and saw that the moon was still high in the sky. As she heard the grunts and snores of the Indians, she paid no attention to them for something had come to her. It was a fragment of a dream, and she tried to bring it back, to dredge it out of the unconsciousness. She was not sure exactly what it was. It seemed that someone had called her name, but she could not even be sure of that.

She lay there, pinched with anxiety about the future, but still there was the matter of the dream if that was what it was. Finally it began coming back to her. It was the memory partly of Good News as he had preached the sermon, and now she could hear his voice, not literally of course but she caught even the tone of it in her spirit: "As Moses lifted up the serpent in the wilderness, even so must the Son of man be lifted up: That whosoever believeth in him should not perish, but have eternal life."

She lay there, and suddenly she was aware that the fear had gone. This came as a great shock, for nothing had changed. Shame and dishonor and pain lay ahead of her, but fear was gone. "What is it?" she whispered, but there was no answer. Still the sensation of peace was upon her. She began to think about the words that Good News had preached. Time and time again he had said, "Look to Jesus as the Israelites looked to their brazen serpent on a pole. He can save you."

Finally a great sorrow came to her, and the knowledge that she had shut God out of her life was quite real. It was as real as any physical pain she had ever had, and she began to pray.

Her prayer was disjointed, and she did not even know, at times, what she was saying in her heart. She knew she was crying out, telling God that she was sorry she had ignored Him. She asked for forgiveness and she prayed many times, "Lord, save Carleen."

She managed to conceal the sobs, but she knew as she lay there underneath the stars overhead that she needed Jesus Christ. She thought of all the invitations she had ignored in church and all the sermons she had paid no heed to, but now she was open, and she knew that God was listening.

Finally she prayed, "I don't know how to pray — but Lord Jesus come into my heart. I'll follow You no matter if someone comes to save us or not. Whatever happens I will be obedient to You."

She prayed like that for a long time, and something like a warmth came to her, not a physical warmth but a sense of inner warmth. She recognized this as peace, and then she began to feel a joy, knowing that God had heard her. She began to thank the Lord God for the first time in her life. . . .

CHAPTER
TWENTY-ONE

Four Bears rode his horse toward the train at a dead run. He pulled him up, his black eyes gleaming with excitement. "Up there," he grunted, pointing to the direction from which he had come.

"How many are there?" Rocklin asked.

"Nine. It is Santana. I saw him myself."

"That's bad news," Rocklin murmured. "They're probably the best of his warriors, too."

"They're not the best right now," Bear grinned. There was a ferocious quality about the Comanche. He had the spirit of battle in him, and his reputation was great among his people.

"Why did it take so long?" Rocklin demanded, his eyes fixed on Four Bears.

"They took time out to go on a raid. I got close enough to hear them talking. They came back with horses and firewater and two captives. They were starting to put the captives to the knife when I left. They'll be at it for awhile." He grinned broadly. "They're drunk though, and we can kill them all."

"What about my sisters, Bear?" Mark demanded.

Bear shrugged his beefy shoulders. "They are alive."

"Have they been harmed?"

Four Bears did not answer but turned and fixed his gaze on Rocklin, waiting to hear his decision.

Rocklin's mind worked quickly. He glanced at Mark saying, "This is good news. If they had made it back to the village, we would have had real problems."

"But there are nine of them. There are only four of us."

"They won't be looking for us, especially if they are drunk," Rocklin said. Something changed in his expression, and Mark saw a determination that was usually covered by an indolent manner. "This is what we're going to do. . . ."

Jori had tried everything she could think of to drown out the sight and the cries of the captives. The Kiowas had staked them out and done horrible things to them. She had heard that the Indians could endure torture silently, but one of the Pawnees could not. His screams had echoed and gone into her like a knife. She had put her arm around Carleen and said, "Cover your ears up. Don't listen."

The two of them had sat like that for what seemed like hours. Finally the cries died away, and when Jori eventually gathered up her courage and looked, she saw that both of the men were dead. She could not bear to look at it, but she turned her eyes on Santana. The biggest of the Kiowas, the one called Fox, was arguing with him, and instantly Jori could tell he was asking Santana for permission to take her. Fox's eyes came to her continually, and he gestured in her direction with guttural words falling from his lips. Santana did not move, but only his will kept Fox from taking her. Jori well understood that.

Carleen had huddled closer to her. She had endured the horror of the raid better than most adults, but now she buried her face against Jori's breast and whispered, "I don't want them to know it, Jori, but I'm afraid."

At that moment Jori was aware that the encounter she had had with God in the darkness was real. Ordinarily she herself would have been paralyzed with fear, but even though she was still in the presence of death, and her own faith was highly questionable, there was a peace in her that enabled her to say, "God is going to help us."

"Aren't you afraid, Jori?"

"I was, but last night I talked to God."

"Did he promise you we'd get loose?"

"It was nothing like that. It wasn't so much what he promised me but what I promised him."

"You promised him something?"

"Yes. I promised him that I would trust him no matter what happened. He's going to take care of us. I really believe that, and you must believe, too."

"Let's both pray then."

"I think that's a good thing." Jori held the girl tightly, and the two of them called upon the God who they were now trusting to deliver them.

Four Bears held up his hand and put his finger to his lips. He made a motion and slipped off his horse. "We tie horses here and go on foot. They are over there behind those trees."

As they tied their horses, Rocklin questioned Four Bears about the situation. The Comanche was sure about the number, but

Rocklin was bothered. "They'll have guards out."

"No, not with whiskey," Kicking Bird grinned. His eyes were dancing as if he had been invited to a party of some kind.

Mark could not understand it, and he kept his eyes fixed on Rocklin. "How are we going to get them free, Chad?"

"It'll have to be quick," Rocklin answered at once. He had been thinking about this all the way on the trail and now had no doubt. "The first thing they'll do when we hit them is try to kill the girls."

Mark was alarmed. "Then how will we save them?"

"I've got two pistols. Here, take my rifle." He handed it to Mark. His voice was clear and steady, and, as he studied the man, Mark knew suddenly that this was the element that he himself lacked. They were about to kill human beings, yet Chad Rocklin showed only a determination to get the job done.

"I'm going to go on ahead and creep up as close as I can. All of you take position and get ready. When I get close enough, I'll kill Santana with the first shot. That'll leave me one more. As soon as you hear my shot, open up on 'em — and don't miss. If they have time, they'll kill Jori and Carleen."

Mark was struggling with the plan. "You're just going to kill him without warning — Santana, I mean?"

"That's what I'm going to do."

"It's not civilized."

"Wake up, Mark." Rocklin's voice was rough. "Think what will happen to Jori and Carleen if we don't save them. You think I can go in and have a debate with them, that I can talk them out of this? They're drunk, and they want scalps. This is our only chance. If you can't do it, say so now."

It was a moment of decision for Mark Hayden. Balanced against him was the life that he had led — soft, easy, and careless. Now he was about to be thrown into a battle in which the lives of his sisters — and, perhaps, his own — were at stake. He saw that the three men were watching him closely, and suddenly anger burned in him. "Don't worry about me. I won't miss. Give me your rifle." He reached out and took the rifle and saw that Rocklin seemed satisfied.

"Good man," he said. "This will be all right, Mark. We'll have them back soon." He nodded and turned to move toward the camp.

"Come. We move in closer," Kicking Bird said. "We get scalps tonight."

Four Bears was studying Mark. "You

ever kill?"

"No."

Four Bears suddenly laughed soundlessly. "It is good to kill your enemies. Come, and do not miss!"

The Indians were completely drunk now. They were dancing and shouting unearthly cries. From time to time one of them would go over and use his knife on one of the corpses.

Jori was watching Santana and Fox. She had been observing them for some time. Finally it had become clear to her that Fox was bargaining for her. She could not understand their language, of course, but the Kiowa's glittering eyes came back constantly, and more than once he gestured to her. He held up several fingers and she guessed that he was offering the war chief horses for her and Carleen.

"What's he talking about, the big Indian?" Carleen whispered.

"I don't know, Carleen." There was no point in alarming the girl. There was nothing she could do about it. Her hope was in Santana although she could not have said why. He had drunk some of the whiskey but not enough to make him wild, as were his warriors. Still, there was somehow a difference in him. At first he had brushed Fox away roughly, but now he was listening, and when Fox held up nine fingers his eyes came over and met those of Jori. Jori held his eyes and saw him smile. He suddenly laughed and took another drink of whiskey from the jug.

He called out, "Now we will see if your Jesus God will save you. You will be Fox's squaw. Take her, Fox."

Jori's blood seemed to freeze as the burly Indian laughed, straightened up, and lifted his arms to the sky giving a wild cry. He turned then and started toward her. He said something in his own language that made the other Indians laugh. Several of them had turned to watch the little drama. Jori moved away from Carleen and could not speak. Fear was outside of her pushing to get in. She saw the lust in the Kiowa's eyes and knew there was no mercy in the man, but she called out, "Lord Jesus, save me and my sister!"

Santana laughed. "Now we will see if Jesus God is strong."

Fox laughed also. There was a cruelty in his features and in his expression. He reached out for her, and Jori knew there was no point in running. But before his hands touched her, a shot rang out, and Jori saw a black hole appear exactly in the center of Fox's forehead. His eyes opened wide for a moment, and then he began collapsing. His legs seemed to be turned into rubber, and he fell to the ground bonelessly.

Almost instantly Jori saw Santana leap to his feet and make a wild grab for his gun, but immediately shots rang out. The Kiowas were grabbing for weapons now, but at least three of them were on the ground.

Things happened so rapidly she could not understand. She saw that the two Indians and another man had leaped into the area and were hacking at the Indians with tomahawks and knives.

She whirled to see Santana grab a rifle and swing it toward her and pull the trigger. The shot, so close to her, was over her head, and it seemed she could hear the hissing of the bullet. She threw herself to the ground, pulling Carleen with her, and a movement caught her eye. She saw Rocklin appear suddenly. He put himself between her and the Kiowa war chief.

Santana ignored the melee of battle going on around him. He pulled a knife from his belt and called out, "You kill my son, but now you will die! I will die happy, knowing I have killed you!"

Santana lunged forward, the blade held

out in a sweeping right and left motion. Jori saw that Rocklin had no gun, but he whipped out the knife that he always carried at his side, and his face was fixed as he faced the charge of the Kiowa. Santana feinted, but when Rocklin moved his knife to catch the blade, he threw himself forward. Rocklin grabbed his wrists and with one swift motion drove the knife in the throat of Santana. A crimson flood burst forth, spraying Rocklin, and a cry was cut short as Santana fell backward.

Rocklin turned, the bloody knife still in his hand and his shirt covered with the blood of the dying Kiowa. "Are you all right, Jori?" he cried out.

"Yes." Jori could barely speak, and she was aware that the noise of fighting had died down. Suddenly there was the scream of one of the Kiowas who threw himself forward. She saw him rising up behind Rocklin and lifting a club. Jori tried to cry out, but it was too late. The club came down on the top of Rocklin's head, and he collapsed, falling face forward.

Before Jori could move, Kicking Bird had leaped forward and brought the sharp edge of his tomahawk down. It caught the Kiowa in the head, making an awful sound that she would never forget. The Indian dropped, and then she heard her name being called.

"Jori — Carleen, are you all right?"

Jori turned to see Mark, his face pale as parchment, running toward her. His arms were out, and she fell into them, and Carleen joined them. He held them, and she saw that he was weeping. "We're all right," she said. She pulled loose and fell on her knees beside Rocklin. He had been wearing his soft hat, and when she removed it, she saw the terrible wound. The top of his skull was indented, and the bones of his skull were shown whitely.

"Chad —" she cried but could say no more.

Kicking Bird had stooped and ripped the scalp off the Indian who had struck Rocklin. He looked at it with satisfaction, then came forward and looked down. He saw the terrible wound in the top of Rocklin's skull and shook his head. "He will die, but he died bravely."

"No, he won't die!" Jori cried. She held his bloody head to her breast and repeated defiantly, "He won't die. God, You mustn't let him die!"

Mark looked down at his sister. He, too, could see the wound and had no hope. He put his hand on her shoulder but could think of nothing to say. He looked down at

Carleen and saw that her eyes were wide with shock. Kneeling down, he put his arm around her.

"It'll be all right, little sister," he said. But he knew in his heart that it would not.

Chapter
Twenty-Two

A rising flood of clear and brilliant sunshine touched the prairie, and for a time, it seemed to Kate, the world was bathed in morning's freshness. She had learned to love this time of day, the "cobwebby time" she sometimes called it, and now she stood peering to the east, longing to see the sign of someone coming. For a long time she stood there watching the gray blades of light slice away at the darkness and glancing up at the stars. She thought that they seemed cold and brilliant and somehow ominous. A strange feeling came to her, and a faint distant memory had its way with her for a moment.

"I guess I could have one of those biscuits if you can spare it."

Kate turned to look at Leland, who was standing with his tin plate in his hand. He looked worn and tired in the early morning light, and when she gave him another biscuit he nibbled it without much sign of appetite. "I keep thinking I need to go look for them."

"That wouldn't do, Leland. What good would you be? You couldn't track anything more than I could."

"I know it, but I want to do *something!*"

"We all do, but our job right now is to hold on here." She moved closer and put her hand on Leland's arm. "Waiting's the hardest thing to do. Always easier to be doing something, but right now we just have to seek God and pray and believe."

Leland gave her a faint smile. "I was never very good at waiting."

"No, you were always good at doing things."

"It's a lot easier to do religious things than it is to be religious."

"What a strange thing to say!"

"Well, it's true enough. You just think about it. Remember when the Harrisons' house burned down? That poor family that lived on the other side of town. Members of our church, you remember."

"Yes, I do. What about them?"

"Why, the whole church was galvanized into action. Everybody was there. You brought two of the children to stay with us for a few days until we could find another house for them. People were bringing food and finding a place for them to live." He took another bite of the biscuit and shook his head saying mournfully, "It's a shame that the church's finest hour has to be when somebody's house burns down. But that's the way it is. You try to get everybody to come and pray all night. See how many volunteers you get. I never could understand how people could pray all night. Why, I could pray for everybody I know in thirty minutes, then I'd just be repeating myself."

"I don't pray like that, Leland."

"What do you mean?"

"Why, some prayers are pretty formal. We put them into words. 'Lord, help me to get that piece of property I want.' We can say it again, or we can say it ten times, but I think the things I really prayed for I didn't put into words more than once perhaps."

"What'd you do the rest of the time?" Leland was interested. He seemed to forget the biscuit and stared at her. "How'd you pray if not in words?"

"I think it's just being aware that God is there, that we said our prayers." She smiled faintly and said, "I think it's kind of like a mother that has a young baby although I've never had one. But they tell me they're always conscious of that baby even if they're not thinking directly about it. There's part of them that's always in that crib no matter what they're doing — washing dishes, washing clothes. Their mind is always open and they never really forget it. That's the way it is with me when I'm really praying for something. God knows our prayers, and He knows we care, and we've got to keep telling Him that we love Him and we trust Him."

Leland's voice was shaded with admiration. "I admire you, Kate, I truly do. You've been the one that held the family together after we lost your sister."

They were interrupted when Callie came up saying, "Could I have some of the grits and bacon and a biscuit or two?"

"There's plenty."

"I thought I'd take them to Paul. He's been standing guard all night. I know he's hungry."

"Here, I'll fix you up a plate." Kate filled the plate and then watched the girl as she left. "I don't know what'll become of Callie. She has nobody. God will just have to look out for her."

Paul turned and saw Callie as she came with a plate in her hand. She carried a cup of coffee in the other hand. "Here, I brought your breakfast."

"That sounds good," he said. He laid the rifle down on the ground, took the plate and the coffee, and sat down cross-legged. He began to eat, and she sat down beside him. Silence seemed to flood the earth at this early morning hour. They could hear the restless movements of the mules, and one of them gave a hoarse cry that split the silence. Finally Callie said, "They've just got to come back, Paul, they just have to!"

Molitor took a swallow of the coffee, then he shook his head in a slight movement of disbelief. "Good things don't happen too often, Callie."

"But sometimes they do."

Molitor studied the girl. She had taken off her hat, and now the early sun touched her hair. It was as black as the blackest thing in nature. As he studied her, her lips made a small change at the corners as something touched her mind. She made a little gesture with her shoulders then turned to look at him. "Don't you think Rocklin will get them?"

"If it can be done, he'll do it."

Callie reached down and pulled up a blade of grass. She brushed across it with the tips of her fingers and said, "I've had a lot of bad things happen in my life, but I still hope. I still believe God can do anything."

"I'm glad you feel like that, Callie," Paul said. "It's the way a person ought to feel, but then I —"

"Listen," Callie said, springing to her feet. She was looking toward the east, and after staring, she cried, "It's them! I see the Indians!"

The two immediately ran and joined the others, who were coming together in a rush.

Kate had been talking to Good News when he heard a shout, and whirling she saw the party coming across the prairie. "It's them!" she said. "Praise God, it's them! Come on!"

They rushed out and were joined by Leland and several of the teamsters.

Leland outdistanced her, running and crying out the names of his daughters. They ran to him and collided, hanging onto each other. Leland was laughing and crying at the same time. "You're all right — you're all right! I can't believe it. Praise the Lord."

Kate stood back, letting them have their moment. Mark came to stand beside his father. He looked pale in the morning light and somehow seemed more mature.

"Where's Rocklin?" Kate asked.

"He's been hurt," Mark said. He turned and waved toward a travois. "The Indians made that stretcher thing that's hooked onto the horse."

Jori broke away from her father, and when she embraced Kate, she said, "He's hurt so bad, Aunt Kate. I'm afraid for him."

Jori moved toward the travois, and as Kate followed her, she saw that both of the Indians had bloody scalps on strips of rawhide tied around their horses' necks. Kicking Bird looked at her and laughed aloud and held up the string of scalps. "Plenty scalps."

Kate ignored him and knelt down beside Chad and looked into his face. He was utterly still, and his mouth was open as he breathed heavily. "It's his head right on top. You see? He got hit by a club."

Kate bent forward and peered at the skull. She saw that there was an indentation there. "His color's not good."

"No, he's worse than when we started, but we didn't know what to do," Jori said.

"Bring him into the camp. I'll go make a bed up for him. Be careful how you move him."

Mark nodded as Kate whirled and ran away. "I knew it was dangerous, Father, but we didn't know what else to do."

"I want to hear all about it, but we'd better take care of Chad first."

Fifteen minutes later Chad Rocklin was lying on his back. Blankets were under him and over him. He was in the shade of the wagon, and Jori was kneeling down and looking at the wound. "Can't you do something, Aunt Kate?"

Kate heard the frantic quality of Jori's voice and said reluctantly, "There's nothing I can do with a wound like that."

Soon the whole train was buzzing with the news. The teamsters all wanted to know the details, and Mark told them as best he could.

Herendeen listened and said, "What about Rocklin? Is he gonna make it?"

"I don't think so, Grat. It's pretty bad."

"Too bad," Herendeen shook his head.

"What do you care? He beat the tar out of you," Stuffy McGinnis said.

"That don't mean he's not a good man. Shut your fool mouth, Stuffy!"

Callie had stayed on the outskirts of the area where Rocklin lay under the blankets. She watched as Kate and Jori went to him, trying to think of something to make him more comfortable, but she had seen enough life to know that there was little hope. Finally she heard Leland Hayden exclaim, "If we only had a doctor here, he could do something!"

At those words Callie suddenly straightened up. A thought had come to her, and she turned at once and glanced around the circle. She was looking for Molitor, but he was not there. She tried to think when she had seen him. Everybody had come when the party had returned, but there was no sign of Paul. She thought, *He's probably taking care of the animals.* She got up and went to where the herd was staked out and asked Pedro, who merely shook his head. "Haven't seen him," he muttered.

Callie began to circle the camp. He wasn't with any of the wagons. He wasn't with the animals. They had stopped beside a small stream where the water had been sufficient for the animals and for their own use. Now she ran quickly and almost at once found Molitor standing between two spindly cottonwoods. He turned as she came up to him, and his eyes seemed sunk in his head. "Is he dead?" he asked almost harshly.

"No, he's alive, but he needs help."

Molitor turned and looked back down into the small stream. His shoulders were slumped, and a silence wrapped itself around him.

"You can help him like you helped me with my shoulder," Callie said. She came to where she could look up into his face, and she saw the bleakest expression she had ever seen on Molitor's features. "You can help him, Paul."

"This is a lot different from putting a dislocated shoulder back." He suddenly lifted a flask she had not seen and took a drink.

She smelled the raw odor of whiskey and said quickly, "Getting drunk won't help, Paul."

He swallowed the alcohol, shuddered as it hit his stomach, and then turned to face her. "Neither will killing a patient. I've done that once."

For one moment Callie did not understand what he was saying, and then it came to her. "Patient? You've had patients? That means you're a doctor."

"Not anymore."

Callie caught his arm. "You *are* a doctor, aren't you?"

"A long time ago. Now leave me alone, Callie."

"Paul, you can't let him die. None of us know what to do. You're the only one who can help."

"I can't help anyone — not even myself. Now leave me alone." Suddenly Molitor tore his arm free from her grasp and walked across the creek. The water splashed, and he emerged on the other side.

Callie stood watching him, then called out, "Paul, you can do it. You've got to do it!" He did not answer, and she turned slowly and made her way back to the camp. She was thinking all the time, *What can I do?* Finally she knew she had to tell someone. When she got to the camp, she saw Jori kneeling beside Rocklin and Kate standing at his feet watching the pair. For a moment Callie hesitated, then she said, "I just talked to Paul. He's a doctor."

Both women looked at her, and Jori's eyes flew open. "What do you mean?"

"He told me. He used to be a doctor."

"Well, why isn't he here?" Kate cried. "We need him."

"He says he used to be a doctor but he's not anymore."

Jori got to her feet. "I've got to find him."

"He waded across the creek. He was headed out on the prairie."

"Wait a minute," Kate said. "It sounds like he's got a problem. I've always known there was something in that man. He's not like most of the men we see."

"He told me he got drunk and killed a patient when he operated. He said after that he couldn't be a doctor anymore."

"Well, we've got to pray that he will. It's Chad's only hope," Kate said. "So, just start praying, and then we'll see."

Molitor had fled the camp. He could hear only faintly the sounds of voices now. He walked upstream aimlessly. Finally he was as miserable as he had ever been in his life. He drank the rest of the liquor in the small bottle and threw it away with one swift, vicious motion. It hit an outcropping of rock and shattered.

"Paul, are you there?"

Paul Molitor turned quickly and saw Jori Hayden coming toward him. He knew at once that Callie had told her what he had said, and now he braced himself for what he knew was coming.

Jori stopped immediately in front of him and said, "You've got to help Chad, Paul. You just have to. There's nobody else."

"You don't understand, Jori. I'm no better than a murderer. I got drunk, and I tried to operate and killed a woman. She's dead, in her grave, because of me."

"That was a terrible thing, but, don't you see, this could somehow make up for that. You can't bring her back to life, but you could save Rocklin's life."

"No, I couldn't. Look at my hands. They

tremble just thinking about operating on someone, and an operation like he would need would take a skilled surgeon in a hospital somewhere."

Jori's eyes were fixed on Molitor's face. "While the Indians had me, I had just about given up hope. And then in the middle of the night I began to talk to God. I didn't make any promises except to follow Jesus, but I know somehow he heard that prayer, and he brought Chad and the others to save Carleen and me. You need to be saved, Paul, just like I did. God has given you a gift, and you're throwing it away."

"I can't do it, Jori, I just can't!"

"Yes, you can. I can't make you do it. No one can. But I want you to know that no one would hold you accountable if the operation didn't save Rocklin. He's going to die. He looks worse every minute. What kind of operation would it be?"

"It's called a trephine. The bones of his skull have been crushed. It needs to be lifted and maybe a steel plate put in there. It's a very delicate operation, and look at me — I'm nothing but a drunk."

"I believe God's put you here for a purpose. That was the way it was with Esther. She was in the one place at the one time that her people were all going to be killed, but she was in the palace and had the king's ear. That's when her relative told her, 'Thou art come to the kingdom for such a time as this.' I think you are in this wagon train for that purpose, Paul."

Paul Molitor stood there, his head bowed and his eyes almost closed, trying to shut out what Jori was saying. She continued to speak softly but firmly and urgently. Finally he heard her say, "This is your chance, Paul. You can do your best. That's all any man can do, or any woman. Will you try?"

Paul Molitor stood in the morning air. It was as if he were on a high wall about to fall either to the right or to the left. Which way he fell would be the way he would be for the rest of his life. He thought back over the bitterness of the years when he had left the practice. What a painful and miserable life it had been. He thought of the joy that he had had when he was a young man just beginning to practice medicine. He felt then that life was good, but since the day that he had lost Marie Anders, there had been no happiness. Suddenly a resolve came to him. It was a resolve born of desperation. He straightened up, pulled his shoulders back, and looked down at his hands. "Jori, I don't think I can help him, but I'll try."

Jori let out a glad cry and threw her arms

around him. "Thank God!" she exclaimed. "You'll have to tell us what to do. I'll help."

"You know what that fella's gonna do?" Stuffy McGinnis was staring over at the scene in the center of the wagons. Charlie Reuschel and Jesse Burkett had constructed a table, of sorts, using whatever material they could. Rocklin was lying on the table with a blanket over him, and Jori and Kate stood close.

"He's gonna cut the top of his head off and mix his brains all up until they're fixed."

"That won't ride. That'll kill that fella," Eddie Plank said with astonishment. "I never heard of such a thing."

"Come on. I wanna see this," Stuffy said.

He moved forward, but he was met by Herendeen, who said, "You keep out of there. Let Molitor do what he can."

The men all obeyed Herendeen, but they could see and they could hear very clearly everything that was said.

Molitor looked around the circle and said, "We're going to have to have a plate. When that bone comes out, I'll have to put something in."

"What kind of a plate, boss?" Addie Joss was standing there.

"Something about this big, about the size of a silver dollar, very thin. Better if it were made out of silver."

"I can do that!" Addie Joss exclaimed at once. "I can take this silver dollar and beat it out."

"Do it now, Addie."

As Joss left, Molitor looked around the circle. His black bag, which he had carried all the years since he had left practice, he had brought with him. He never could understand why, since he never used it, but it was the one tie to his old life and, perhaps, a symbol of what might happen one day. Now it was happening, and Paul Molitor looked around at the faces. They were all hopeful, and he said, "I'll say this again. I don't think this will work."

"Tell us what to do," Jori said quickly.

Molitor reached into the bag and pulled out a brown bottle. "This is ether. He's got to be absolutely still. Jori, somebody has to put a few drops on this. It'll put him to sleep, and if he gets restless, you'll have to add some more."

"I can do that," Jori said.

Molitor bent over and studied the wound. "His color is bad, and his breathing is erratic. There's a lot of pressure on his brain, but if we can get that bone out of there and relieve the pressure, I think he'll be much better."

"When do you want to do it?" Leland asked. He was standing farther back and had no inclination to watch. He was squeamish about this kind of thing.

"We might as well start now. It'll take awhile." He looked up at Kate and Good News. "I guess you two are the champion prayer warriors on this train, so I'd advise you to get to it."

"I already started," Good News said. "I like to shout when I pray, but I figure now wouldn't be no time for that."

"No, I need everything as quiet as I can get it."

Molitor straightened up and took a deep breath. There was something different in his face. Everyone saw it, and Callie at that moment smiled at him. "You can do it — just like you did my shoulder."

"I wish it were that easy," Molitor said. He hesitated and then began to lay out the contents of his bag. "Kate, you hand me these things when I ask for them. I don't know the names of them. I'll point to them, and you just hand them to me. Now we need to wash up as well as we can."

Everyone watched as they washed their hands thoroughly in a basin with strong soap. Molitor came back and said, "That's a scalpel. Give it to me with the handle toward me."

Kate picked up the scalpel carefully and handed it. Molitor bent over and looked at the wound, then he lowered his hands and began to make his cut. . . .

It was a much slower process than any of them had thought. Molitor worked very carefully with tweezers and scalpel, pulling out fragments of bone. No one said a word, and Molitor had apparently forgotten his audience. Twice he had to say, "A few drops more of ether, Jori, about three or four."

Jori put the cloth over Rocklin's face, placed the four drops on it, and felt his breathing grow steady. She was not watching the operation itself but kept her eyes fixed on Rocklin's features. She wanted to reach out and put her hand on his cheek, but there were too many people watching. She was praying constantly, as she knew others were.

Finally Molitor said, "Joss, you got the plate?"

"This be all right, boss?"

Molitor took the rounded piece. It was about an inch and a half in diameter and smooth, without a sign of a scratch. "How'd you get it so smooth?"

"I'm a blacksmith, boss. I do things like that."

"It's just right." Kate watched as he inserted the plate and then said, "Hand me that needle. I'll be putting the sutures in now."

Kate handed Molitor the needle and watched as he stitched the scalp together. Finally Paul cleaned the wound and moved around so he could look in Rocklin's face. He was still for a moment and then turned to face Jori across from him. "That's all I can do, Jori."

"His color is better, I think."

"I believe you're right. We'll just have to see." He turned and walked away and began to wash his hands. He felt a touch and turned to see Callie standing beside him. Her eyes were like stars, and there were tears in them.

"You did so good, Paul! You did wonderful!"

At that moment Paul Molitor felt better than he had in years. He studied the face of the young woman and said, "If you hadn't guessed that I was a doctor, it wouldn't have happened. Rocklin would have been lost, and I would have stayed lost the rest of my life. So, I guess you saved my life, Callie."

"I was proud to do it!"

The time passed so slowly that Jori lost track of it. She sat beside Rocklin and seldom took her eyes from his face. It was two hours after Molitor had closed the wound that he suddenly blinked his eyes. Instantly she called out, "Paul, he's waking up!"

Molitor was there. He took Rocklin's wrist and exclaimed, "His heartbeat's much better!"

"And his color. That dreadful pallor's gone," Jori said.

Kate, Mark, and Leland came closer, and Good News took Kate's hand and held it. She looked at him, and he smiled. "Don't give up prayin'," he whispered, "but I think God's done reared back and worked a miracle!"

Jori felt the tears rise in her eyes, and she could not stop them. They overflowed and ran down her cheeks. She suddenly felt her father's hands on her shoulders. He had a handkerchief, and he wiped the tears away. "He's going to be all right, daughter, I just know it."

"He has to be, Papa — he just has to be!"

At that moment Leland Hayden knew that his daughter's life was tied in with this man who lay before them. He squeezed her shoulder, and the two stood there looking down at the still face of Chad Rocklin.

CHAPTER
TWENTY-THREE

The darkness dissipated, disappearing like fog drawn away by a soft wind. It had been a warm, friendly darkness, comfortable, and one that he hated to leave. As long as he was in the dark there was no pain, but the light brought the pain with it. Several times he had almost come to the brightness, but the pain had been so intense that he had allowed himself to sink back into the black velvet night that enveloped him. He was like a swimmer who floated to the top, but something dreadful appeared to be there so he had allowed himself to sink back into the depths.

This time, however, the light seemed to touch his eyelids with fingers so gentle as to be almost unfelt, and there was sound too. He had known sounds before but always the sound of voices. This time the sound was of a bird singing somewhere close by. He listened and could not identify the bird, but he began to wonder why a bird should have such a happy song. Birds couldn't have lives all that wonderful, but the song was as merry, as gay as anything he had ever heard.

Then a memory came shouldering its way into his mind, almost like a big strong bully pushing his way among weaker people. It was a terrible memory — violence, pain, screaming, and death. He himself was in the dream, and he could almost smell the burning powder and feel the sweaty grip of his hand on the butt of a pistol.

The dream faded, and he felt something on his forehead. It felt cool and wet. This was no dream! He took a deep breath and was suddenly aware that he was lying down and some sort of light covering was over him. The light was stronger now, and he opened his eyes a mere slit. Something was moving in front of him, and all he could tell was that it was a light blue color. Opening his eyes more he saw that it was cloth, and then he saw a face. Great relief came to him for it was a face he knew, a woman wearing a blue dress.

"Hello."

His voice was weak and rusty and seemed to come from deep inside his throat.

"Chad, you're awake!"

"I guess . . ."

Then he opened his eyes fully and saw that she was holding a cloth to his forehead. He was lying down on some sort of a bed, and the sky was blotted out by an arching cover of some sort. *A wagon. I'm in a wagon.* "Where is this place?"

"Don't try to talk. Let me get you some water. I know you're thirsty."

At her words he was keenly aware of a raging thirst, and he heard the sound of water being poured from one container to another. While that was happening he glanced around and saw that he was in a wagon that was full of all kinds of objects, boxes, sacks, bags, clothing, but a bed had been formed on top of it. He lifted his head and saw that the back cover was off of the wagon. He could see other wagons outside, and now he heard the birds singing louder, and over this was the sound of voices. The smell of wood smoke came to him, and he caught sight of a fire and a woman bending over it cooking something.

"Here, take this."

Rocklin felt her hand beneath his head, lifting it up. There was a moment's pain, but he did not notice, for the water was the best drink he had ever had in his life. He gulped it down, and some spilled over his chin onto his bare chest. He saw that he was not wearing anything, and embarrassment came to him. "Where are my clothes?"

"It's been hot, and you had a fever so we had to cool you off. How do you feel?"

The question confused Rocklin. He squeezed his eyes together, and then the memory came flooding back. "There was a fight with the Indians."

"Yes. You were hit in the head with a war club of some sort. You were very badly hurt."

"My head itches." Rocklin lifted his hand to touch his head, but she caught it.

"Don't scratch it. It's got bandages on it."

Now things were getting clearer. "This is your wagon, isn't it?"

"Yes. You've been here for two days now."

"Two days? That long? I don't remember anything except the fight."

Jori smiled. Her lips were trembling slightly. This was the first time he had come to a consciousness like this. Several times he had awakened. His eyes had opened, and his lips had moved. But now she felt he would be all right. Joy came to her, and she gave him another drink of water. "Drink it slowly now. You need to drink all you can, Paul says."

"Paul? You mean Molitor?"

"Yes."

"Anybody else get hurt?"

"Just Santana and his band. They're all dead, but none of our men got hurt except you."

Rocklin lay there and studied her face for a moment. The heat caused her to perspire, and the thin dress clung to her figure. She had a fine layer of perspiration across her top lip, and a lock of her hair had come down over her forehead. He wanted to brush it back, but instead he said, "I must have been hurt pretty bad."

"You were dying, Chad. If it hadn't been for Paul, you would have died."

"What did he do?" Rocklin lay there while she explained how Molitor had come out of his shell and revealed that he had been a doctor in a past life. She told about the operation and how fine it was and how most had expected him to die.

"Well, I disappointed them, I guess."

"Do you think you could eat something?"

"I reckon I could." He was suddenly aware that he was hungry.

She had cleared a partial path to the back of the wagon, and now she filled the glass and said, "Here. Just sip it. I'll be back with something for you to eat."

Rocklin watched her go and then lay there listening to the sounds of the camp. It was all coming back now, and he could remember the wild light in Santana's eyes as he lunged forward with the knife. He could almost feel the grate of his own knife as he had plunged it into Santana. Beyond that he remembered turning to see that Jori and Carleen were all right and then — nothing.

"Well, look at you."

Rocklin looked down to see Paul Molitor framed in the opening of the wagon. He watched the man scramble up and then move along to where he could look at him. "Let's see about your pulse." He felt the pulse, put his hand on Rocklin's forehead, then pulled the bandage off that covered the top of his head. "It's healing real well," he said. "You're gonna be all right, but you won't be doing much for awhile."

Rocklin stared at him. "So you're a doctor."

"I used to be." A look of wonder came into Paul Molitor's face. "I guess I will be now. They probably need doctors in Santa Fe. If not, I'll go on to San Francisco."

"How much do I owe you, doc?"

Molitor laughed. "I'll put it on your tab," he said. "Now, Jori's coming in with some soup. I want you to eat all you can and drink all you can."

"We need to get out of this place. Those

Indians might come back."

"Don't worry about it. We're all standing guard twenty-four hours a day, and Four Bears and Kicking Bird are out there. They'll let us know if there's any Indian trouble."

"There'll be water trouble. Water's pretty scarce."

"Grat Herendeen's rode out. He's already found water for the next stop. Grat said we could fill our water barrels up there."

"It looks like I've lost a job."

"For awhile. You just take it easy." He turned suddenly and nodded. "You're doing great. I think if any man has a right to thank God, it's you. I'll come and check on you later."

Molitor was gone then, and Jori was back. She had a saucepan full of something that smelled delicious. She propped his head up with a pillow and said, "Here, I'll have to feed you. Open up."

"I feel like a blasted baby," Rocklin grumbled. But he opened his mouth, and she gently gave him a bite of the delicious stew. "That's great. What is it?"

"That's what Kate calls her 'What is it?' stew. She claims anything that comes along goes in it, so just enjoy."

Rocklin ate the entire bowl and then suddenly became very weary. "Thanks for taking care of me," he muttered and then dropped off so quickly it frightened Jori. She felt his pulse and was relieved when it was strong.

"It's all right, my dear, you're just tired," she whispered. She sat there for a long time watching him. She was very tired for she had stayed up most of the night, too. Finally she got up and left the wagon. As she stepped down, she saw Herendeen standing there hulking large in the morning sun.

"How's he doin'?"

"He's doing fine, Grat."

"That was somethin', the way the doctor took his skull off and scrambled his brains."

Jori suddenly laughed. "Yes. It was something."

"The doctor tells me we can leave in a couple of days if we take it easy."

"I think it is time to move on. How's Mark doing?"

Herendeen grinned, his wide mouth twisted slightly. "You know that tenderfoot fooled me a lot. He's growed up on this trip. He's still green as grass, but I could make a mule skinner out of him if I had time. Maybe I will." He hesitated, then said, "When Rocklin wakes up, you tell him not to worry. Everything's being taken care of."

"I'll tell him, Grat."

Rocklin had made spectacular progress, and Paul Molitor had reluctantly agreed to let him sit up in the wagon seat. Rocklin had protested, "I can't lie down anymore, doc. Just let me sit up."

"You sure you're not having any pains in your legs anywhere?"

"Wasn't hurt in my legs."

"I know, but you got nerves that run all the way up to your brain. One of them could have been hurt. As a matter of fact, you could have been totally paralyzed."

Rocklin was sitting on a box beside the fire. He was wearing the lightest weight shirt he had, and his color was good. "I'm fine, doc. I'm going to bring you lots of customers." He reached up and laid his hand lightly on the bandage on the top of his head. "I still can't hardly believe it that I'm packin' a silver dollar in the top of my head."

"Don't fool with that. It's got to heal completely, and please don't get hit on the head again. That wouldn't be good."

"I'll do my best."

Molitor lifted his head. "Looks like we're starting up. I'll check you at noon. That's probably as long as you need to sit up for awhile. Then you can lie down and rest during the nooning."

"Sure thing, doc."

Molitor left, and Jori climbed up in the wagon seat. "I'm surprised you talked the doctor into letting you sit up and ride."

"It feels good to me. Thanks for the cushion." Jori had made a cushion of blankets. Rocklin was sitting there loosely. He was alert now and keen-eyed. "I sure hope somebody's taking care of my horse."

"Callie's taking care of him. He's all right."

At that moment Mark went by. He stopped his horse and lifted one eyebrow. "Well, the patient's sitting up. How do you feel, Chad?"

"Better than average, Mark. I had a good doctor and a good nurse."

Mark studied the face of the big man and said, "I don't want to think too much about what we did with Santana's men."

"I've got memories like that. I keep them locked up in a big box. Sometimes you have to do things for other people, and that's what you did, Mark."

"Yes."

"Just think about Carleen and what would have happened to her if you hadn't come."

"I've had nightmares since we've been back. I guess it was just shooting that Indian

421

without giving him warning."

"You don't give Kiowa warriors warnings. You're dead if you do," Rocklin said. He saw that the young man was troubled, and he said, "I hear you're in charge of this outfit now."

Mark laughed. "Don't be foolish. I'm just helping Grat. He's the boss until you get back."

"Not what I hear. He rates you pretty high."

The praise reddened Mark's cheeks. "I'm learning," he said. "I hope I don't get us lost."

Rocklin laughed easily. "Well, if you miss Santa Fe, you'll know it because you'll run into the ocean. If you do, you just turn around and come back."

Carleen came scrambling into the wagon, climbing up the wheel. She clamored over Rocklin and sat down between him and Jori. "What are you talking about?" she demanded.

"About naughty little girls that interrupt," Mark said. He laughed and pulled his horse around. "I'll see you when we stop at noon."

"Let me see your head, Chad," Carleen said.

"Look all you want."

"No, I mean the hole in your head."

"Carleen, will you hush!" Jori said. "You have no manners whatsoever."

"I want to see the silver dollar."

"You can't see it. It's covered up."

"I seen the whole thing, Chad. I seen Paul pullin' bones out and messin' your brains around, and then I saw him put that silver dollar in. It was really something. Maybe I'm going to be a doctor when I grow up."

"I thought I told you that there are no women doctors," Jori said with a smile.

"There'll be one when I get growed." She reached over and took Chad's hand and held it in both of hers. "Tell me again about the raid. About how you found us and how you got us away from that old Santana."

"Not much to tell. We just came and got you. Couldn't do without you." He squeezed her hand, and she looked up and smiled at him.

They heard Mark give a call, and the wagons began to move forward. "When we get to Santa Fe, Carleen, I'm going to take you to a fandango."

"A fandango? What's that?"

"It's what the Spanish folks call a big ball."

"I've never been to a ball."

"Are they nice?" Jori said.

"Well, they're not much like the balls you have in Little Rock, but you'd enjoy it, I think. I hope you like Santa Fe."

Jori was thinking, *He's all right. He's not going to die.* A great relief had come to her over the last few days. She thought back to the time when she had leaned over him in the Indian camp and seen the horrible wound in the top of his head. She breathed a prayer, *Thank You, God, for Your tender mercies.*

The country had taken on a different look. It was a long land but not a level one. It looked to Jori like a land that time had somehow forgotten — vast and empty with endless sand and clumpy grass and sun. It reminded her that the earth was a large place, and she had seen only a small part of it. There seemed to be no end to the country, as day after day they moved ever westward. The sun, of course, was a pale source of heat, but it was a pitiless heat.

As the days passed, Rocklin grew stronger, and he would point out the spots on the trail — Round Mount, Rabbit Ear Creek, Point of Rock, Wagon Mound. They all looked about the same, the scenery changing little. They were headed almost due south and finally, after many days, Rocklin, who had begun riding for short periods now, had come to sit beside her on the wagon. He pointed ahead saying, "San Miguel is up there. We'll cross a little river there, the same river that comes around close to Santa Fe down through the Sangre de Cristo Mountains."

"Sangre de Cristo. What does that mean?"

"The blood of Christ. I don't know why they call it that except sometimes the sunset there is red as blood."

Two days later Jori was aware of a changing scene. The vegetation was changing. Mostly it was composed of a small bush, dark green. "What kind of bush is that, Chad?"

"Piñons. You'll see a lot of them. The Spanish can't do without 'em. They burn the wood and eat the nuts."

That night they made a fire over piñon wood, and it gave off a pungent odor that she liked. They cooked steaks over it, and they had a delicious flavor.

As they ate, Callie had joined them along with Molitor. The two had spent a lot of time together, and now they sat there talking quietly, eating the steaks. "What'll you do when you get to Santa Fe, Callie?" Paul asked.

"Work, I guess."

"Work doin' what?"

"I'll find something."

Molitor grinned at her. "You know, I think I'd better take you to raise. Kind of like you was my kid sister."

"I'm not your sister!"

Paul lifted his eyes at the vehemence of her answer. "Well, I know that," he said. "Maybe I'll be kind of like your daddy. You might need a switching once in awhile."

"You're not my daddy either!" she said shortly.

"What are you mad about?"

"Nothing."

"Look, I just want to help you. If it wasn't for you, I'd still be a drunk ex-doctor. How about this? I'm going to set up there as a doctor. Won't make much money, but it's a start. Maybe you can be my housekeeper, and I'll teach you about nursing."

"Me be a nurse? I couldn't do that."

"Sure you could. What do you say?"

Suddenly Callie turned her face away. Paul stared at her. He saw that her shoulders were trembling slightly. Quickly he reached out, drew her around, and saw tears in her eyes. "Why, you're crying. What's wrong, Callie? I didn't hurt your feelings, did I?"

"No. You didn't hurt my feelings." She smiled brilliantly and said, "I feel just fine. Now, tell me some more about how it will be when we get to Santa Fe. . . ."

■ ■ ■ ■

Jori had noticed that Kate had been unusually quiet. She was a quiet woman anyway, more or less, but there was a despondency about her that was very unusual. Kate Johnson had always been a cheerful woman, able to put up with almost anything and keep her smile. She thought about it and several times almost asked Kate, but instead she observed the woman closely. She saw that Kate was always happy and laughing when Good News was around, but as they grew closer to Santa Fe, she seemed to be losing this. She also saw that Kate's eyes followed Good News wherever he went, and finally she put two and two together and found the time to talk with Kate.

It was late at night, and Kate had stayed up sitting by the fire. Almost everyone was asleep except the guards and those watching the animals. Jori came and sat down across from Kate, picked up a stick, and began to poke the fire. She watched the sparks fly upward and then said, "You're not happy, are you, Aunt Kate?"

"I'm as happy as most, I guess."

The answer was short, and Jori threw the stick in the fire. It began to burn, throwing off the acrid odor that burned her eyes. She moved around, sat down beside Kate, and put her arm around her. "I know why you're unhappy."

"I tell you I'm not unhappy."

"Yes, you are. You're unhappy because you love Good News."

Kate started and shook her head violently. "That's foolishness!"

"No, it's not. I've been watching you. You've been different around him. I've never known you to take such an interest in a man."

"I don't want to listen to this talk."

"Well, you're going to, Aunt Kate. Remember the talks you gave me? Remember when I fell in love with Ronald Barker, how you sat me down and talked to me like a dog?"

"Well, you deserved it."

"Yes, I did. So, now it's my turn. You listen to me. Good News loves you."

"No, he doesn't."

"Yes, he does. You're just being bullheaded and stubborn. That used to be me. He loves you. It's written all over him."

"Then why doesn't he *say* something?" Suddenly Kate seemed to collapse, her shoulders slumped. "I've been waiting for him to say something for a long time. I think he likes me, but he never says anything like that."

"Don't you know why?"

"He doesn't love me, that's why."

"No. He thinks you're better than he is."

"Better?" Kate came up. "What are you talking about?"

"He doesn't have any education, Aunt Kate. He doesn't have any money."

"Neither do I."

"But you come from a good family. To him that's money. You're educated."

"Not all that much."

"Aunt Kate, stop arguing with me. I'm telling you he loves you, and you're going to lose him if you don't do something."

"A woman can't do anything about that."

"Yes, you can, and here's what you must do. . . ."

Good News had wandered down the length of all the wagons and then had taken the rifle out in the hope of potting a prairie dog or something to eat. He had found nothing, and he was surprised to see Kate come walking toward him. "Hello, Kate," he said. "What are you doing out here?"

"I came to talk to you."

Surprised, Good News lowered the rifle and put its butt on the ground. "Sure," he said, "what is it?"

"Good News, I want to marry you."

If Good News had taken a shot directly in the stomach, he might have been more surprised but not a great deal. He opened his mouth to speak but said nothing. He stared at her wildly for a moment and then stuttered, "Why — why — Kate —"

"I've grown to care for you on this trip, Good News. I'd like to spend the rest of my life being as good a wife to you as I could. Will you have me?"

Good News dropped the rifle, and it fell to the ground. He leaped forward and grabbed her shoulders and held her. "Why, Kate, I don't know what to say."

"Say yes or no." Kate was looking up at him, and there was a hurt expression in her face.

Suddenly Good News shook his head. "I'm a blamed fool, that's what I am, makin' you ask like this. Why, Kate, I've cared for you for weeks now. There's never been a woman like you, but I couldn't ask you to marry me."

"I know that. That's why I asked you."

"Think what people would say. An educated woman from a good family. I'm nothin' but an ignorant mule skinner."

"I don't care about that."

430

"You don't?"

"No, I don't. I care about you."

Good News was not an educated man, but he had a deep wisdom, and it came to him suddenly what a tremendous thing this woman had done. She had always been one of the strongest women he knew, but he realized it had taken every bit of determination to come and say what she had. "Why, it's with you like it is with me, ain't it, Kate?" He reached forward, and as he pulled her closer, he saw a small smile loosen and soften her lips. He saw the pride in her eyes and the vitality and knew that she was the kind of woman that could, if necessary, draw a revolver and shoot a man down and not go to pieces afterward. She had courage, but at the same time it was a woman's courage and not a man's. He pulled her forward, kissed her firmly, and said, "Kate, I want to marry you more than I ever wanted anything in my life. Will you have me?"

"Yes!"

Then he put his arms around her and drew her close. At that moment Kate felt like a sailor who had reached port after a long, hard, and dangerous journey.

CHAPTER
TWENTY-FOUR

Jori never forgot her first glimpse of the Sangre de Cristo Mountains nor her arrival at Santa Fe.

The mountains were towering, and Chad told her they were five thousand feet high. The air was so thin it made her breath short for a time, but as they made their way into the towering heights through the passes, she found a beauty in the majestic snow-mantled peaks. They crossed a body of water that was the Pecos River, but it seemed more like a creek to her. It was icy cold when she got down to drink it, and Rocklin looked up at the peaks and said, "Snow makes it that cold."

They wound their way through the peaks, passing through San Miguel, which was merely a group of small houses straddling the Pecos River. Everything was made of adobe bricks, a mixture of earth and straw that was stacked into walls when it was dried.

The houses were the color of earth, so the small town seemed to grow out of the earth. The people were friendly and seemed happy enough, and Jori said, "I'm going to have to learn Spanish."

"It'd be a help. I'm too lazy myself," Rocklin said.

Finally they began to climb, and the animals had to labor. They had to double-hitch up the pass, and it was a punishing trip. But it was worth it to Jori.

They crested the top of the hill, and in the blink of an eye, she got her first sight of the entire valley of the Santa Fe Plateau. Her eyes could not take it in at first.

"Well, you've come eight hundred miles, and there it is," Rocklin said. He was sitting beside her in the wagon and was pleased at her reaction. "Right pretty, isn't it?"

"It's beautiful!" Straight ahead in the distance was a great range of mountains. "What's that?" she said.

"That's the Jemez."

To the south the plain was broken by an enormous mountain that seemed to blot out the sun. "That's the Sandias," Rocklin informed her. "And there to the north, that's the road to Taos."

"It's beautiful. I love it!"

"Glad you like it. Think you might stay?"

"I think I could be a Santa Fe woman without any trouble." She was sitting so close to Rocklin that she could feel the warmth of his body. It gave her a feeling of completeness. She sat there studying the country as they descended to the floor of the basin. It was beautiful, different from anything she had ever seen. Once she had thought it was a hard, merciless country, but there were people here and houses and fires and a river with trees.

Finally they passed into Santa Fe itself. Columns of smoke were rising to the sky, hazy and drifted by the breeze, cottonwoods were plentiful, and the streets were lined with mules and horses and burros. She saw young women with painted faces and young Spanish men, graceful as anything she had ever seen and vain, apparently, from their costumes.

She turned to Rocklin and said, "You know, I think you'd be miserable in this place, or else you could learn to love it."

"I've always liked Santa Fe. There's somethin' about it."

For a moment the two sat there and did not speak, but something passed between them. She expected him to speak, for she already knew that she loved this man, tall and lanky. When she had had to care for him like an infant, it had been a joy to her, and she knew that she would love him when they both became old. But it was up to him to speak. Suddenly she thought, *I told Kate to say her mind to Good News, but it's different for me.* She waited and saw a sentence form itself, something coming into his eyes, but then he said, "Well, let's get into town. We've got goods to sell."

Mark Hayden and his father were sitting at a table in a café. Before them were the remnants of some of the hot spicy food that they both had ordered, and Leland Hayden was looking down at a tablet where he had totaled up a line of figures. "Look at what we got out of our goods. We sold at least two-thirds of it."

"Why, Father, I reckon we're rich."

"Seems almost immoral to charge this much."

"No, glad to get it. We're doing them a service."

"Well, we made it. Only lost one man. I think we had a good trip."

"We almost lost Jori and Carleen. I'll never stop thanking God for that."

"Nor me either."

The two men sat there loosely, and Leland studied his son. This was a different young man from the one that had pulled out of Little Rock. His cheeks were tanned, his muscles were taut, and there was an alertness and a pride in him that had been lacking. "The trip has been good for you, son."

"I thought it was going to kill me at first, but it's been the best thing I've ever done."

"Well, we'll have to make some plans, like going back for another load maybe. But not today."

"No," Mark grinned. "I'm not ready to start yet. I want to go to that fandango I've been hearing about. I hear they're really something."

The two men sat there talking idly, and Mark said, "You know, I've been thinking about all those mules the Indians had. There must have been three hundred of them, and we got them for practically nothing. Why couldn't we buy some trade goods, take all of our drovers and mule skinners, and go buy a huge herd."

"Of mules? And do what with them?"

"Why take 'em to Missouri and sell 'em, of course. You know how prices are going up on mules, at least so I've heard. Then we keep the best of them and bring another train back. Maybe a bigger train, ten, twelve, twenty wagons."

Leland suddenly laughed. "You're bound to be rich."

"I doubt it, but I'm thankful to God for what He's done for us."

"So am I, son."

"Well, let's go get ready for that fandango."

Jori saw Callie walking along the main street looking at the stalls in the shops. She came over to her at once and said, "Are you going to the fandango, Callie?"

"I reckon not."

"Why? It'll be fun, at least they tell me."

"Not much for partying. As a matter of fact, I've never been to a real one."

An idea came to Jori, and she said, "Come on. I've got a purse full of money, and we're going to go shopping and buy ourselves fandango outfits."

"Me? Not likely."

But Jori would not take no for an answer. She laughed and pulled the young woman into a store and said to the Spanish storekeeper, "I want to see the two prettiest dresses you've got in your whole shop."

"Sí, señorita. I have the beautiful dresses. Every man in the fandango will fall in love with both of you!"

■ ■ ■ ■

Paul Molitor had little enough money, so he had simply worn the best he had to the fandango. He had never seen anything exactly like it, but he had quickly discovered that the Spanish people had a great fondness for jewelry, dress, and amusements. As he walked down the street, he studied one of the dresses of the women. They were different from any dresses he'd seen. Most of them consisted of a skirt, a colorful blouse, and a scarf called a reboso around the head and shoulders.

As for the fandango itself, he discovered that this was a waltz of sorts. He stood for awhile watching the dancers, and finally he moved toward a stand that sold food and wine. The food was remarkably cheap and delicious.

More than once a woman would stop and smile at him, but he had no money and did not feel comfortable. Finally he made his way toward the end of the street, taking in the sights. He brushed against a young woman and touched his hat saying, "Pardon me," and would have continued, but then he heard his name. "Why, Paul, don't you know me?"

Molitor turned quickly, and his eyes widened when he saw that it was Callie.

"Why, Callie, it's you!"

Indeed, it would have been hard for anyone to have recognized Callie. He had never seen her in anything besides the shapeless men's clothes, and now her trim figure was outlined by the colorful dress. It was a white dress with a loose bodice, scooped neckline, and short sleeves outlined in red trim. The skirt was full and had bright colors in stripes such as red, green, orange, yellow, and blue to the hem, which fell to her ankles.

"Why, you look beautiful, Callie."

"Thank you, Paul. Jori helped me pick the dress out, and she actually bought it for me."

"Well, you two did a good job." He stood looking at her in admiration and then said, "Some of this food's good. Do you want to sample it?"

"Yes. I am hungry."

He took her to one of the stalls and kept stealing glances at her. She was pleased, and her lips stirred, her smile a small lightness around her mouth. Paul Molitor was shocked at how feminine she was.

"It's going to be a little bit hard for me to think of you like this."

"What do you mean, Paul?"

"I mean like a woman."

"Why will it be hard?"

"Because you never dressed like one or acted like one — but you should."

"I never had a chance before."

The light from the lanterns ran over the curves of her shoulders, and it was kind to her, showing the womanliness of her figure. She was smiling at him now, and her face was a mirror as her feelings changed. A small dimple appeared at the left of her mouth, and her eyes suddenly danced. "I think I like dressing up like a woman. Maybe I can get a job in a saloon."

"Callie, don't be foolish!"

She laughed with delight. "I was just teasing. Of course I won't do that."

The two stood in the middle of the swirling crowd, and she said, "I'll have to find something to do here."

"Why, you could do what we talked about." She waited for him to speak, and he said hurriedly, "You could learn to be my nurse. I'll always need a good nurse."

"That would be —" She could not put it into words, and she turned suddenly. "Let's walk a bit." They walked, and she was like a child, delighted by the colors and the dance. He tried to get her to join the festivities, but

440

she said, "I don't know how to dance."

"Well, I'm a good teacher. Before the next one I'll give you some lessons."

Callie was laughing as they approached the wagons. "I'll have to find a place to stay. We can't live in the wagons."

"No. Maybe I can get a place with an office and rooms over it."

"Why, I couldn't stay with you there. We're not married."

Paul hesitated then said, "We'll find you something."

The two stood silently, and there was something awkward in Callie. She was like a young colt in a way, awkward but full of the promise of true beauty.

Suddenly Paul reached out and took her hand. "I don't know much about women, Callie. I had one once, but she left me."

"Where is she now?"

"Dead," he said.

She caught the sound of something in his voice. "You didn't ever want another woman?"

"No, that is —" He hesitated then looked down at her. "Not until now."

She did not answer but stood looking up at him. "All my life I've been lonely," she said simply.

"So have I, Callie. Maybe we could help each other." He reached out, embraced her, and kissed her lightly on the lips, but it turned into another sort of kiss. At that moment the shock of the softness of her lips came to him, and suddenly he was aware of the wild sweetness that was there. He was aware of his own needs, and something passed between them then — something that took the loneliness, the incompleteness, and the emptiness out of him. When he lifted his lips, he could not speak for a moment. "You're so sweet, Callie, but I'm too old for you."

Callie reached up and put her hand on his cheek. "No," she whispered, "you're just right."

Suddenly a great joy came to Paul Molitor and he laughed. "You can be my bride. I can marry you and raise you right so you won't have any bad habits."

"And you'd teach me how to bring your boots and wait on you hand and foot."

"Exactly."

"I think I'd have something to say about that."

There was a lightness then that came to both of them. Each knew that they had passed some point and could never go back to being what they were before.

"Stay here in Santa Fe, Callie. A woman needs to be courted. I'll come courting, and we'll find out if we can make it through a lifetime."

Callie Fortier knew then that this man loved her, and she knew that she had loved him for longer. She put her hand on his chest and whispered, "All right, Paul, I'll stay."

"Well, blast it, Chad Rocklin, you're so contrary you'd float upstream if I threw you in the river!"

Leland Hayden was staring at Rocklin with displeasure. He had just paid him and had immediately begun to talk about future plans for establishing a trading business. But Rocklin had brought him up short, saying, "I don't think I'd be interested, Leland."

Leland had known that his daughter loved this man, and now the question in his mind was why Rocklin would not want to pursue her. She was lovely enough for any man, he knew that, but he saw something in Rocklin he could not identify.

"Look, Mark has a good idea. We take all our men back, get mules from the Indians, take them and sell them in Missouri. Then we can bring a train back. Why, we could make a good thing out of it."

"I think you and Mark can do that without me."

"No, we can't. We need you, Chad."

"I've been thinkin' about goin' trapping. Maybe prospecting."

There was something different in Rocklin, and Leland wanted to blurt out, *What's the matter with you, man? You've got it all right in front of you. My daughter loves you, and you'll never find a better woman.* He knew this would not do, so instead he set out to convince Rocklin to join forces, to go into business with him. But Rocklin would not agree, and finally Leland watched the big man walk off. "What's wrong with him? I wonder if he's got a wife stashed away some place."

Carleen came to find Rocklin who was still camping out at the wagons. "What are you doing out here, young 'un?" he asked fondly. He felt a great wave of affection for this young girl and smiled as she said, "I came looking for you. Papa says you're going to leave."

"I've been thinking about it."

"No, you can't leave." She came up and took his hand and pulled at him. "I don't want you to leave, Chad."

"Well, I don't want to leave so much, but I've got other things to do."

Carleen stared at him for a minute. "You'd be too old for me by the time I'm old enough to marry, but you can marry Jori."

"You are the nosiest young woman I ever saw! Jori is a fine lady, and I'm a mule skinner and a mountain man. She would never marry me."

"Yes, she would," Carleen nodded emphatically. "She's in love with you."

"Don't be foolish!"

"She is. It says so right here." She opened a small book that she had brought with her and read a line out. " 'I love Chad so much, but he doesn't care for me. That's obvious.' She wrote that yesterday. See the date?"

"Carleen, this is Jori's journal!"

"I know it. I read it all the time, but she doesn't know it. I brought it to show to you because you need to know she loves you. Now, read that."

Against his better judgment Rocklin took the book. He felt a sharp twinge of guilt, but his curiosity overcame his scruples. He began to read and for several minutes stood stock-still. Then he closed the book and looked down at Carleen, who was watching him expectantly. "I guess I see what you mean, Carleen."

■ ■ ■ ■

Jori heard Rocklin's steps. Their family had rented a house on the edge of town, and she thought it was Mark or her father returning. The knock on the door startled her, and she muttered, "Who can that be?" When she opened the door, she found Rocklin standing there. He took his hat off and said, "Hello, Jori, can I come in?"

"Why — of course. Come on in."

As soon as he was inside, Jori turned to him. Her lips were drawn together into a firm line. She said very stiffly, "I understand you're leaving for prospecting or something."

"Well, that was on my mind."

"I suppose you came to say good-bye."

"Well, that was my intention, but I've been thinking. It's a dangerous thing for a man to walk away from a situation."

Jori stared at him. "What do you mean?"

"I can look back at two times in my life when I had a chance to do something and instead of doing them I just walked away."

"Were they women that you walked away from?"

"One of them was. I was only nineteen. What did I know?"

Jori wanted to ask about the woman, but she was upset and asked merely, "What was the other time?"

"I was at a revival meeting when I was sixteen. God spoke to my heart that day, and I should have been saved. Instead I got up and ran out. I ran from God for a long time. That was a big mistake. I walked away from the best thing in life."

"I'm sorry to hear it."

He took a deep breath and said, "Jori, I can't walk away because it would ruin your life."

"Ruin *my* life! What are you talking about?"

"You love me so much, Jori, that you'd never get over it if I left. You'd wind up an old maid and be miserable."

"Why, you insufferable —" Jori stuttered and could not think of a thing to say that would put him in his place. "I think I could survive the loss if you left. What makes you think such a thing?"

"It says so right here."

She had not seen the object Rocklin had been carrying in his hand. When he held it up, she gasped, "That's my journal!"

"Yes, I've been reading how much you love me here. It says right here, 'I love Chad so much I don't even know how to put it into words, but he's the only man I've ever loved or ever will.' "

"You give me that!" Jori grabbed the journal, her face flaming. "I know where you got this. Carleen stole it and gave it to you!"

"Yes, she did." He moved forward, saying, "I'm sorry. It's a bad thing to read a private writing like that, but it made me see something."

"What did it make you see?"

"That you care for me. I didn't think you could, not like I love you, Jori." He reached forward and saw the fire and the spirit in the soft depth of her. There was a sweetness in her and a gentleness and a goodness. She was rich in a way a woman should be rich, and he said quietly, "I don't know when I first fell in love with you, but I know I do." He pulled her into his arms and kissed her. Her mouth was firm when he touched it, but the firmness dissolved and he felt the goodness of her. Old hungers suddenly rose in him. It was like falling into a softness, and he held her, unwilling to turn her loose. He felt her lips returning his caress, and, as he kissed her, it was as if she was saying what she had written in her journal. The feeling of a deep need satisfied ran through him.

"I don't keep a journal, Jori, not on paper, but if I did, I'd write in it, 'There's only one woman in the world for me. She's beautiful and true as steel. If I don't have her, I'll be miserable for the rest of my life. But if she'll marry me, I'll have the world right here in my arms.' "

"Oh, Chad, do you mean it?" Jori dropped the journal and put her arms around his neck. He kissed her again, and then suddenly a voice broke in.

"You see, Chad, I told you she was in love with you."

"You — you varmint!" Jori screeched. She pulled away from Rocklin and made a wild grab at Carleen, but Rocklin beat her to it. He snatched the young girl up and put his face against hers.

"Why, I can't let you do it, Jori. She's a favorite of mine, you see."

Jori watched as Carleen smiled and put her hand on Rocklin's cheek. "You need to shave, Chad. Your whiskers hurt." She turned and said, "I want you to make him shave every day after he marries you, Jori."

And then Jori laughed — a full, free laughter that came from somewhere deep in her heart. She came over and put her arms around the two of them, and then she said,

"Well, it'll take both of us to raise him, Carleen, but we can do it together."

ABOUT THE AUTHOR

Gilbert Morris is among the most popular Christian writers at work today, his books having sold nearly six million copies worldwide. He specializes in historical fiction and won a 2001 Christy Award for the Civil War drama *Edge of Honor.* Once a pastor and English professor who earned a Ph.D. from the University of Arkansas, Morris now lives with his wife in Gulf Shores, Alabama.